chain of being

First published in the UK in 2005 by
Dewi Lewis Publishing

www.dewilewispublishing.com

All rights reserved

Copyright ©2005
For the text: Khan Shafqat
For this edition: Dewi Lewis Publishing

ISBN: 1-904587-21-6

Design & artwork production: Dewi Lewis Publishing

Printed and bound in Great Britain by
Biddles Ltd, King's Lynn

2   4   6   8   10   9   7   5   3   1

First Edition

chain of
 being

 Khan Shafqat

 dewi lewis publishing

Waiting for miracles is the only way to preserve your sanity in Pakistan. Of course, the miracles never happen, but that does not matter. One keeps believing that one day, as one awakens from a long night of mosquitoes, or sultry afternoons of flies, that things could be different. *Chain of Being* is an attempt to make a miracle independent of the belief in hope.

Chain of Being is a fictional portrait of today's world, described by a man who believes in magic. This man – Mohammed Khan – represents a collective mindset whose genesis lies in autochonous myths and extrinsic beliefs. This is the same mindset that puts limits on what can and cannot be taught, the same mindset that creates confusion about one's role in this world, the same mindset that produces leaders of controlled democracy, and sometimes leads to religious fanaticism epitomised in Al-Quaeda.

I started this novel a few years ago, with a friend called Tariq: I a hopeless romantic, he a detached observer of life. Somewhere down the line he moved on, though this book belongs to him as much as it does to me.

I dedicate this book to the indifferent triad: my wife, my daughter and my son. Thanks are due to Baber the Pal and Farooq the Buddy. Cheers, fellas.

Khan Shafqat

Prologue

Then shed the blood of the pagans wherever you find them, and seize them and besiege them and lie in ambush for them.
 (Al-Quran, 9:5)

And mine eye shall not spare, neither will I have pity.
 (Ezekiel, 7:9)

Hast thou not seen how thy Lord dealt with the Army of Elephants? Did We not foil their stratagem and sent flocks of birds to pelt them with clay-stones and render them like green blades devoured.
 (Al-Quran, 105: 1-5)

Prologue

Those were the days of uncoiling answers.

In his backyard, where shade was scarce, there spread a tree. It was the tree of answer.

His mother believed it was the tree of danger. She had heard that a seventy-foot long python lived on it, though no one, including Mohammed Khan, ever saw it. Still, it did not deter mother from believing in it because she saw things only through her heart.

It was a family tree. When Mohammed Khan's great grandfather migrated from the mountains, he found it here. Mountains were in the rugged north, the only place in the Indian sub-continent where the sun did set on the British Empire. North had its own private sun: a bright, cruel, blistering orb of fire accustomed to bounce off rugged hills and breccias. The place was scorching in summer and icy in winters and Mohammed Khan's ancestors lived through the melting and freezing of time. They'd been living there ever since God commanded E to equal MC^2 and continued to live there until golden men, who wore red uniforms and did not wash their buttocks after defecation, came waving black cannons, and stormed their village at the crack of dawn.

Mohammed Khan's ancestors knew their religious duty in times of aggression. They besieged the army of pagan soldiers, took their women as concubines, confiscated their uniforms as war bounty, then cut off their limbs and displayed them in the main square of the village. Mohammed Khan's great grandfather was a certified reverse engineer. He dismembered enemy cannons and built his own version that fired stones, arrows and spears. When the men of gold returned, they faced a barrage of tiny rocks raining from the sky. They retreated with a pledge to write epics about the episode.

Mohammed Khan's great grandfather was a wise and cowardly man. He had learnt the remodelling procedure in his dreams and read about the victory in a book of predictions that also predicted that the enemy would return with new-model cannons capable of intercepting his arrows in mid-air and throwing them back on the turbaned warriors. The book cautioned that this time there'd be no identified or unidentified flying objects to shower rocks on the advancing forces. On the night when the villagers celebrated the victory dedicated to his name, the wise man took his family and dissolved into the darkness of the night. In the morning, the betrayed villagers collected his wisdom, his honour, his victory, his dream, his cowardice, his fears; and buried them without due burial rites.

Mohammed Khan's ancestor walked two hundred miles south until he found the Valley of Gandhara. Here land was green and aplenty, and a thick, smooth grass covered the earth like a layer of soft emeralds. In this place was neither burning sun nor cold severe. The blissful shade of towering trees came down low and clusters of fruit bowed upon them, easy to reach.

The king of the Valley was mighty hospitable. The family of Mohammed Khan's ancestor was served in vessels of gold and in goblets that seemed to be crystal but were actually made of silver. They were given a drink of ginger tempered with the water of the softly flowing fount and allowed to partake of as much as they desired. All around them were blooming youths who looked like scattered pearls and when the famished outlanders looked at them, they saw only bliss and a realm transcendent.

"This is thy reward, Mohammed Khan's great grandfather," the king said, giving the tidings of the great grandson who would one day inherit the earth. "Thou hast suffered long and hard during thy journey through the night. Here in my kingdom, thou wilt live in everlasting bliss. It is a refuge for the wise, the cowardly and the agnostic. From now on, thou wilt live by the river and under the tree of unanswered question. Now go and embrace its trunk."

The tree was there since the beginning. Mohammed Khan's great grandfather sighted it and accepted its eternity. Gandhara was the valley of acceptance. Things were made to happen here with fated dynamism. This way of life was acceptable to those who accepted it, testing for those who wished to continue it and hard for those who wanted to live it.

"Thou wilt be given an abode for thy family," the king said to him when he had overfilled his heart with the ginger drink.

"I will construct it, Lord of valleys and deserts," said Mohammed Khan's ancestor, his pride conspicuous in his humility. "I am a man of talent and a man of brain. During the Mountain Age, I built shelter for my family and performed reverse engineering for my tribe. People across the oceans have written treatises about me."

The king smiled mysteriously. When Mohammed Khan's distinguished ancestor returned to the corner plot of land he had chosen for building his house, the house already stood there and the last of the working angels was disappearing into the windy, dusty lanes of the village.

His new abode was a structure of pearls, built upon the ruins of a rugged mud-house that had once balanced itself along the ridges of flattened mountains. It was on the bank of the river flowing with fresh milk and imported honey. When Mohammed Khan's great grandfather first drank from the river, he fell on his back and slept for nine days. His wife recalled that there was a constant smile on his face and he no longer snored as he had done when he lived amongst the people of fire. His body emitted the fragrance of musk, which no one else was able to smell.

Many things happened to him in the Valley of Gandhara. He turned fair, his face now looked like the fourteenth-day moon. His eyelashes turned black like the night shining with moonlight on a clear sky. His pupils, formerly dull and dilated, turned black and sharp. His sclera once hosted by red snakes, became white as butter. His skin grew radiant and free of wrinkles, caressed by cool shade and nourished by apples, peaches, and olives. He became seventy times more powerful, and seventy-two times more handsome. His wife became thirty-five times more fragile and thirty-six times prettier – confirming the divine law regarding the man-woman parity of 2:1.

Book I

Coming of the Oracle

*Jesus said: "I have come to the world to prepare the way
for the messenger of God, who shall bring salvation to
the world. But beware that ye be not deceived,
for many false prophets shall come.*
(Gospel of Barnabas, 72:5)

1

Every kingdom divided against itself is brought to desolation; and a house divided against a house falleth.
(Luke, 12:17)

Then Allah brought down their buildings from their foundations, then the roofs fell down upon them from above and He brought down agony upon them.
(Al-Quran, 16:26)

More than two centuries went by and the great ancestor continued to live. He spawned a large clan of men and women, out of which many expired waiting for his demise so that his property could be distributed among the heirs and the era of private ownership be ushered in with unsuitable fanfare.

"The old man is hanging by a worn-out thread," the optimists claimed as they grappled with hovering doubts. "It'll be any year now that funeral ceremonies are held and the new era dawns."

"Don't be absurd," the pessimists retorted with a firm belief in the futility of hope. "The old man drank from the fount of eternity. He'll still be alive when heaven turns into molten brass, the moon splits asunder, mountains disintegrate into tufts of wool, and seas burst beyond their bounds."

"Who cares whether he dies right now or lives until the next millennium," those who did not stand to gain from either outcome would mutter.

It turned out that pessimism was the correct way of thinking in this land. Mohammed Khan's great grandfather continued to live and prosper. The news of his prosperity travelled back to the mountains and several thousand refugees arrived in the Valley, claiming to be his nephews, nieces, cousins, aunties, uncles, brothers-in-law, sisters-in-law, grandmothers, grandfathers, great grandfathers and great grandmothers. They came in tens, then in hundreds, finally in thousands, to dwell in the valley, some tillers of the ground and keepers of sheep, and others terrorists-in-the-making. Mohammed Khan's great grandfather took pride in their number and delight in their prosperity.

"You look for treasures beneath the earth, but your real wealth is your ancestry," the old man would tell his sons and grandsons. "The people of your clan are your arms and legs. They are your strength. Look after them and they will give you their lives in return."

The clansmen never forgave him for his favours. Their cryptic intrigues started as soon as they found food to eat and a place to sleep. First came whispers: hushed, surreptitious, spreading like hot air. Whispers found ears and ears inspired tongues, creating a conspiratorial affinity from which the great ancestor was excluded. He continued to enlarge his clan and alienate himself. He died a lonely man, spending his last years in a house that had thirty rooms and ten times the emptiness. His death arrived in the form of a freak incident involving a gun that went off fortuitously while his trusted servant, suspected by many to have accepted a bribe from his heirs, was cleaning it. His nineteen children, along with the entire clan, rushed to watch him pass on. Mohammed Khan was five years old when it happened. Within a span of three fateful minutes, he saw his great grandfather turning from an unwanted reality to a haunting myth as the villagers gathered around his dying body that no longer had a heart, for that is where the bullet had found its mark. No one breathed during the entire episode, firm in their apprehension that the great man never had a heart and the bullet fired by a force more powerful than their lineage had gone on to hit non-existence. All forebodings proved wrong in the end. The doctor from Hazro Municipal Hospital inspected the stiffening body, counted his fee and withdrew from the dead. He motioned his assistant to put the instruments back in the medical bag and made a sad face that promised to usher in the era of happiness.

"The great man is dead," he announced with solemnity. "And the world still breathes? How far away can Doomsday be?"

People gasped and let their lungs exhale their fears with such force that trees were uprooted, tin roofs flew in the air to land upon unsuspecting women washing clothes on the other side of the river, and a power breakdown darkened the valley for days. His heirs secretly celebrated the great death and publicly shed modest tears. When the burial ceremonies were over, everyone rushed to contact their lawyers and the gushing flow of lawsuits and preemption proceedings against a lifeless ancestry compelled the Provincial High Court to set up a special bench in the Valley.

During those days of dark nights enkindled by the flickering light of smelly lanterns, Mohammed Khan heard his father, Rahim Ullah Khan, question the wisdom of the great ancestor.

"The nocturnal journey was a mistake," he would tell Mohammed Khan, who had heard the story so many times that his memory declined to retain its details. As a result, it was a new story every time and a new pain. "Back in the mountains, we had gardens of mint and saffron growing on rooftops, and girls were born only to the people of low caste. Here, I am burdened with seven daughters and five brothers who are out to grab my lands with the connivance of a faulty legal system."

Brothers were not the only problem for him. There were thousands of uncles and cousins camped outside the High Court, waiting for the verdict about the division of land. But nature had other plans. Before the High Court could deliver its judgement in favour of some and against the rest, it was announced through the mosque loudspeaker that the village was on a geological fault. A holy man identified the most likely path of the crustal fracture with his wooden staff and soon, as suspicion turned into belief, several earthquakes hit the village, creating chasms that zigzagged through every house, dissevering rooms, verandahs, yards and gardens. People rushed back from the court and grabbed whatever they could.

"This is the third and final division," Mohammed Khan's father told him. "We divided the land once, then divided it again. Now nature has taken over."

Mohammed Khan was slowly becoming aware of nature's grand design. On the day of the earthquake, he awoke to find everything struggling for space. The ceilings of his house had descended so low that his father who stood six foot three without the shoes he rarely wore, had to permanently stoop during the rest of his living days. Their house had shrunk to one-sixth its original size as his five uncles claimed their share. The division was so illogical that every brother had to pass through the other's house in order to get on to the streets that were encroached by squatters waiting in vain for the High Court's decision. Mohammed Khan came out of his house after walking through his elder uncle's bedroom where he was busy making illicit love to his maidservant, and discovered that the long and winding village streets through which he used to run after donkeys, or utilise as an escape route when his father chased him with a stick, were choked with the smell of the present. The open land, where he had flown kites and played marbles, had vanished, the trees he'd climbed in order to pluck apricots were felled, and the well from which he had pulled water had dried. Everything looked dark and cold, as if an unnatural chill had penetrated the walls, the ceiling, and the dust of which everything is created.

There was a reassuring predictability about life-before-the-earthquake. All day long, Mohammed Khan ran through the dusty streets, jumped from one rooftop to another, entered any house he wanted to, and invited strangers to have lunch with his parents. Once he spotted a Canadian hippie passing through the village and took him home. The hippie was over seven feet tall and an impressive goatee hung from his chin.

"You want food?" Rahim Ullah Khan asked his guest.

"I want hashish," the hippie said.

Burdened with the heavy weight of hospitality, Rahim Ullah Khan travelled all the way to Afghanistan to bring high quality hashish for his guest. When he returned, he found the Canadian saying prayers in the village mosque.

"I have converted to the truth, my honourable host," said the Canadian, whose converted name was so difficult that he spent his remaining life trying to learn its pronunciation, without success. "I no longer smoke hashish. I now drink buttermilk and breathe fresh air."

Mohammed Khan often recalled those days of freedom with tearful eyes. In those days, he could freely exercise his right to pee next to a drain or against a wall or facing a tree, and watch the hot stream of urine create rainbows. He would spend most of the time roaming the streets or playing indigenous sports: *gulli danda*, a primitive version of cricket; *pithu garam*, a ball game in which the pitcher targeted the buttocks of other players; *kokla chhapaki*, where boys sat in a circle and a player ran after another, hitting him with a knotted cloth on his back until the runner completed the round; *kabaddi*, a game of agility and strength in which one player attempted to outsmart the opponent team as it tried to stop him from getting back to his side.

There were other forms of entertainment too: shoving a wooden staff up a donkey's ass, tying a tin cup to a buffalo's tail, throwing rocks at dogs and chasing them as they ran yelping, climbing trees in search of kite's eggs, digging a hole in the ground and waiting for someone to trip and break a leg or twist an ankle. Sometimes he would tease a deranged man who roamed the streets, uttering obscene words, which many believed were expressions of a mystical power of ominous prediction. Frequently, the holy man would show his erect member to chador-clad women, who would lower their gaze in respect and pass by. The man's member was exceptionally long and its cleft looked like the eye of a reindeer. He disappeared after the earthquake. Mohammed Khan suspected that he fell in one of the several cracks carved upon the earth by the tremor, but Maulvi Sahib who led prayers in the village mosque, had another interpretation.

"He bared the root of all sins before us and warned us about the consequences of phallic indulgences," Maulvi Sahib said during Friday congregation. "Alas we did not listen, for what are we but deaf, dumb and imbecilic, living on a land condemned to disintegration. No Chief can save us now – be he Chief Justice, Chief Election Commissioner, Chief Martial Law Administrator, Chief Rival, or Chief Executive."

Like others, Mohammed Khan soon felt the full effects of the great earthquake on his life. His day now began with waiting for his turn to use the toilet, as his father Rahim Ullah Khan would sit stiff on the toilet seat and wrestle with his prostrate within the claustrophobic confines of the bathroom, built after the land became scarcer and meadows were encroached by trespassers from other lands. Mohammed Khan would stand outside the door, trying to hold his aching bowels that screamed for the freedom they no longer had. The ritual of eating was also performed inside because they were forced to cut the mulberry tree and sell its wood to finance the construction of a formal dining room equipped with a dining table, chairs, napkins, and cutlery. Mohammed Khan reminisced with nostalgia about the liberating experience of eating with hands and the superfluousness of a formal dining room. Things were equally bad outside. Streets were choked with undernourished children, and drains overflowed with putrefied sewage carrying the stench of modernisation. He could no longer talk to strangers because it was not safe anymore.

"Don't go near anyone who's not from your own faith, son," Rahim Ullah Khan warned him. "With so many unwanted children inhabiting the earth, you will soon see men with alien faiths come from strange lands to kidnap our children and sell them to the sheikhs of deserts."

He was right. Every week, strangers posing to be locals would come and offer sweets of dubious character to children to put them to sleep. They would stow the sleeping children in gunnysacks, take them across borders into waterless deserts and sell them to wealthy Arab Sheikhs for the price of a goat. In the deserts, where tents were pitched and wine was splashed on the bellybuttons of belly dancers, the children were tied to the bellies of racing camels and their bodies were thrown in dried wells when the race was over and the belly dancers had returned to Egypt.

Mohammed Khan hoped that some day things would get better.

Hopes were like Fazal Mahmood, the fast bowler who had won them the first ever cricket test match against England. The Oval Hero, they called him. Mohammed Khan had spotted Fazal's photograph on the inner side of the shopping bag made from a month-old newspaper, when he bought peanuts. Fazal beamed toward the camera, his smile contorted by the crinkles on the newspaper. Still, he was the hero. The Oval Hero. Emerging from the bag of peanuts. They no longer used newspaper-paper to make shopping bags; perhaps that was the reason they did not make heroes any more.

Hopes were also like Barkat Khan who arranged weekly mouse hunts. Barkat was a tall man with a white complexion and blonde moustache. He was the only person in the village who owned a mousetrap, which he claimed, had been handed down to him through several generations of mouse hunters. The mousetrap was a big ugly mother made of thin plates of rusty iron, but it must have appeared completely innocuous to the mice because they kept getting trapped. Maybe it had magical powers over those red-eyed rodents. Like a good villager, Mohammed Khan believed in magic.

Barkat Khan was a gracious man. He lent the trap to anyone who needed to clear his house of mice, but he imposed one condition: every mouse entrapped belonged to Barkat Khan and he alone would decide its fate. He made that decision every Friday after main prayer and it was always the same.

He would dress appropriately for the occasion: in white shalwar and cream-coloured kamiz, the shamla of his starched cotton turban standing erect above his head with the pride of an African cobra. His servant, Yaqoob the Cobbler carried the mousetrap with mice scrambling to climb its walls as if height promised deliverance – though they kept falling.

"Come on, boys," Barkat Khan said. "The hunt begins. We have to finish the game before Zuhr prayer."

Barkat Khan led the party to the jungle. They took slow, deliberate steps to the green and humid jungle where sand sparkled under the sun, beaming through the foliage, bringing their shadows closer to the ground. Mohammed Khan, like everyone else, didn't like the sun.

Yaqoob the Cobbler put down the trap on the sand and withdrew a couple of feet. The boys moved in and surrounded the cage. Mohammed Khan looked closely at the mice, moving his gaze from one to another. They looked alike.

Yaqoob the Cobbler kicked the cage and it went rolling along the ground. He kicked it again, like a footballer, which he was not. The trap fell into a puddle of water and the cheer of anticipation rose. Boys moved in closer but Yaqoob the Cobbler warned them away. "Get back," he commanded. "Let me supervise."

Boys moved back. The mice struggled inside muddy water that was now beginning to fill their lungs – if they had lungs. Even if they didn't, there was something inside them that did not like to be filled with water. Stomach? Mohammed Khan wondered. Must be stomach.

"Now," Barkat Khan commanded his servant who hurriedly pulled the mousetrap out of the puddle and held it high for everyone to see.

"Okay," Barkat Khan said. "Get your clubs and rocks ready, boys. Let the bloody intruders loose, Yaqooba."

Yaqoob the Cobbler, reduced to Yaqooba by the oral decree of Barkat Khan, opened the trap. The mice came out; their movements sluggish like a group of drunks on a Friday night.

The first out was a giant reddish-brown mouse who survived the first rock by a few inches. "Hold it," Barkat Khan ordered. "Don't be impatient. Let the intruding pig run a while."

Other mice, reduced to pigs in status by yet another oral decree of Barkat Khan, came out. The third in line was not so lucky. A rock, thrown by Yaqoob the Cobbler landed on it. Even though the blow didn't prove fatal, it slowed it down. Yaqooba removed his shoe from his foot and hit the mouse on the head. The soft, moist sand gave way under the combined weight of the mouse and Yaqooba's heavy leather shoe. For a few seconds, it seemed to be a part of the sand – a sculpture in the sand – but life returned. It struggled to revive itself, which made Yaqoob the Cobbler laugh out loud.

"Why, you son of a pig!" he said and slammed down his shoe again.

2

As for the women, you may take these as plunders for Yourselves.
  (Deuteronomy, 20:14)

You women who are so complacent, listen to me; you daughters who
  feel secure, hear what I have to say.
  (Isaiah, 32:9)

Men are protectors over women on account of that by means of which
  Allah has made some of them eminent above the others.
  (Al-Quran, 4:34)

Mohammed Khan returned home from the mouse hunt to find his mother crying. "Your sister will leave for her home on the fourteenth of next moon," she told him amidst sobs. "The date has been set."

"But this is her home."

"Not after she's married," his mother said.

"Why does she have to get married?"

"Because she's already twelve. It's time for her," mother said. "Now go take a bath, you smell like a dead rat. In the meantime, I'll get you some tea."

Mohammed Khan felt an inexplicable uneasiness, then everything stopped. Time went by without announcing its passing existence. The tea remained untouched, turning tepid and finally cold. The warm Valley sun arched over to the west, losing its brightness in the process as evening fell and finally gave way to night. Mohammed Khan continued to sit in the semi-darkness of his room until he heard his sister calling him for supper. He came out and hugged her so tightly that she yelled in pain. Mohammed Khan laughed uncontrollably and tears spilled from his eyes.

"Ha, ha, ha. He's a girl, he's a girl," his sister squeaked. "Mohammed Khan cries like a girl."

"Hold your tongue, girl," mother admonished her. "Don't you be calling my son a girl. He followed seven of the likes of you, and may his offspring be all male. May his back remain erect and his shoulders unburdened."

Mohammed Khan had followed seven sisters. The eldest six were married and lived in lands about which he knew little. They never visited their parents and it did not occur to him to ask why they had forgotten the home that once was theirs. But those were the days of acceptance: it would be some years before questions would start uncoiling.

The marriage preparations gained momentum when the new moon appeared on the horizon. Mother made seventy sets of bridal dresses laced with golden threads, ten sets of gold bangles weighing three tolas each, thirty rings studded with precious stones, dangling earrings supported with thick gold chains, glittering teekas and jhoomer, ruby-studded nose-pins, and gold necklaces so heavy that when the bride-to-be tried them on her neck flexed under their weight and nearly snapped.

As the wedding date drew close, Mohammed Khan began to look at his sister from the perspective he'd reserved exclusively for a young girl who had once lived in his neighbourhood. Mohammed Khan would climb up to the roof and secretly watch her bathing under a hand pump, marvelling at her young breasts that looked like unripe mangoes – until one day he heard that she had been married to a man living in the land of golden people; and was gone. For several days, he would go to the roof and see her shadow, but time eventually erased all shadows. Now he longed to see her bathing under the same hand pump, before another man came and took her away to a place where no one yet wrote letters.

The fateful day eventually dawned. The marriage procession arrived before noon on a cold February morning when chill had attacked the village with a vengeance, but everyone in the baraat – the marriage procession – was oblivious to it in the heat of bashful emotions. The cavalcade was about half a mile long, passing through streets soiled with animal dung and human spit. There was a shroud of stink around the moving cortège and through the reeking haze, Mohammed Khan watched the white horse without a groom gracing its back. He presumed that his impending brother-in-law didn't know how to ride.

The horse's face was covered with garlands of roses and jasmine. Around its neck were more garlands of brand-new rupee notes. Its body was covered with a shiny cloth and a sixteen-year old boy aching to be a man held its reins, leading it towards tents erected in the open fields. Outside the tents, where Rahim Ullah Khan and son waited for the baraat, a local music troupe played shehnai and dhol. A group of young men holding naked swords performed khattak dance to the beat of the dhol while others, not able to muster enough courage to dance in front of the elders, only danced their heads with the rhythm.

Mohammed Khan watched the scene with mixed emotions, trying to empathise with his father amidst the pain of losing his sister to a man who would play with her breasts in the darkness of nights and the haze of dawns. He felt a sense of rage and humiliation, but a look at Rahim Ullah Khan's face made him falter. Although only nine years old, he understood that daughters were beloved guests in their father's house. They were guarded as an alienable treasure belonging to someone who would arrive one day and take them away. Until that moment, parents had to protect their chastity, teach them the finer points of modesty, and train them in the art of domestic chores. The marriage day was a critical test for the father – simultaneously dreaded and welcomed; and for the bride – a painful severance from her familiar environment and a giant step towards a fearfully exciting integration into a new family.

A sound, perhaps wind striking against the tent, made Mohammed Khan look up. In one glance he saw written on his father's face the grief of losing his beloved guest and the satisfaction of successfully carrying out his paternal duty. He was a sad father and a proud man.

The person Mohammed Khan suspected to be the groom was a middle-aged man with a red beard and a potbelly that jitterbugged as he walked. The priest hired to solemnise the marriage was the legendary Maulana Khamosh: the man without a tongue. Legend had it that he had dared to speak the word of truth before a dictator, who ordered that his tongue be cut out and cooked for dinner. A converse version of the legend claimed that Maulana was tempted into the sin of fellatio and his tongue was yanked out of his throat as the punishment decreed by the one to whom he claimed proximity.

Maulana Khamosh solemnised the marriage by mouthing the words from the Holy Book. The audience, now having grown double its original size, listened in reverential silence – their heads bowed in respect for the divine words they could not hear. A large meal followed the nikah ceremony, with over two thousand jaws munching on oily rice and roasted meat. When the food was over, an elder rose from his seat and cleared his throat.

"Rahim Ullah Khan," the elder said in a voice surprisingly loud for his age. "You have given us a befitting lunch on your daughter's wedding. We affirm that it was indeed a great feast and the marriage arrangements are hereby declared successful."

Rahim Ullah Khan hung his head in polite acceptance.

Finally the palanquin carrying the young daughter left for the groom's house. Mohammed Khan watched his sister leaving as he cried alongside his father. Mother fainted with grief, and as if on cue, the leader of the musical troupe that had so far been playing happy songs, brought the tip of the shehnai to his mouth to play the plaintive tune of a popular wedding song they had played on countless occasions to heighten the moment.

> *"Sweet Daddy, I'm leaving my home – my sanctuary;*
> *Four carriers have decorated my palanquin,*
> *Taking me away from my loved ones and from those*
> *I don't know.*
> *Sweet Daddy, I'm leaving my home – my sanctuary."*

When night fell, Mohammed Khan finally blurted out what had been swelling in his chest since afternoon. "I don't like my brother-in-law. He has a big belly and an ugly face."

Rahim Ullah Khan turned his head and looked surprised. "Who are you talking about, my son?"

"The man with the red beard and big belly."

"God forgive you, Mohammed Khan, for that was Maulana Laj Pal. He's not the groom."

"Really? I thought he was my brother-in-law," Mohammed Khan said with renewed hope in his sister's future.

Rahim Ullah Khan looked the other way as mother started to sob and then cry.

"Shut up, wife," Rahim Ullah Khan said angrily. He touched Mohammed Khan on the shoulder and nodded with sincere sadness. "Your sister was not married to a man, my son," he said softly. "She's married to the Book of Customs."

A lot of things disintegrated inside Mohammed Khan. He lost confidence in himself, in his beliefs, in his father, his mother and a book he'd never read.

"When three daughters were born to me in a row," Rahim Ullah Khan continued, "I made a promise to God that I'd marry them to the Book of Customs if he gave me a son. I married my six daughters to the Book before God heard my prayers and blessed me with a son. I'm a lucky man."

He smiled confidently. "Your sisters have taken holy vows to the holiest of the holy books. They live in the convent of age-old Customs. They are happy. My heart tells me."

Mohammed Khan found it difficult to search for his voice in the stillness of betrayal. "The man with the big belly plays with their breasts," he screamed. "He's going to play with Seema sister's breasts too."

Rahim Ullah Khan's face turned the colour of his untainted Aryan blood and he slapped his son with the force of convictions held for centuries. "How dare you speak like that about Maulana Laj Pal? He's the most pious man alive. Go and ask forgiveness of God for I don't want to colour my hands with the blood of an apostate son. May God and Maulana forgive you for your blasphemy."

Maulana Laj Pal finished his isha prayer and cried before God. Finally satisfied that God had heard his cries and exonerated him of all sins committed by him so far, he wiped his face and left the room in search of fresh sins. Marching along a long verandah of desires, feeling his inner purity that needed tainting, he entered the chamber of fulfilment where a dentist's chair stood in the middle. Maulana reclined on his back and closed his eyes.

Four young girls wearing nothing but green veils entered into his privacy and gently undressed him. They combed the hair growing on his chest and on his thighs, shaved his greying pubic hair, pruned his beard, and dyed his locks black. Then they soaped his face, his chest and his genitals, washed them with mineral water, dressed him in a green shalwar suit and left.

For a long time, Maulana lay on the chair, relishing the memories of soft hands on his body. Eventually, he got up and retrieved a tablet of Viagra from the side pocket of his shirt. He gulped it down with Seven Up and marched towards the bridal chamber.

He entered the chamber, looking forward to all the erotic elements of meeting a stranger at his mercy – lifting the veil to see a fresh face, relishing her shy resistance, and finally consuming the gift of virginity.

He moved closer to the ornamental bed made of rounded wood and coloured in varying tones of virginal blood. He felt the bride shrinking within herself with every step he took. He stopped: she stopped shrinking. He took another step: she shrank further into her shyness. Maulana Laj Pal felt his synthetic erection, and smiled.

The room was lit by a lantern, turning everything pale, including the painted face of the bride. Maulana moved deliberately, feeling the pleasure of anticipation erupting from his loins and spreading in all directions: stomach, heart, arms, head, eyes and hair that stood like thorns on his bearish body. He could barely control himself, the pleasure threatening to be over even before it had started. In the flickering light of the lantern, he saw the phantom of the forbidden triangle and struggled to embrace nudity. "Oh God, oh God," he pleaded under his breath as he tried to control himself, and was soaked with the shame of premature ejaculation.

3

Read in the name of thy Lord who created,
  Created man from a clot of blood
  Read: for thy Lord is the most Bounteous,
  He Who has taught the use of pen;
  He taught man what he did not know
  Nay, but verily man transgresses.
  (First revelation made to Prophet Muhammad, Pbuh;
  Al-Quran, 96: 1-6)

And the Lord God commanded the man, saying, of every tree of the garden thou mayest freely eat but of the tree of knowledge of good and evil.
(Genesis, 2: 16-17)

Mohammed Khan's mother cried for her daughter for forty days. Finally things settled back to an uneasy normality.

Satisfied that he had fulfilled the last of his obligations to God and to his daughters, Rahim Ullah Khan realised it was time to send his son to the local mosque for textual reading of the Holy Book. "I've made arrangements for your education, my son," he proudly informed Mohammed Khan. "As from tomorrow, you'll be going to Maulvi Sahib for knowledge."

Maulvi Sahib was a short, dark man with an enormous mole on his upper lip. He searched his new student without interest and pulled at his earlobe. "Know and accept in your heart that I am the possessor of knowledge," he said. "You, my pupil, can hope to acquire a part thereof if you demonstrate obedience and improve your memory. The intrinsic requirement of being a good pupil is docility. Do you understand?"

Mohammed Khan nodded.

"Don't move your head like a washerman's donkey," Maulvi Sahib snapped. "Say Jee Maulvi Sahib."

"Jee Maulvi Sahib."

"You will learn only if you earn my favour, do you understand?"

"Jee Maulvi Sahib."

"Now cross your legs, place the Holy Book on your knees, and open it. We'll start with the first line."

"Jee Maulvi Sahib."

Ten months later, Mohammed Khan finished his maiden reading of the Book.

"Maulvi Sahib?" Mohammed Khan said.

"What is it, pupil?"

"Can you teach me the meaning of the Holy Book?"

"You've already finished reading it. What else do you want?"

"I want to read its translation. I want to attain knowledge of good and evil."

Maulvi Sahib slapped him hard on the face and Mohammed Khan fell on his back. "Don't be blasphemous, boy," Maulvi Sahib roared. "How do you expect to attain knowledge of good and evil through your tiny mind?"

He slapped him again and brought his index finger close to Mohammed Khan's face until he saw two of them. "Remember the basic rule of learning, pupil," he said sternly. "You will do what I want, understand? You've read the Book in the language that God speaks. All other languages are incomplete and impure. Your tiny mind, polluted by generations of greed for acquisition of other people's land, is not capable of understanding the word of God. If you try to comprehend it without His and my blessing, you will go astray. Now stop talking, and get back to recitation. You have to finish a second reading of the Holy Book."

Gradually Mohammed Khan learnt that reciting each word of the Holy Book would provide him with ten units of sawab, the reward from God that would enable him to walk the bridge over infernal fire. He had heard that the bridge would be finer than a hair and sharper than a sword, and only those who had earned enough sawab in life would be able to cross it in the after-life to enter paradise. He finished the second reading and decided to repeat his request to Maulvi Sahib.

"When will I be ready to comprehend God's message, Maulvi Sahib?" he asked.

"When He wills – which may be never, so in the meantime, I want you to start reading a very important book. It's called *Ornaments from Paradise*. The book contains the complete code of conduct of our religion. You will certainly get a place in Paradise if you strictly adhere to the doctrine given here."

The book was about a thousand pages long, discussing topics like prayer, fasting, religious practices, basics of correct belief, issues relating to marriage, dowry and divorce, menstruation, puberty and ablution, manners of social interaction, recipes for herbal medicines, menus for the distillation of beverages, and instruction about dyeing clothes. The first chapter set out the conditions under which a person must cleanse himself.

"A Believer must perform ablution," the Book said, "if he discharges faeces or urine, or farts either through his arse or through his penis, as can happen under certain medical conditions. (Mohammed Khan was not aware of any such condition). If an earthworm, nematode, a tapeworm or gangrene oozes out of the asshole, ablution becomes obligatory. However, if the worm or gangrene comes out of a wound, or a piece of flesh is torn away from the gangrene, provided no blood flows, ablution is not necessary. If a person pokes his finger in his nose, and blood sticks to his finger, ablution is not required provided the quantity of blood was such that it did not flow down the finger... If a person regurgitates, and his mouth is not filled with vomit, he need not wash himself, otherwise ablution becomes obligatory...."

Mohammed Khan ran to the bathroom and vomited.

On a hot day when Maulvi Sahib had gone to the village of his in-laws to convince his estranged wife to come back, Mohammed Khan secretly went through his books. On the top shelf of the closet, he found three copies of the Holy Book, one of which was translated in a language imposed on the locals by those who had migrated from other places. As he brought the Holy Book close to his face to kiss it, he noticed a bookmark inserted in it. Breathing hard, feeling guilty that he was attempting to read the word of God against all warnings of Maulvi Sahib, he opened the page and read:

> *"When the sun is overthrown,*
> *And when the stars fall,*
> *And when the hills are moved,*
> *And when the camels big with young are abandoned,*

And when the wild beasts are herded together,
And when the seas rise,
And when souls are reunited,
And when the girl-child that was buried alive is asked,
For what sin she was slain,
And when the pages are laid open,
And when the sky is torn away,
And when hell is lighted,
And when the paradise is brought nigh,
Then every soul will know what it prepared for itself.
Oh, but I call to witness the planets,
The planets that rise and set,
And the night when it closeth
And the morning when it softly breathes
That this is in truth the word of an honoured messenger,
Mighty, established in the presence of the Lord of the Throne,
One to be obeyed, and worthy of trust;
For this fellow man of yours is not mad…
Nor is his message the word of any Satanic force…"

That night Mohammed Khan did not return home. Rahim Ullah Khan searched for him throughout the village and in the neighbouring villages, but it seemed as if the earth had sucked him inside its chasms.

4

And when the thousand years are expired, Satan shall be loosed out of his prison, and shall go out to deceive the nations which are in the four quarters of the earth, Gog and Magog, to gather them together to battle.
(Revelation, 22: 7-8)

Until he reached a valley between two walls and found a people beyond the two walls. The people said: O Zul-Qarnain, surely, Gog and Magog are doers of evil in the land. We shall pay thee a tax if you build a wall between them and us. And Gog and Magog were not able to scale the wall, neither were they able to dig through it.
(Al-Quran, 18: 93-97)

Until when Gog and Magog are let loose and they come spreading down from every height.
(Al-Quran, 21: 96)

While Rahim Ullah Khan searched for the lost son, the son walked with unmeasured steps toward the uncertainty in his heart. When he reached it, he was alone. Loneliness followed him like a frisky pet, frolicking at his tired feet. Behind him was a beige trail of shattered beliefs. The trail led back to nowhere. All traces of him were disappearing into the wintry crevasses of an earth grown old.

His arrival went unnoticed. He was clad in obscurity, a boy without conviction, betrayed by those who held power over what could and could not be learnt. His heart was fragrant with the words of truth he had secretly read, yet his brain was sick with the rotting interpretations put forth by Maulvi Sahib.

Morning was still struggling with a hangover when Mohammed Khan arrived at the place of his arrival. Facing him was a seventy foot high wall made with rough hands. It rose above the brittle earth to encircle the existence of whatever lay inside it. Mohammed Khan placed his cheek against its nodulous surface and found it quivering under his touch. He snuggled his nose deep into its warm crevices and smelt the sweet aroma of fresh milk. In a state of exploratory passion, he brushed his eager tongue along the chalky clay and tasted its secretions.

For a long time, he clung to the wall, sniffing it like a passionate mongrel, feeling its warmth, relishing its juices. Suddenly the wall stopped lactating. It went cold and unresponsive.

Mohammed Khan withdrew in horror.

For hours, he circled around it, looking for an entrance. He yelled for attention but only heard silence. He banged his fists upon the coarse surface but the wall remained frigid. He kissed it with a passion fuelled by the fire of suppression and ended up tasting his own blood. He gave up. "You're the Eternal Wall," he finally said in submission. "Deaf, dumb and blind."

He withdrew from the wall and sat upon the steps of what had once been an ancient coliseum. The steps were brittle, ravaged by fixed games of predicted outcomes. He remained sitting there until evening fell and weariness caught up with him. He lay down under a sky blistered with stars, waiting for things programmed to happen.

Night was quiet: only his thoughts screamed out. They were discordant, shapeless thoughts, nagging like the mosquitoes he kept flattening against his face and arms. He wanted to be a part of the wall and yet remain himself without losing his alterity – but there was no reassurance of it, nor any promise of reassurance. The wall was confusing his cognitive balance. He was teetering towards a state of conceptual vertigo.

Sometimes during the night, he went to sleep and sometimes during the same or some other night, a scratching sound emanating from the direction of the wall awoke him. He opened his eyes and tried to penetrate the blurriness of his senses. There was darkness all around him. Stars had moved to some other part of the cosmos where they were needed more productively. He tried to gather his limbs and thoughts, succeeding only partially.

Between him and the wall was darkness hiding behind more darkness. There were layers and layers of murk that slowly disappeared as the scratching sound blew them away. Mohammed Khan moved cautiously, tripping over unknown obstacles. Finally his fingers brushed against something that felt like the wall, though he could not be sure in his present state of sensory blindness.

The touch was magical. The spot he touched began to radiate the lustrous glow of gold. The sound grew louder as well, except that it was not a scratching sound as he had initially misconstrued. It was the slurping echo of something licking the wall.

Suddenly, he started to understand. "Gog and Magog," he whispered to himself in a state of paralysing horror. "The world is coming to an end."

He had learnt about Gog and Magog from Maulvi Sahib. "God sent Alexander the Great to confine them behind a wall of molten brass so the world could be saved from their evil," Maulvi Sahib had taught him. "Since then, they lick the wall with their tongues from dusk until dawn. When it's time for the world to end, they will burst through the wall and destroy everything."

Mohammed Khan stared at the wall in horror. It was not long before it was scraped all the way down to its last layer. It stood there trembling, more diaphanous than the hymenal membrane of a twelve year old virgin, and smelling of fresh onions. In a state of rising appetite, Mohammed Khan reached across his yearning to witness a million female tongues licking furiously at the thinning film. They were women of all ages and eras, each with golden hair, blue eyes, slender waists, long legs, smooth skins, and efficient tongues.

He cried out in joy as he saw among them his sister, and six other faces that seemed familiar despite absence of memories. He ran to the wall, calling the names of his sisters. By now the sun was beginning to show its presence in the East. Mohammed Khan clenched his fists, urging his seven sisters and their companions to hurry, with his cheers and curses, afraid that the light of an unwanted sun might defeat their attempts to attain freedom. The women continued to work with remarkable discipline, impervious to dripping blood and pouring saliva. Suddenly they stopped.

Mohammed Khan screamed in horror. "What are you doing, stupid women? No, no! Don't stop. You're already there. Just another lick."

The tongues started to move back inside battered mouths. "It's only as thick as an onion's skin," the women said in a chorus. "We must rest and come back later to finish the job."

"No, no, you stupid creatures," Mohammed Khan yelled. "Finish the work now."

His voice failed to penetrate the barrier. The women turned and went away.

In a fit of rage, Mohammed Khan attacked the clay membrane with banging fists and a lolling tongue. His fists bled from cuts and abrasions. His mouth was filled with blood and mud and straw, but the wall stood defiant. As the sun arched along its pre-defined path, the wall started to regenerate back into its thick stoniness. Mohammed Khan banged his head against it and cried in despair.

Voices rushed toward him. "There he is," he heard someone say. Moments later, his father embraced him against a trembling chest resonating with the beat of a scared heart. Mohammed Khan looked up and saw his father Rahim Ullah Khan's tear-stained face. He looked around and found himself sitting under the shade of the tree of eternity in his backyard.

"The tree saved you, my son," Rahim Ullah Khan whispered in his ear. "Your great-grandfather is with you. May his soul guide you and protect you from the dangers of life."

Maulvi Sahib appeared from behind his father, a metaphysical smile on his face. He kissed Mohammed Khan on the cheek and whispered in his ear, "Forget about the tree, pupil. Just remember that as long as women remain confined within the four walls of our homes, the world will not end."

5

And we said, "O man! Dwell thou and thy wife in this garden but go not near this tree lest you be unjust."
(Al-Quran, 2:35)

The Satan said: "O man! Shall I point thee to the imperishable tree and a kingdom that never fades?" Then both of them ate of it, therefore their evils became apparent to them.
(Al-Quran, 20:120-121)

Samiree cast their ornaments and produced a corporeal calf. And he said: this is your god and the god of Moses but he hath forgotten.
(Al-Quran, 20: 88)

The miracle rejuvenated people's declining faith in the tree and in Mohammed Khan's great grandfather. Overnight, his illustrious ancestor became a legend, like the python, living on the tree of question.

But there were still those who did not believe in the python or the tree. "It is just a story which people without true knowledge heard from their parents and grandparents, and from minstrels who would sell history for a coin," Maulvi Sahib said with scriptural conviction. "They spread this tale to frighten the young and keep the tree where it is. The tree is just a mark, a creation of God, a wedge between our village and what lies beyond. Trees are only there to give us wood and protect us from summer heat. They are gifts and signs of things believable and unbelievable."

Many shared his opinion. In the evening gatherings at the hujra, men of faith and men of doubt debated the existence of things believable and unbelievable, heard and seen, miraculous and factual. There were those who debated Satanic Verses and those who recited Divine Verses. It was all heard and registered by those upon their right and those upon their left. Topchi Kaka sat on the right and addressed both sides.

"If I ever met him," Topchi said to his audience, "I'd embrace him until his heart would hear my heartbeat and then I'd say to him, 'Brother Salman! Embrace the truth and renounce the Verses you fabricated.' I'd implore him, beg him, but if he didn't retract, I'd chop off his head and claim my reward."

"But he is an enemy of the truth, Kaka," said Alam the Blacksmith, a man with fading optimism in the truth. "If you let your chest touch his, he will send contagions of disbelief into your heart, and you'll be condemned to eternal quarantine for at least ten years."

"My heart is made of molten brass, my child," Topchi said with pride. "It is protected from evil, just as a face inside a veil is protected from shame, and you and I are protected from those living beyond the wall."

Topchi was seventy years old. He had served as a gunner on a battleship during the Great War. Popularly nicknamed Topchi Kaka – Uncle Gunner – by villagers, he had many a story to tell about the exotic lands he had visited and the women with whom he had copulated. The stories of Topchi's sexual exploits not only established his machismo credentials, they also became a source of shared pride for his audience that one of their own had conquered the women of their masters.

The village elders showed their disapproval of Topchi Kaka's erotic details. They knew of the inherently dangerous nature of human sexuality and its infinite potential to cause moral degradation. A dispassionate public discourse on sex and women was a taboo, though in extreme situations, sex was used either as a part of the abusive vocabulary between adversaries, or as a humourous indicator of intimacy between friends. The elders did not fit in either category and tended to avoid Topchi's company. Some would get up and leave when Topchi Kaka arrived in the hujra.

Topchi was also among those who did not believe in the python or the tree. He would piss on its trunk to show that it held no magical powers.

"Python? What python?" Topchi demanded contemptuously. "There is no python. It's only a distorted legend described in a superseded book."

"It's real, Kaka," someone from the audience said. "It coils around you and squeezes the life out of you."

"No ordinary python can do that, my child. It's the job of a golden python: the mem," Topchi responded. "Let me tell those who are willing to listen about the real python. Be informed that I have been burnt by the golden flames."

Topchi was a magician. With one sweep of his veined hand, he could collect disparate ornaments of their desires and create a golden woman that looked and sounded real. Her voice was the transcendent sound of a nightingale with the haunting quality of a flute playing from the far side of the jungle running parallel to the village.

"A golden woman is the most beauteous and lustful creature on earth," Topchi would tell his audience, waving to the golden curves of his creation.

No one doubted him. They had savoured the distant sight of gold-skinned mems, seen parts of their sensuous bodies with surreptitious glances, smelt their fragrance, scenting the air as they passed like queens through bazaars and railway platforms and threatened their manliness by their aggressive femininity and lustful gait. They were inaccessible – fairies from a distant land who should have been in the tents, untouched by man or jinn before the deserving made the final choice.

"How would it feel to touch a mem?" Alam the Blacksmith wanted to know. "Imagine touching that ivory skin."

"I have touched a golden woman," Topchi Kaka said with the pride of a man of dust and bone and negligible military skills. "I have kissed her too. I am among you who drank of saltish honey."

The odour of jealousy hanging in the air thickened. "This can't be true," Yaqoob the Cobbler said sceptically. "They won't let a subaltern touch them."

"They're made of gold and live in the land of gold with men of gold, my child," Topchi said. "I touched their men and was turned into gold. Did I tell you that I saw a golden triangle too? She laid it bare before me, begging me for zina."

"Intercourse?" Alam the Blacksmith repeated incredulously with a mouth full of craving saliva. "Tell us about it, Kaka! I've heard they have three breasts."

"Three?" Yaqoob the Cobbler objected. "How is it possible? Golden folk lived in an age when mankind didn't know how to count."

"They did," Topchi said. "I taught them how to count."

"That's bullshit, Kaka," said Alam the Blacksmith. "If you taught them the wisdom of our ancestors who discovered counting when Europe was in darkness, how come you're still alive? Why didn't they kill you? Why didn't they build your shrine to revere you as a saint for learning and prosperity?"

"Because I developed a Pythagorean fascination for the number six, my child. Those people invented more digits than I wanted to learn and it saved my life."

"Still a mem can't have three breasts," Yaqoob the Cobbler objected again.

"Of course they do," Alam the Blacksmith said. "Didn't you hear the famous couplet about mems?" He placed one hand against his left ear and was about to recite it when Maulvi Sahib started calling the faithful to prayer through the mosque loudspeaker.

Everyone laughed, felt ashamed and prayed for forgiveness before dispersing for the isha prayer. Mohammed Khan felt intrigued. There was a vibrant sensation coiling in his loins. It was time to leave and be embraced by the truth. He heard Maulvi Sahib's call and walked toward the tree, weighing his faith in his mother, in his mother's mother and in all those whose blood flooded his veins.

The tree looked uncannily like Barkat Khan's mousetrap. No tree ever looked like a mousetrap – but this one did. Its branches were so close to the ground it virtually had no trunk. The branches seemed to lift from the earth and curve inward, until they clasped each other like human ribs.

Mohammed Khan hugged his family tree: the tree of question. He clung to it involuntarily, sighing and panting, holding on longer than he expected, loosening and tightening the grip as he penetrated deep into the folds of the wooden primordiality, spent and exhausted. He was not a man among men, not a woman among women. His soul was discharged, sensations emptied – in a numb bliss, breathing his last. The embrace left marks of the ancient rings of the tree trunk on his chest and arms. The tree floated and swayed in the wind.

It was at this moment – though not for the first time, but certainly not for many centuries – that the python emerged from the depths of the tree roots and slowly coiled around his body, moving from below. It pushed him forward, squeezed him and blew emeralds and onyx into him. Mohammed Khan surrendered helplessly, floating on primal waters. His body liquefied and he breathed his last, snoring the snore of his great grandfather who was distinguished for snoring before migrating to the valley of acceptance.

"You're snoring," his mother said. "No one has snored in this house since your ancestors left the mountains." She took a closer look at the marks on his chest and arms, and her eyes widened. "What are these marks on your body?" she demanded. "Did that lowly Maulvi beat you? How dare he? He eats from our kitchen, lives in our hujra and look what he has done to my son, Rahim Ullah Khan?"

"Mohammed Khan is not doing well in studies," her husband said by way of explanation. "I told Maulvi Sahib to give him proper attention."

The marks became more visible by noon. Maulvi Sahib was nearly evicted from the mosque for inflicting more than necessary corporal punishment upon Mohammed Khan. The local hakim whose medicine was known to work magic, failed to dim the marks. They gradually turned into hieroglyphics which only Mohammed Khan could read.

6

*And anyone who has sexual relations with an animal must be
put to death.
(Exodus, 22:19)*

*If a man entices a maid that is not betrothed, he shall surely
endow her to be his wife.
(Exodus, 22:16)*

*Every sin that a man commits is outside his body, but he who
commits fornication, sins against his own body.
(Corinthians, 6:18)*

Eureka!

Mohammed Khan read himself under the cool shade of the tree through long and lonely summer afternoons when sparrows, kites, crows and vultures would disappear inside their strawy nests to fool the lashing sun. For hours that sometimes seemed to stretch into years, Mohammed Khan ran his fingers all over his skin, listening to the fables and stories hidden beneath the somatic emblems etched on him. His fingertips became his eyes and senses, open to each hieroglyph and its countless interpretations.

In the evening gatherings at the hujra, Topchi continued to dazzle everyone with his narratives. Mohammed Khan secretly suspected that Topchi was a liar but could not bring himself to face his suspicion. Topchi helped him reach across.

Topchi had a premeditated opinion on every subject under the sun and beyond, ranging from economic management, cosmology, nuclear physics, politics and sexology to firearms and military strategy. While others gave their ideas on a topic, Topchi would tell the related story with a rare gift of narration. Topchi existed in his narratives. He was a narrative written in the past and incessantly interpreted in the present. No one saw him before or after his verbal performance.

Topchi knew what had happened in the world before it reached *now*, and had a fairly good idea of where *then* was located. He had witnessed the rise and fall of great and tiny empires. He had seen the atrocities committed during the War of Cracks, and knew every tiny detail of the Great Civil War of Silence that was to follow many years later between the followers and detractors of Mohammed Khan. He had on his fingertips the devastating details of the Great Flood that would nearly submerge the Valley. He knew about Ram Babu and his library though he was reluctant to divulge the secret of his one thousand missing books. He could list every major scientific breakthrough since the beginning of the beginning, and had inside knowledge of the humble circumstances that led to great inventions. It was through the story of one such invention that he sent Mohammed Khan to the next stage of evolution: adulthood.

On a hot afternoon – said Topchi – when the sun had descended to the Valley, a young boy discovered an unrecognisably mutilated corpse lying in the ditch with a carrot thrust in its mouth. The complete absence of life, accentuated by the advanced stage of *rigor mortis*, made the boy aware of his own existence and he laughed uncontrollably.

The corpse was several days old and it reminded everyone of someone they knew but could not recall. "I saw this man feeding carrots to his donkey," the boy who discovered the corpse told those who failed to discover it. "Then he took off his trousers, went behind the donkey and did something shameful. The donkey kicked him in the stomach and he fell down. The donkey turned around and inserted a carrot in the dying man's mouth."

He couldn't tell them exactly when it happened but he knew the name of the dead man. "It was Ditta, the washerman, and it was his donkey that killed him," he informed them with puerile conviction. Everyone laughed and rebuked him for such a lewd lie because they knew that Ditta's donkey did not like carrots.

The villagers' own investigation revealed little so they executed the donkey and decided to stage demonstrations against drycleaners whom they suspected of having murdered the washerman. When the violence on the streets threatened to get out of hand, the Superintendent of Police, Major

Charles Devereux arrived on the scene. He rode a black horse. His red face was aflame like the hot July sun in its full fury. His body was big and strong and chiselled like mountains.

Major Charles Devereux got down from the horse and stoically walked over to the dead man who waited in the ditch for his arrival. He saw the corpse with a long red object thrust in his mouth and his racial dilemma was immediately solved.

Major Charles Devereux went on to invent oral sex.

Before Major Devereux's times, there was vaginal sex and anal sex. The Major performed occasional vaginal sex on his wife who would dutifully pretend to enjoy it even if she had a headache. His native batman performed anal sex on him: revengefully but with diligence. It was the Major's orders.

Major Charles Devereux was not satisfied with either activity. He was more interested in the native women but a concern for spermatozoic purity kept deterring him from allowing the racial fluids to mingle. He was an old fashioned man determined to keep the liquid secret of power to himself. In this way he felt himself the fittest for the job at hand.

Major Devereux was a limitless man. He stood seven feet three inches, weighed three hundred pounds, and had fists the size of an Afghan melon. The officers of his artillery unit originally stationed at Bombay called him Big Paw Charles. His wife called him Little Dick Charles. He wanted to know what other women would call him.

Major Charles Devereux returned from the crime scene with a Newtonian sense of purpose. He sent his wife to Rawalpindi, dismissed all servants for the day save his housecleaner who was a dark young woman in her early twenties. He called her to his chamber, made her clean the room and the attached toilet, and finally displayed his best-kept secret to her. "Pretend it's a lollipop," he ordered her with the vigour of a fatigued army man.

The cleaner was dumbfounded. The broom fell from her trembling hands. Her eyes eclipsed with shame and horror.

"What?" she asked apprehensively. "Sahib Jee, it is an impure thing and my mouth is pure. With my tongue I utter the names of everything that has been named. If I obey your command, the names will be defiled and I'll fall sick. The natural refuge of this white devil is in the impure cleft specifically designed for it at lower levels. When this impure lump of flesh finds its natural refuge, it will beget more lumps and grow in strength. It will then earn a name for itself."

Major Devereux felt pity for the housecleaner. She had lost the golden opportunity of drinking from a historical fountain whose archaeological authenticity had been confirmed by a well-preserved family tree. According to it, Major Devereux's great-grandmother had had a romantic encounter with a prisoner at St. Helena when she came to clean his jail cell. She gave birth to a daughter who she swore was the progeny of the man in the jail cell whose name she didn't know, but whom subsequent research identified as Napoleon Bonaparte.

Major Devereux secretly hoped that like his illustrious great-grandfather, he would one day overthrow the King and assume his position. With that ambition in mind, he chose his wife carefully, a woman who fitted his ideal of a queen. He trained her to burp Madam Rochas and fart Chanel No. 5, and managed an assignment in the Royal Palace so he could watch the Queen's mannerisms in great detail. At night, he would note important points of royal punctilio in his notebook and hide it inside his rectum so no one, not even a Prussian spy, could find it.

Unfortunately, Major Charles Devereux, during a spell of diarrhoea that lasted nineteen days and left him nearly dead, misplaced his notebook. After he recovered he started behaving like a captain. At other times he acted like a king – though there were lonely moments when he was both the king and the queen. The army psychoanalyst recommended him for the Victoria Cross, for defeating death. In the end it wasn't awarded to him, but the recommendation itself went a long way to him regaining his natural form. He became impeccably Anglo-Saxon, walking with an extruding chest and a stooped back.

The housecleaner's refusal made his soul restless. Major Devereux felt guilty. In the process he became more curious about native women and their mouths. He next approached his barber's daughter, and repeated the order refused by the housecleaner.

The barber's daughter cupped him in her hands, kissed him, rubbed him gently on her eyes and started caressing him so reverently that the Major lost all steam.

By now the Major was mad and desperate. "These women, they are idiots. Their intellect resides in their bloody heels," he yelled. His voice reverberated momentarily through the house, before escaping through a cracked ventilator like a wounded bird in search of water. "They don't know anything about great ideas and their role in history. They are ignorant of genealogies, ancestries, the secrets of power, the decorum of status, and the genetic implications of the unity of opposites. They have no bloody souls."

He dismissed the barber from his service, fired the house-cleaner and with a mind finally at peace, thought about other options. That evening, he visited Kasai Galli, the red light district in Rawalpindi.

The Naika, a retired prostitute who trained young whores and managed the whorehouse, was a woman in her early sixties. She welcomed Major Charles Devereux with a bow and showed him in. The dim sound of music and the ankle bells of the dancing girls in some other room titillated his sensations of the impending encounter. The Naika entertained Major Devereux with paan and beeri before she asked him with smiling eyes: "What has brought the Sahib here to this humblest of places?"

"I want to meet a good, intelligent girl," the Major replied. "Good and intelligent," he emphasised.

The Naika clapped her hands and four hundred young maidens appeared, each prettier than the other. They passed in front of the Major, saluting him by touching their foreheads with the tips of their fingers, smiling shyly with downcast eyes. The Major signaled to the one he supposed was good and intelligent, and went inside the room with her.

"I'm an inventor," he told her. "I invented fellatio so that my racial purity can remain intact. I'm here to let you benefit from my invention."

The girl smiled. She amorously undressed the Major and then herself. She kissed him from the top of his head all the way down to his toenails, giving delicate attention to his hair, forehead, eyes, cheeks, chest, navel, and toes. She touched Major Charles Devereux where he badly wanted to be touched and surrounded him with her lips. Major Charles Devereux, even in that state of raw ecstasy, had the good sense to give up his plan to patent his invention because the young tawaif had obviously been there before him.

The tawaif kissed her way back to his mouth while her fingers ran up and down his spinal column. The Major was helplessly ecstatic. He was immensely impatient to go beyond all boundaries but did not know how to wrest the initiative from her. The girl brought his head close to her navel and the Major's tongue was nearly sucked in from its root. The Major farted silently and fainted.

Only two things lurked in the Major's consciousness about the visit: he had lost his wallet and had problems getting a full erection after that.

For several days, Major Devereux searched for a cure to his latter predicament. He finally found it in the words of a quack who stood under a tree, which he claimed was the tree of knowledge of disease and cure.

"Gugga Pir was the king of snakes," the Major heard the quack say to his audience of young boys, mature men and senior citizens. "Gugga Pir, last of the great saints, was Chuhan by caste. He would go into the jungle and draw a line on the ground with his stick. The snakes would fall into a queue, clasp their hands behind their backs, and follow him obediently. At night he would make a bed of snakes and sleep without a pillow. In the morning he would cut them into pieces with his sickle and eat their hearts. One day the chief of the snakes called an emergency meeting and confided in his fellow reptiles that if Gugga Pir kept killing at the current rate, their race would become extinct like the dinosaurs.

"My respectful listeners!" the quack took out a cane basket and thundered, his face red with effort, cartilage and bones showing underneath his attenuated skin burnt by sun. "That chief of snakes who conspired against Gugga Pir is here in my little basket. It is the most venomous of snakes. It has a crown of flames on its head and shaving foam in its mouth. It is so poisonous that with one breath it can set fire to rain forests and make holes in the ozone layer. A man stung by this snake cannot even ask for a glass of water; he only wants Coke. If you desire to see it, take off your shoes, move forward three feet, close your eyes and recite the name three times. God save us from the bite."

Major Charles Devereux took three steps forward, closed his eyes and recited the name of the King three times.

"My valuable listeners," the fake doctor thundered. "My ustad Hakim Nur Din has prepared this powdered eyewash using the chief snake's crown as its ingredient. If at midnight you or any member of your family or the neighbours feel sudden pain in the eyes, just put a little powder in your eyes and you will feel a cool sensation as if your eyes had been kept in the refrigerator. This potion is only for one rupee, one rupee, one rupee . . ."

Major Charles Devereux opened his eyes and ordered the quack's arrest. "Bring him to me in cuffs and shackles."

The quack was produced before the Major; his hands tied with the band of his shalwar. The Major searched him with the eyes of a man who had failed to win the Victoria Cross or be the King. "Leave us," he ordered. The police left.

"Have you any cure for half-erection?" he asked the quack.

"Yes, Gora Sahib," the hakim said proudly. "My eyewash is an elixir. Paste it on the symbol of your magnitude in the morning when you have an empty stomach and you will attain everlasting greatness."

Major Charles Devereux applied the powder as directed and in three weeks, he stopped wearing glasses. Considering it merely as a side effect of the medicine, he persisted with it and six weeks later, the cleft of his member turned into a half-opened eye. The major could not stand the horrible sight and reportedly committed suicide.

"Did you see the penis-eye with your own eyes?" Topchi asked Major Charles Devereux's batman.

"No I didn't," the batman said. "But I know. In any case, even if I did, I wouldn't tell you. I know you, Topchi Kaka. You're not bothered about the moral of the story! You just want to show off that you know why Major Sahib died – if he did die. You want to tell everyone about blowjob and claim you invented it. I can't let you violate Major Sahib's intellectual property rights. Besides, your listeners may talk about oral sex to their wives and mistresses, and who knows – they might compel them to do blowjob on them."

"So let them do it," Topchi smiled. "Our men should benefit from Major Sahib's pleasurable invention."

"What are you talking about, Kaka?" the batman said angrily, wiping his nose with Major Devereux's favourite napkin. "You want loss of Believing Sperms and decrease in Believers' population? You're Devil's Disciple, Topchi; perhaps the Devil himself. I pity myself that I told you all I knew about Major Sahib. I wish I had not divulged the secret of my patron… I wish it had not happened…Well, actually it did not happen. I was only carried away by your keenness, so I fabricated this unpleasant and possibly untrue story. You led me astray, Topchi. You tricked me into the sin of the tongue. Words fly on the wings of Satan: I pray we both lose our memory of the recent past."

"I wonder why Major Sahib committed suicide?" Topchi said to Mohammed Khan. "Every Holy Man is blessed with Dionysian vision. Don't you recall the holy man who forewarned us of the earthquake?"

He lifted his shirt and dropped his shalwar. Mohammed Khan found himself looking at the eye of a hognose snake. When he returned home and inspected himself in the privacy of his bathroom, he realised that he too had turned holy.

That was the day when Mohammed Khan became convinced that he was destined for great heights.

Topchi eventually died. His furious brother-in-law slew him when Topchi divorced his third wife and asked for her younger sister's hand. The estranged brother-in-law finished Topchi with a single blow of an axe bought specially for this purpose from the best axe-maker in the neighbouring town of Hazro. He then cut off Topchi's member and thrust it in his mouth. They found a dead Topchi performing oral sex on himself.

They buried him in the graveyard next to Ram Babu's library in the neighbouring town of Hazro.

7

The judges of the Supreme Court today took fresh oaths under the Provisional Constitutional Order issued by the country's military ruler, and pledged to uphold every order of the General.
(A news item in the Pakistani press)

And God taught Adam the names of all things, infusing the knowledge of them into his heart.
(Al-Quran, 2: 28)

Ram Babu was a clerk in the Governor's office in Calcutta – the seat of learning in the days of Sir Rabindranath Tagore. Ram Babu was there when Tagore's *Gitanjali* was unveiled in a private ceremony. He cried with each poem and swore he would devote his life to learning, which he did. Instead of spending his pay on cigarettes, paan and women, Ram Babu spent half his pay on buying books and half his time reading them. When he retired as a clerk in the Governor's office, he had collected and read a thousand and one books.

Babu read every book carefully. He would open the book with great care, read it slowly in many sittings, concentrating on each phrase as if it was the Governor's noting on a Most Urgent file, and put it back in a niche of the house which he mopped several times a day. After his retirement, he returned to his native town of Hazro where he contested and won the election for membership of Hazro Municipal Committee by getting all the Hindu votes and not one Moslem vote. He took the oath of loyalty to His Majesty the King, to his Queen, their succeeding generations, to other members of the Royal House, to Major Charles Devereux and his third-eye, to law and the people of the land, to the coming of a holy messenger, to the making and unmaking of law, and to splits and wholes.

"Oaths are sent down upon people to instill in their hearts all that is sacred and must be protected," he said in his opening speech. "Oaths are important so that boundaries are not transgressed. Oaths are violated by those who take other oaths, but there is no harm in inventing new oaths. We know there are times when it is necessary to do so and I hereby take the oath to invent new oaths when I know it is time. Bhagwaan save the Supreme Court!"

No one understood him and they clapped for just short of forever. They stopped when their hands could no longer move.

When Ram Babu left Calcutta, he had a thousand and one books. When he arrived at Hazro, he had one. He desired to make a library for it.

A room was selected in the Municipal Committee School for his library. The school was next to the town's Moslem graveyard which men visited during the day and women visited at night. The school was there since the beginning of remembrance but its existence was often ignored like an unpleasant memory. A brick wall, broken in several spots to provide makeshift entry points, encircled it. Two rooms, one still incomplete, stood awkwardly against the western end of the wall. The unfinished room was a stopgap toilet, which ladies visiting the cemetery used at night, while the other room remained locked for want of a conceivable use. The Municipality converted this room into the library and named it Ram Babu Memorial Library.

Special funds were allocated for the project. It was furnished with furniture made of shisham and polished by the best craftsmen from Rawalpindi. Solid-wood tables and high-back chairs woven with cane were set in the middle of the room, surrounded by shiny cabinets, one of which proudly displayed the solitary book. People seeking refuge from the sweltering heat sat through long afternoons under the cool air of ceiling fans specially imported from Gujrat and watched the book. No one visited the library in winters.

There were many legends to explain how a thousand and one books decreased into unity. Some believed that Babu lost the remaining books while shifting back to Hazro, others asserted he never possessed more than one book, and still others said that Babu's books were burned during a Hindu-Moslem riot in Delhi. A minority, citing none other than Babu himself, claimed that after reading many books he found that only one book remained the same every time he read it. A friend of Ram Babu was convinced that Babu had destroyed all other books when he came to know that distorters had distorted them. The idea of donating books, selling them to a secondhand bookshop, or simple theft did not occur to anyone.

Mohammed Khan stumbled upon the library by chance. He saw the building but didn't think it was a library because he didn't know that such a phenomenon existed. If he had, it was doubtful that he would have gone in.

He was looking for a place to urinate. He had heard about the room in the school which ladies used as latrine at night. Since this was daytime, there was no likelihood of a female presence.

When he entered the room, he was embarrassed to find a man in checkered dhoti and white shirt sitting on the floor among bookshelves.

"I…I…," Mohammed Khan stuttered.

The man in checkered dhoti smiled. "You… you!… You were looking for the book."

He looked like a nice person and Mohammed Khan hated to contradict him. He took a step forward and mumbled, "Well…"

"The book is here," the man reassured him. "I am also here and it seems that so are you. I'm not quite sure who you are, but I know who I am. I'm Ram Babu, the librarian of this library. It was made in my memoriam."

Mohammed Khan looked around the room. The empty bookshelves had been neatly wiped, with not a speck of dust allowed to settle anywhere on the surface. There was a desk and chair designated for the librarian but he sat cross-legged on the floor, facing the book.

"What is this book?" Mohammed Khan asked, pointing to the object inside the glass casing. "Can I see it?"

Ram smiled. "Yes, you can see it," he said genially. "It is there to be seen. But you can't touch it unless you have the right intent and purity of heart."

Mohammed Khan hesitated. "Babu Sahib, I came all the way from my village Behbudi but I didn't come here with any intent to read. I was actually looking for a place to pee and I thought perhaps this was a toilet."

"Do you want to pee or read the book?" Babu demanded suspiciously. "Make up your mind because we don't have toilet facilities at the library. I myself have to walk into the fields on the other side of the town when nature calls, and at my age it calls so very frequently."

"Now I want to read the book," Mohammed Khan said. "I'll piss later."

Ram Babu thought for a long moment during which his face changed from yellow to red and finally swarthy. "Your honesty impresses me, young man. I'll let you read. This is the end of your journey. There are no more supper tables to sit around, no more mountains to climb in search of burning trees, no more female clothes to steal from the river, no more Banyan trees to sit under, no more caves to seek refuge in, and no more deserts to cross in the middle of humid nights."

He lifted the glass casing and reverently picked up the book. He kissed its leather cover and settled the book gingerly in front of him. "Here," he said, "Sit beside me and read."

Mohammed Khan sat on the floor and opened the book. His eyes traced the unfamiliar writing inscribed on decayed pages smelling of history. "I cannot read it," he said. "What language is this?"

"The language of the Name," Ram said from behind. "Once you've learned all the names, you'll be ready for the world."

"I only understand my mother tongue," Mohammed Khan confessed. "I can read the language of God, but I can't read the language of the Name."

"Sure you can read it: if you have the desire."

Mohammed Khan looked again and recognised some marks. He went through the first passage and stopped. "What does it mean?" he asked again. "What is the language of the Name?"

"Read on, young man," Ram urged him. His breath brushed the side of Mohammed Khan's neck. "Read on and you will understand."

"But I can't," Mohammed Khan said.

Ram wrapped his arms around Mohammed Khan and enveloped the boy's torso with gubernatorial potency. "The meanings of this language are in the reading and reading is the meaning," Ram said. "Those who know the Name will also know the names of the Name and reach the root of the tree whose branch they're holding. Everything comes out of the Name, my boy, and ends in it. Name gives power and weakness. Name is the oath, the law, the land and the splits and the wholes. It means what it means."

He released Mohammed Khan from his embrace and went back to a place from where he could see the young man and flash a smile at him. Babu had a toothless smile, his teeth gone with his years. His red gums sparkled when he opened his mouth. "You'll know the meaning when you read it. Those who unread it do evil things in the name of the Name. Name is you, me and that which you embrace and which comes from below and lives on the top."

He paused momentarily and smiled out his gums. "To confirm it you will travel long distances, meet people, hear them and see them do what they must. Soon you will see the prophecy come true."

Mohammed Khan tried to persuade Ram Babu to let him borrow the book but Babu insisted that reference material was not available for borrowing. Mohammed Khan returned disappointed and was about to board the tonga back home, when he heard Babu yelling after him.

"Wait," Ram Babu screamed breathlessly. "I was wrong. I judged you unfairly. I should have known that there are people who are not hindered by the vicissitude of the seasons, or scared of that which surreptitiously lies coiled in their way, or troubled by the distance that exists between them and their destiny. They are wise even outside of that in which they will enter one day. Here, take the book, but make sure you return it within fourteen days to avoid a fine."

Mohammed Khan had little idea what Ram Babu had said for the most part, but he accepted the book gratefully.

He hid the book inside the band of his shalwar and let his long shirt cover it. It was not a good arrangement. When he went to the mosque with the book hanging next to his crotch, he faced considerable difficulty performing the physical rituals of the prayer. As he bent down in rukku, the book slipped from the grip of the band and fell forward, making a tent in his shalwar. Mohammed Khan pressed his thighs together, trying to hold the book tightly between them and got his virginal erection.

After prayers, he carried the book home and hid it under his pillow where mother immediately found it.

"What have you brought home, Mohammed Khan?" she demanded suspiciously.

"It's a book, Maanjee. I got it from Ram Babu Memorial Library."

"That Hindu's stock of evil? What are you planning to do to yourself, my son?" she said.

"I'm planning to read, Maanjee. The man in dhoti told me to read."

"Read what? Pagan knowledge? Hindu faith? Heathen writings?"

"No, Maanjee. The language of the Name."

He had trouble reading the book at first. He was not used to reading anything that was outside the Holy Book. Going beyond settled boundaries was painful and exciting. It was a dizzying experience during which his senses dulled to the point where familiar words also lost their meanings. Eventually, words and their melodious sound remained the only things living inside him.

Mohammed Khan continued to read. He read lying in bed, and sitting on the rooftop, but never felt so contented as when he sat under the tree in his backyard. He developed a fascination for the tree and its shadow that was so conducive to reading. He read all things about the Name.

By the time he finished his fifth textual reading of the Holy Book, he knew all the names too. Maulvi Sahib thought that Mohammed Khan possessed a pure heart and fine memory, and suggested that he should become a hafiz. "Your memory will never desert you if you commit the Holy Book to your heart. From then on, anything that gets into your memory will be forever," the priest said. "You'll then be blessed with eternal memory."

On the first day of the Month of Restraint, Mohammed Khan commenced the sacred task of memorising the Holy Book. He finished the task in two years. The entire village came to congratulate his father.

"Rahim Ullah Khan," Maulvi Sahib said to the proud father. "Your son has learned the words of power and he shall soon discover the power of words."

He turned toward Mohammed Khan and patted him on his cheeks. "As long as the words are with you, no harm will come to you, Mohammed Khan. Let yourself be possessed by them, then go out and spread them among believers so you may ascend to the top of the tree of ultimacy."

Mohammed Khan nodded without understanding. Maulvi Sahib kissed him on both cheeks and smelt musk on the young man's breath. Maulvi Sahib's breath smelt of smouldering thaapies.

Mohammed Khan loved the aroma of burning thaapies – dried cakes of buffalo dung. His mother would gather buffalo droppings, she would flatten the dung in her small, chafed hands, deftly convert it into a round thaapy, and paste it on the outer wall of the house to dry. Dried dung was the chief source of energy in winters and a mosquito repellant in summers.

Recently, a sizeable percentage of villagers had started using oil and gas as fuel instead of thaapies. Mosquito coils also became common. Strangers from other lands visited the village: some came to count the number of mosquitoes; some wanted to know why people were using coils and not thaapies; and others arrived in order to sell coils and teach people how to use them.

Mohammed Khan's friends went in search of other novelties to lands across the waters where it was rumoured that trees still bowed to strangers. In Gandhara, things were consistently deteriorating. The river had become polluted, though its water was still drinkable. Apple trees were still laden with fruit and they bowed down to the people albeit more out of burden than hospitality. Peaches no longer grew here and Mohammed Khan sometimes suspected that perhaps they never did. A few sporadic olive trees did sprout on the other side of the jungle but no one ever saw olives on the branches. The sounds of birds that used to chirp on trees at the time of his great grandfather were completely replaced by the bark of stray dogs.

Every day he felt lonelier. He had memorised the Holy Book, read the book of the language of the Name; and when he finally went back to return the book, he was told that a great fire had burned down the library, transforming Ram's body to ashes. His family members had taken the ashes and fled across the Ganges to survive ethnic cleansing. Maulvi Sahib also disappeared mysteriously. The police searched for the body and finally gave up. The Station House Officer of Police Station Hazro wrote in his final report that he had no clue about Maulvi Sahib's fate though he believed that that was his fate. The Station House Officer knew what would happen and what would not happen because it was recorded in the FIR – the First Information Report. The SHO also knew that one day Maulvi Sahib would return because he had a great memory.

"Forgetfulness is your prime enemy," Maulvi Sahib used to say. "If you forget, you will disappear."

8

Belshazzar the king made a great feast, they drank wine, and in the same hour came forth fingers of a man's hand and wrote over the plaster of the wall.
(Daniel, 5: 1-5)

And I will pray to the Father, and he shall give you another Comforter.
(John, 14:16)

If there arise among you a prophet, or a dreamer of dreams thou shalt not hearken unto his words and he shall be put to death.
(Deuteronomy, 13:1-5)

On the first day of August, when the last century of the millennium was three years short of half its life, the villagers awoke and saw graffiti carved on the adobe walls of their houses.

They dismissed them as cracks. For a full week, donkeys carried bags of brittle earth on their backs from the riverbank to each house where labourers and masons worked furiously to fill the cracks and remove the words. By morning, cracks would reappear, reaffirming the earlier belief that the village was indeed on a fault.

Rahim Ullah Khan received a book by special delivery from a French archaeologist who had conducted research about cracks in Moenjodaro ruins. At night, when the donkeys had tired and the labourers and masons were wearied from their monotonous failure, he read out the book to villagers in a voice that travelled to each woman and child in their divided rooms and verandahs. Sitting under the tree, waiting for a sign, Mohammed Khan heard his father's voice narrating someone else's words.

"No, not really," the familial voice came to him through the thick foliage glistening with moonlight. "It was no writing they saw in the Mount of the Dead. There was no need for this anonymous form of public communication in a community so arrogantly uncritical of its own existence.

The cultural context indicates that it was the age of miracles, and people searched for the unusual – this was an existential strategy for finding meanings in the given. When they failed in their search, they looked for miracles in their own being. Against this social setting it was natural that someone should read some sort of a message into the cracks in the walls."

Mohammed Khan moved uneasily under the tree. He was surrounded by darkness and foliage and confusion. The day before yesterday, he had taken out Ram Babu's book and read it from cover to cover. Yesterday, he had recited the Holy Book from the first word to the last. Today, he had recalled every story and fable that Topchi had narrated in the hujra. All this time, he had sat under the tree, embracing its trunk and hoping for emeralds. When darkness fell, he took off his clothes and tried to reread the hieroglyphs on his body but still remained barren. Then the voice came, telling him about cracks and the fault and the Valley where the researcher had spent countless days researching the cracks so that he could justify his sabbatical.

He let out a laugh that went back all the way to the hujra. "How come the fault, so determinedly zigzagged through every house, dividing rooms, all which should not have been halved?" he demanded from no one. "These are not cracks," he yelled, addressing no one either. A bird fluttered inside the branches and reluctantly flew away. Mohammed Khan felt the cold drop of a tear caress his cheek and trickle down to his lap.

The cracks started to change colour – from muddy to beige, then sienna, tan, bronze, russet, tawny, scarlet, cerise, green, vermilion and finally the colour of bloodshed. Mohammed Khan spent days looking at changing colours and deepening fissures, intoxicated by a semantic wine flowing in his veins and smelling on his breath. He saw the cracks, then deciphered the words, but between the cracks and the words was a line sharper than a sword and thinner than a hair and impossible to cross in his present state of confusion. But his faith in the graffiti finally opened his heart to its sense. He felt it and interpreted it. He laughed. People gathered around him, some fascinated by his laughter, others horrified, some amicable to him, others hostile – but Mohammed Khan transcended their enmity and their friendship. He was obsessive and hesitant.

"It's the writing on the wall," he whispered to himself so no one should hear him. "And my heart is the witness to the happening."

In true rural tradition, the villagers soon forgot about the cracks that pockmarked their walls and the fault that divided their houses.

The cracks continued to spread and weaken the walls. The first to fall was Rahim Ullah Khan's side of the house. Fourteen days after the appearance of the first crack, it came down with a soft thud, raising a dust storm that set out to choke every throat. By the midnight of the fourteenth of August, a cyclone of soot rose from across the jungle and landed on the village, destroying every house and every hujra, uprooting every tree and every bush, and killing every snake and every python. Mohammed Khan found himself naked under the black sky as the family tree above him was uprooted by the fury of the cyclone and thrown across the Indus.

For several days, the villagers remained occupied, walking in circles. The earth below them turned into fine dust. Then rain came and converted the dust into mud so they could no longer move their feet. By now they had buried their dead and there was nothing left to bury. They had searched for their valuables and there was nothing left to search for. They had mourned the departed and there was no one left to mourn. They had cried over their loss and nothing was left to lose. They had divided everything and nothing was left to divide—at least not for another twenty-four years. They sat down in a circle, feet tied to the earth, heads bowed toward it; quiet and discontented.

Mohammed Khan walked into their midst, displaying the imbedded hieroglyphs on his chest and on his stomach, across his back and his neck, along his legs and his arms, around his circumcised penis and his shaven testicles. No one paid any attention to his nakedness: the hieroglyphs on his body saved him from the shame of exposure. He stood among the dressed, unnoticed and untaunted. "They are words," he roared, pointing toward the graffiti on his body. "They are cracks infused with the spirit of the words."

No one heard him and he waited patiently for their inner noise to go away. The people lay under a rain that continued for as long as anyone could remember, and when the memories were exhausted, it stopped. The clouds went away and the sun came back.

Everything looked changed. The debris of their homes had been washed away into the river. The graveyard had been flattened and all traces of their heritage were gone. Some cried over the loss, others celebrated it.

The earth ultimately freed them of its viscidity. They opened their eyes and ears and gathered around Mohammed Khan, looking curiously at the marks on his body. Their movement was sluggish; they dragged their feet in the glutinous mud.

"Yes, they are words," they said when Mohammed Khan's voice finally reached them. Their speech was heavy, their voices had merged into a collective whisper. "Who carved them on your body, O Mohammed Khan? The jinn or a man?"

Mohammed Khan found his nakedness curiously exalting. He felt their looks prying his body but made no move to hide it. "Does it matter if they were made by jinn or ins?" he demanded of them.

The crowd moved closer until their chests made a ring around him. He heard their heartbeats, smelled their sweat, felt the heat of their bodies, and a portentous ecstasy squeezed him in its fold.

"They are colours," they cried in wonder.

"They are the colours of the sacrificial soul," Mohammed Khan roared. "They've come from within and are visible to those who look within. Those who look towards the wall or the body are misguided. They'll never see anything because what is a body? Nothing but an adobe wall. A lifeless, soulless, wordless pile of inorganic material. It's a miracle that it has been blessed with colours and it's also a miracle that I've seen them and now display them, but it's no miracle that I can read them because everyone knows I can read. I have read the Holy Book and the Book of Names, and the time has come for me to compile the Book of Words."

A ripple ran through the crowd. "They're the colours of the awakening soul," Mohammed Khan thundered in his nakedness. "The wall trembled under the burden of its void and cracked. It was, after all, an old wall built by a government contractor whose palatial house was completed much earlier than every wall. He stole cement and steel from the site and used it for the base of his own house. He was a dishonest man. He changed everything when he changed the past into present. In the past, people were honest. They led a simple and frugal life. Nothing was more and nothing was less. Existence was in equilibrium along the heavenly axis but its axiality was shaken by people of the curve. Do you know who are the people of the curve?" he demanded and got no answer. "They are the ones whose spirit has been slouched by the jingle. And what is this jingle?" he demanded again and still did not get an answer. "It is the tinkle of the mettle that has divided mankind into those who know counting and those who do the counting. Let it be known that numbers are a sign. They have been sent down so man should recognise things, name them and remember them. With numbers they should count their children, their miseries, their bounties and their sperms, but not calibrate their testicles or compute the number of breasts of women of any colour. The jingle is a snaky treasure hidden underneath the tree and cursed to constriction. It is a pythonic vibration but alas, they know not the boundary between vibration and zero-order stillness. They are condemned to de-eroticised orgasms. They demand fellatio but know not the entire range of its pleasures and mistakenly think that Major Charles Devereux invented it. They should know that all inventions belong to the first Inventor and He alone holds the genuine claim to them. They should also know that fellatio is not sex and sex is not about pleasure but about power. You are powerful because you have the ability to penetrate. Sex is a partible item: the superior takes it and the inferior gives it. Man is superior because he can enter, so be a man: do not forsake claims to manliness.

"The cracks are transformations, my people. If you believe me, then follow me to the wall and see for yourselves beyond the wall. Only then will you know what transformations are and from where they emanate. They're all around us. Inside and outside. On the flesh and in the heart. I've read the accounts of bygone nations. I've gone through the record of their deeds and misdeeds and the stories of their life and their death. Those who denied the power of the cracks disintegrated and those who recognised signs in the cracks ascended the throne of the blessed."

He closed his eyes and whispered. "Power lies in the correct and melodious pronunciation of the word. So pronounce correctly and derive power. In olden days there were rains, floods, famine and deaths. In our days there are sins and defilement, excessive noise and Viagra."

He paused. His body stiffened and his eyes rolled back. He clenched his fists as pleasure ran through his soul like a hot current of the river flowing with honey. When he opened his eyes again, they were red with gratification. "That which must be veiled is laid bare and the revealable is concealed," he thundered. "I have, therefore, *come*!!!"

"Why do you speak like that, Mohammed Khan?" the voice of Yaqoob the Cobbler rose from the crowd. "You speak as if you are the only one who has the ability to speak, despite the fact that your ability as a mouse-hunter was rather deficient."

Mohammed Khan bowed his head in veneration. "Yaqoob the Cobbler! I seek refuge in the Word from arrogance. I narrate what is shown to me and the shown must be narrated. It is not my speech that counts but the message, and the message is written on the wall. I am merely repeating it."

"On what authority do you speak, Mohammed Khan?" Barkat Khan challenged him from the other corner. "You don't flaunt baldness nor does your belly protrude."

"My son you're too young to see what was seen by the elders," Mohammed Khan's maternal uncle, Musa Khan added gently.

"I honour the elders and their words of wisdom, my uncle," Mohammed Khan cried with solemnity. "What I say is not different from their saying. Verily the elders knew the meanings of the cracks but you have forgotten them."

Silence swept through the crowd. The Valley went silent. Then the silence was broken by an uproar.

"You are a mad man, Mohammed Khan," Uncle Musa Khan shouted. "We are the elders and we haven't forgotten the ways of the more elderly. You are a liar. Your voice croaks. Your throat vibrates like a sodomised rectum. You talk like a bachelor who no longer enjoys masturbation. You speak like a politician who is eternally numb outside his speeches. You talk like a whore who has no shameful memories. You orate like a priest who doesn't have the courage to divide belief into sects. Go and get psychiatric treatment."

"No, no. He's not psychotic," Yaqoob the Cobbler intervened. "He's possessed. Let's call the exorcist."

"Yes, yes. Pir Bukhari knows how to castrate the jinn by blowing chili smoke into his nostrils," suggested Achoo, the low-caste minstrel-cum-genealogist, in his fleeting moment of glory. A loud laughter lightened the charged atmosphere but was soon dampened by the sound of a blow Achoo the Minstrel received from Mohammed Khan's paternal uncle, Isa Khan.

"You son of a dog. Don't you dare say anything against my nephew," the paternal uncle yelled in a voice burdened with the obligations of family solidarity. "If his father is dead it doesn't mean that he is without relatives."

"My father is not dead," Mohammed Khan protested.

"Then why is he not beside his son at this moment of judgment?" Isa Khan roared and slapped Achoo the Minstrel again.

"Don't you dare touch my protégé, Isa Khan," Mohammed Khan's maternal uncle Musa Khan yelled back at the paternal uncle. "Achoo the Minstrel lives under my protection. His wife also lies under my protection. So does his daughter and *inshallah* her daughters when they come of age. That slap you hurled at his face was a slap on my face."

"Stop it, stop it," someone from the crowd pleaded. "Do not fight among yourself, Musa Khan and Isa Khan. Don't cause cracks in your lineage."

"It will not be stopped. I have not forgotten how Mohammed Khan's father forcibly took control of my pastureland. The day has come. It is the day of settling an old score, paying the debt I inherited from the bygone members of my family," Musa Khan said. His face had reddened with the stains of blood of the unknowable murdered men. "Let the battle begin," he shouted.

There was no way to stop the war. It was fought in everyone's backyard. The warring factions faced one another with clubs and bricks and stones. They were surrounded by singers, musicians, dancers, acrobats, poets and image-makers enveloped in their own shadows. In this war that had yet to be waged, everyone joined to be a participant and a witness, and everyone was apprehensive of victory. No one recognised anyone; no one knew what the day would bring. They were dressed in their hopes and their hopes were naked, leaving them with a strong sense of shame in optimism.

They finally gathered in the main square of the village. They were friends and relatives, and enemies separated from friends and relatives. They knew each other but tried not to recognise the affinity. Storytellers and mythmakers gathered, ready to collect pains and agonies and sighs and heroics. Men of matter appeared in great spirit and men of spirit mattered much. But conspicuous among them were those in between, weighing the scales of victory and defeat and counting the spoils they would acquire and the losses they would suffer if they took or did not take sides. They were the people with numbers.

No one tried to stop the battle. No one wanted to. There was no holy man to intercede; no coward to run for life; no ambitious general to engineer a bloodless coup; no hypocritical strategist to plan a strategy for minimising human losses; no brash sinner to detect virtue in the honourable display of manhood; no virtuous soul to promise distant rewards for valour and martyrdom. It was the most appropriate and timely action taking place in the right place. Its propriety was its own justification, its timeliness its motivation. The Valley was the perfect setting for a happening impervious to historicisation and shielded from the evaluative ravages of the chroniclers. Only Topchi knew it all and he could talk, but Topchi was devoted to silence and he only hummed from his grave.

The war eventually started. One man with a double-bladed sword stepped forward. Another from the adversaries moved ahead to meet him in the middle. They were big men, both of them: big and strong, their limbs shining, eyes radiant. They did not utter a word but each part of their body was eloquent, declaring what it had to declare.

For a hundred days, the two warriors stood facing each other in heat and in cold and were consigned to history by deadlock.

Historians say that Mohammed Khan was the sole survivor of the Great War of Cracks, and that his was the only reliable account of the events though he himself did not remember much about it. They also say that he was its evaluator, its cause, its victor and its victim, and he wished that his uncle had not reacted so violently to Achoo the Minstrel. He wished he had more leisure time to wait for further cracks to appear in the wall. "Will they survive the war, the cracks? Are they forever?" He had no answers. He was not sure about the question either. He only believed in his own self, his eyes, his heart, and his uncle's commitment.

Mohammed Khan had fainted just before the start of the battle when a dancing eunuch, in a moment of hallowed ecstasy, kicked a rock that hit Mohammed Khan on the temple. In a state of semi-consciousness, Mohammed Khan vaguely recalled the day's proceedings. He knew he had had an argument with someone and he had seen his uncle approaching the adversary from behind. He also remembered the ancient tree being felled and the python dissolving in disappearance, but that was all he could glimpse in his last moments. Before he passed out, he prayed to be resurrected in the land of his prayers.

Book II

Flight of the Oracle

*Moses entered the city at a time when it was neglected
by its inhabitants, and he found therein two men fighting,
one of his own and the other of his enemies; Then the one who was
his own asked him for help against the other, Therefore, Moses smote
him with his fist and finished him. And there came a man from
the far side of the city and said: "O Moses! The chiefs are in council
regarding thee in order to kill thee, therefore get away."
So Moses got out of the city.
(Al-Quran, 28: 15-21)*

9

*Every shopkeeper and restaurant owner has been directed to close business by 7.00 p.m. this evening. Anyone attempting to celebrate the new millennium will be arrested at the spot.
(Chief Commissioner Islamabad)*

*Baton-toting members of Jamat-i-Islami will patrol the city streets to break the legs of those who dare celebrate the new year.
(A news item in the Pakistani press)*

The Great War created a chasm in time. The epochal chain broke in two discrete parts. One existed in memories, the other in dreams. The survivors kept travelling from past to future and back, never touching the middle ground. The past reminded them of a lost pride and the future made them uneasy. Some left the Valley to escape the past, others stayed behind to escape the future, and many remained undecided between options.

Mohammed Khan knew he must leave the Valley to save his present. The elders, angered by his iconoclastic speech, had placed a price of one thousand rupees on his head and every unemployed male in the Valley would soon be looking for him. While the war raged in the Valley, Mohammed Khan emulated his great grandfather and left under the cover of a sneaky night.

He walked in the company of his thoughts that were so concentrated as to cast a moving shadow on the road. He followed a circular path, travelling during the night and hiding during the day, and it was on the seventh night of his exodus that he realised he had been walking in circles. The realisation made him wiser to the laws of circular geometry but did little to bring him closer to his destination.

On the tenth night of his attempted flight from harm, he bumped into a squatting man who was busy urinating on the roadside.

"Hey, watch where you're going," the man yelled as he fell forward into the foaming puddle. "I fell into my urine and now I can't even say my prayers."

"Forgive me, for I didn't see you in the dark," Mohammed Khan quickly apologised, scared that bounty hunters might hear him.

"I doubt if you're capable of seeing in broad daylight either," the man said in a mysterious tone that bordered on sarcasm. "Verily, you need a leader to show you the way."

Mohammed Khan found the urinating man's voice curiously familiar and he took a couple of steps forward to see his face. "Who are you, sir?" he asked, as he tried to determine the shape of his facial contours. The darkness separating them was too dense. "Do I know you?"

"Do you know yourself?" the man demanded angrily.

"No," Mohammed Khan admitted.

"Just as well," the man said as he searched for a stone to dry the tip of his penis. "Fuck," he cursed. "What a place. You can't even find a decent stone to dry yourself. It's high time they imported toilet paper."

"What?"

"Never mind," said the mysterious man. "You'll come to know about toilet paper and learn its uses and misuses if you leave the Valley and go to America."

"America? What is America, kind sir?" Mohammed Khan asked eagerly.

"It's another planet where local baseball teams play amongst themselves and still insist on calling it the World Series."

"A planet? You mean like the sun or the moon?"

"Something like that," the man said. "From a distance, it is as shiny as the sun."

Mohammed Khan shook his head in complete awe. "How come you know so much about unseen things, sir?"

"Because I am a foreign employment promoter," the man said with a touch of pride. "I send people to foreign lands and other lives."

"Including America?" Mohammed Khan asked.

"Including America," the man confirmed.

"Can you send me to America, sir?"

"Only if you're a heretic, a Laodicean or a terrorist-in-the-making," the man said.

"I am willing to be a bit of all three."

The answer pleased the man, for he reached out and hugged Mohammed Khan, soaking his senses with the smell of urine. "You've made a wise choice, my son," the foreign employment promoter said. "In America, you'll prosper if you're willing to do all the menial jobs and promise not to criticise their foreign policy. Now, come with me to Islamabad where I'll arrange a fake American visa for you."

"A fake visa?" Mohammed Khan frowned. "I'm not comfortable with the idea of fakery. With a fake visa I might end up in some fake America."

"That's a real possibility," the promoter said. "I know of a group of people with fake visas who were sent on a big boat to Dubai, and after travelling in the seas for several days, they ended up landing on some deserted shore of their own country."

"Then?"

The promoter shrugged but said nothing.

Other men followed Mohammed Khan's example and left the Valley in search of alternative options. Eventually, only women were left behind to survive sultry monsoons. They collected their memories and buried them in a mass grave at the edge of the village. For forty days, they sat around the grave, tending it with tears. On the forty-first night, at 0001 hours, they changed into silk and taffeta and declared independence.

The independence party was held under an open sky littered with stars. Women danced with other women and in the process created history, which many believed should not have been created. Others argued that history's abode was the pages of books and burning them was also a part of Mongol history.

The independence celebrations were marred by violence. Members of a devout Islamist party misconstrued the festivities to be a New Year party and they attacked the proceedings with a brimming resilience not to let the New Year set in. They came with hockey sticks, cricket bats and staffs made of wood slashed from trees growing in the jungle of bearded ghosts, and bashed each female on the head until alien thoughts bled through their ears and noses. Police watched the spectacle in appreciative silence because deep down in their hearts they too were against the dawning of the New Year. The bashing continued until daybreak when Maulvi Sahib's son called the faithful to prayer and clubs were returned to the mosque. After breakfast they gathered together again and erected a seventy-foot high wall made from loam collected from the riverbed. The wall grew of its own justification and encircled the existence of all women to protect them from the

Mediterranean influence. At night, women heard the breeze pant, and during the day, they waited behind their veils, praying for Mohammed Khan's safe arrival in America.

Mohammed Khan resurrected in the land of white people with blonde hair. The place was so colourless that he had to purchase sunglasses to see hues and tones.

He reached that place hidden in the bowels of a ship, eating rats for breakfast and mice for dinner. He escaped both plague and drowning as his ship sank three thousand miles off the shore of his destiny. Mohammed Khan swam through the salty waters and arrived at a coast covered with snow. As he came out of the freezing waters, he was captured by men in uniforms.

"Hey," they yelled at him as he came out of the ocean. "Are you Osama bin Laden?" the taller one asked.

"Who? No, not at all."

"Are you Fidel Castro?" the shorter one demanded, looking suspiciously at his ruffled beard.

"I am Mohammed Khan."

"Are you a Cuban refugee trying to enter our country?" the two asked in unison.

Mohammed Khan assured them that he was not a Cuban and that he had never even heard of such a country. The men guarding the coast relaxed and became friendly. "Do you have a valid visa for entering freedom, sir?" they asked him in a friendly tone.

"Freedom resides inside me," Mohammed Khan said. "Come in and take a look. But tell me one thing first: is this the real America or a cheap replica?"

"Afraid I can't answer your question, sir," the officer said. "An answer to your question would be against the procedure, and if we let you come too close to us, it might taint our racial purity. However, if you grease our palms and promise not to report us for our negligence, we'll pretend you didn't exist."

"You don't need to pretend, for indeed I don't exist without the lineage I left so far behind," Mohammed Khan said with a smile whose sadness made the men in uniform burst into tears. While they were busy wiping their dripping eyes, Mohammed Khan disappeared out of sight without either greasing their palms or making a promise of silence. The men in uniform later convinced each other that he indeed did not exist because he was from nowhere.

Mohammed Khan walked many miles in the snow. After nine days of persistent toil, he reached a town whose architecture was tropical. He knocked at a door and a man answered. He had a familiar face but Mohammed Khan's memory had frozen due to the arctic cold, and he could not recognise the man behind the face. There were other men in the house, each looking familiar without being recognisable. They all had sunken cheeks with eyes devoid of consideration. They took him into a dark room reeking of the collective smell of about fifty men jammed in there.

"We'll soon make arrangements for your legality in the land of illegal opportunities," he was told. "Our service charge will be $500."

"What's a dollar?" Mohammed Khan demanded.

"It's the name of the local currency."

"But I have no money," Mohammed Khan cried.

"We gladly accept credit cards, personal cheques and IOUs. We're even prepared to buy you as a slave."

Mohammed Khan stayed there for three days. On the fourth evening, when a blizzard had whitened everything outside and made the world even more colourless, he was taken to another room where a man as colourless as the snow greeted him. He went so far as to embrace him and kiss him on both cheeks. The man's mouth smelt of greed.

"Welcome to freedom, Mohammed Khan," the colourless man said. "You're in the land of the relatives and friends of the golden people who your great grandfather conspired to defeat through his trickery once upon a time. We'll make sure that you continue to stay among us without becoming a terrorist."

"I have no desire to stay," Mohammed Khan said dryly. Then tears filled his eyes. "I wish I had not left home in the first place."

"Ha, the cultural shock," the colourless man laughed. "It happens with every legal and illegal immigrant. Eventually, you'll learn to love this place: it's like an arranged marriage."

He patted Mohammed Khan on the shoulder and smiled again. "We have located your wife whom you married five years ago. She's ready to testify before the INS authorities about your sexual prowess."

"But I am not married!"

"Of course you are," the colourless man said. "You are what I say you are. Without me you don't exist in this land."

He clapped and in came a Mexican woman in her early thirties with black eyes that had prematurely lost their shine.

"I am Sylvia," she said. "I am your wife, my husband."

"I've never seen this woman before in my life," Mohammed Khan protested.

"See through your third eye and everything will fall into perspective," the colourless man said. "Now go with this woman before someone else claims her as his spouse. That would complicate things for all of us."

The woman named Sylvia led Mohammed Khan into another room where she briefed him in detail about their earlier life as man and woman. "We were paper-married in a chapel in the Biggest Little City in the World. That happened ten years ago."

"The man said five years," Mohammed Khan objected.

"He confused your case with another man whom I paper-married separately," the woman said. "We have two children from our wedlock and I'll produce them before the Immigration guy provided you give me a legal undertaking that in the certain event of our divorce, you'll not ask for their custody."

"If you're my wife, can I have sex with you?" Mohammed Khan asked eagerly.

"That's not part of the contract," the woman said. "If you want to include a clause for sex, you'll need to pay extra because I don't find you attractive enough to do it for free. When you have seen as many men as I have, you don't find any man attractive, Gregory Peck being an exception... but he's dead in any case."

She got to her feet. "I think you'd better sleep now. You have your interview scheduled with the INS tomorrow. You should look your best when you go there. Wear your finest costume and make sure your mouth doesn't smell of hope."

Mohammed Khan watched her get into bed with him. Before he went to sleep, he felt her arms tightening around his chest with a strength that made him gasp for air. When he awoke next morning, it was with a sense of confidence that he would do well in his interview with the Immigration authorities.

"I slept with civilisation," Mohammed Khan said. "I resurrected Sylvia from sexual asceticism and inscribed my experience with the eternal ink of spiritual semen on the hymenal tablet so she could be read. Then I slept the post-coital sleep. In my dreams, I experienced more dreams and after I awoke, she told me to get ready for this interview."

"That's not exactly the kind of an answer I had in mind," the Immigration Officer said gently. He was a man in his late thirties whose face was a fertile ground for ripening pimples. He kept scratching them with his index finger, targeting the one perched on his nose until it started to bleed. Mohammed Khan reached for a box of Kleenex and offered him a tissue.

"I wasn't really replying to your question. I was satisfying my own curiosities and your suspicions," Mohammed Khan said as the Immigration Officer dabbed his bleeding pimple with the tissue. "I was doing a catharsis," he added.

"A what?" the Immigration Officer frowned. He neatly folded the tissue and placed it in his pocket.

"A catharsis," Mohammed Khan repeated. "A private lustration. An inner cleansing. An emotional purge."

"Jesus!" the Immigration Officer exclaimed irritably and broke another pimple with his nail. "Are you trying to teach me English? You've got a lot of guts for an alien, you know?"

Mohammed Khan moved uneasily in his chair. "I don't understand," he protested mildly. "The men at the shore said I did not exist. You tell me that I'm an alien. Who's right and who's wrong?"

"I'm right," the Immigration Officer said with statutory conviction. "Alien's more legal. I am a legal-minded person who's here to serve the law."

"Indeed," Mohammed Khan nodded in agreement. "Law serves those who wield power and when the weak become powerful only then do they discover why they needed power. I discovered that when I sat under the tree and it spoke to me."

"Trees don't speak, mister. You've gotta be crazy."

"I'm not," Mohammed Khan said as gently as he could. "It's crazy to believe that the moon is made of cheese or counting is superior to evaluation. It's crazy to believe that the God of Earth causes the apple to fall and not the God of Tree."

"Who's the God of Tree?"

"You'd better ask the Tree itself and everything that comes out of its depths and coils around you. It's been there since E was ordained to equal MC^2."

"Since when?" the Immigration Officer scowled.

"Since the Beginning… when there was nothing. Then there was something. And then there was more of something: the River, the Egg, the Tree, the Snake, the Python, the Word, the Line. I went to the end of the line and found emptiness. So I recycled my experience and evaded extinction."

"There I agree with you one hundred per cent," the Immigration Officer nodded vehemently. "Recycling's the only way to avoid extinction."

"There are other ways too," Mohammed Khan muttered. "Like making sequels."

"Sequels? You mean like *Return of the Jedi*? Or *Batman Forever*?"

"And *Godfather II*," Mohammed Khan added. "*Godfather* was created from dust and blood and made part of history. Then recollections were brought in to mingle with the present. Now he stagnates at the summit of evolution where he will live forever until I annihilate everything – which isn't too far because I have arrived."

The Immigration Officer leaned forward and eyed him suspiciously. "Are you suggesting that the sequel's not as good as the first part? The sequel also got a five-star rating in the Blockbuster Video Guide."

"Sequels depend on recollection and recollection leads to hunting, killing and burying. It's the exit. Sylvia's not satisfied with my efforts – she probably wants more children from our wedlock – but she doesn't realise that if satiety is not dressed it loses its essence and becomes hunger. I told her that if she continued to run after things, she'd become a thing herself."

The Immigration Officer shook his head in confusion. "I'm not sure I understand you. Why're you suddenly talking about dress and hunger? Are you in the restaurant business? Or a dress designer, perhaps?"

"You are what you eat and what you wear," Mohammed Khan said. "Dress is nakedness. You dress to tell others you're naked. Those who are naked tell others they're not naked."

The Immigration Officer thought hard for a moment and his face brightened. "Now that's what I call a good interview answer," he said. He stamped Mohammed Khan's application form with his signatures and smiled broadly. "Okay, Mr. Khan. Your case for elevatory immigration is hereby approved in the Dress Designer category."

He handed a coloured card to Mohammed Khan. "Here's the light Green Card, Mr. Khan. Wear it all the time on your lapel and no harm shall come to you. You're now a potential citizen of the one and only nation on God's earth. We believe in democracy, and by God, we'll make sure you agree with us. If you don't," he added with the erection of his forefinger, "we'll declare you a terrorist and condemn you to eternal exile in Afghanistan where they will shave off your head if you try to play soccer in shorts."

Mohammed Khan did not agree in his heart but he said, "Yes sir," and kissed the card with all solemnity and reverence. "I'll wear it all the time," he said. "This is my land: I was allotted to it through the great lottery along with fifty thousand other souls. I belong to this land. I was born here. Even if you don't admit this fact or your records show otherwise, I tell you with certainty that I grew up here. If you think this too is not correct, then know the prophecy that says I'll grow old here. I've met you before. If not in body then I definitely met your soul and trillions of souls like yours and mine. Don't you recall that sublime occasion when we all gathered and said, 'yes'? The event has been recorded in the Holy Book."

The Immigration Officer nodded happily. "Yeah. Sure, I remember. The Republican convention."

Mohammed Khan left the office wearing the Card against his chest, experiencing the inner elevation. Others looked at him with dignity as he walked away from nowhere. He was not himself; never was. Intuitively he knew it was all unreal. Not his reality.

10

*Look to your actions and abstain from women for verily the first sin,
   which the Children of Israel committed, was because of women.
   (Sahihul Bukhari)*

*Prophet Abraham was circumcised when he was eighty years old.
   (Abu Hurairah quoted in Sahihul Bukhari)*

*The line between love and lust is often blurred.
   (Anonymous)*

Mohammed Khan was hired by the Mayor's office to sweep streets and alleys and when he had made enough money to pay Sylvia and the colourless man for their services, he moved to another town that had no name. He found work in a café on a numberless freeway. Each night, he thought of his noble lineage blessed with chefs and servers and dishwashers, and cried in shame. It was a private shame: no one from his village knew that he was doing these menial jobs. He was away from those who used to do these jobs for him and his family – those ugly, undernourished, unsmiling, nosy servants: inefficient, uncooperative, jealous of his riches and always up to some trick. There was no one here to play tricks: only his ambition.

For the next two years, Mohammed Khan continued to do all sorts of low jobs as he hitchhiked from one town to another. One day, after two years had passed, he appeared in a town on the western side of the country. The only witness to his arrival was a woman named Sue Mangan.

 He came into town shivering from a cold that pierced through his heavy clothing and bit him like guilt. Sue watched him descend from the Greyhound, her eyes evaluating him from outside and inside. He was a man of pale complexion and average height but his bouncing gait made him look taller. His saltative hair was ebony, reaching his curved shoulders. His chest was broad, his stomach curved in nice and flat, and he had criss-crossing legs built like sculpted logs. A scar started from his left temple and ran down to his sunburnt cheeks. His body was tattooed like the truckers and bikers that stopped in her Granddad's bar and drank themselves into brawls, but he was surely no trucker or biker. He had alien features and he was neither a skinned person like her nor a skinless man like Samuel whose memory defined her world.

Samuel was a fantasy, or perhaps the memory of a fantasy, cherished in the present or maybe inherited from the past so that she could be led to a predictable future. Whatever the reality, she knew that the time had come to unravel it and replace it with another fantasy: more real, more tangible, more visible.

They met in the County Medical Center. She was there because she needed treatment for flu. He was there because he was trying to donate his blood, which the hospital would not accept on the grounds that he was from nowhere.

"I'm sorry, sir," the doctor told Mohammed Khan in a monotonously polite tone. "We can't accept your blood. I told you it's the hospital policy not to accept blood from nowhere."

"It's not a hospital," Mohammed Khan reasoned with himself in desperation. He came to doubt the hospital's existence, its essence, its essentiality. In the process, he disbelieved everything: his surroundings, his life, his being – and his blood.

Someone touched him and his delusions. It was the woman. She had come to him laterally and silently, and before he could hit his head against the wall in desperation, she held his hands with a strength that surprised him. The moment he laid his eyes upon her, he had a flash of orgasmic intuition that she was the woman for him. He reached for her, leaned over her and kissed the scar on her forehead. Sue felt the metaphysical warmth of an extrinsic presence that made her forget her hot-tempered mother, her poor, popular, prayer-saying, carpenter father and the names of her six brothers and sisters.

They came out of the hospital into the darkness of the burgeoning night. All architectural marks dissolved behind their back into the anaesthetised fog through which street lamps were starting to faint into balls of blurred light. Everything seemed to be evanescing into everything else, into its own formlessness.

"I'm Mohammed Khan," said a rugged voice with stony edges.

The words melted into an illusive eternity.

"I'm Sue Mangan," the other voice said.

Even if it was not said, it was nonetheless the voice of someone falling in love.

This was the second time she had fallen in love. The first was with Samuel Joseph, an unmedaled hero of an unchronicled war, a skinless, and a nothing. She had met him when she attained puberty and decided to marry him.

When she told her Dad about her decision, he was stunned. "But he's a skinless guy, my child," he cried in horror and revulsion. Gruesome scenes of his horrifying end flashed before his eyes. "You can't afford to marry him."

She brushed aside her Dad's concern with a smile. Dad was an old man with failing eyesight unable to see the unreality of the skin.

"His skin glows like night, Dad," she said. "He's not without a skin. He just got it black."

Her father guided her by the elbow to a broken mirror hanging on the wall. "See for yourself, Sue," he said in a trembling voice as he pointed toward her ivory skin. "This is the only skin that matters, my child. All other skins and colours have been condemned to nothingness."

"Dad, when you look too deep into the skin, it turns into a white mask," Sue cried.

"The masks protect our honour from getting tainted, Sue. Stay away from Sam, my child."

"I'll hire the best of plastic surgeons, Dad," she tried to reassure him. "He'll become a skinned folk like us. Michael Jackson has succeeded, hasn't he?"

"You don't have that kind of money, Sue."

Sue's mother, who hated the skinless and hurled obscenities at children passing in front of her home, screamed and threw a glass of wine that smacked against her daughter's forehead and knocked her unconscious. When she regained her senses, everyone was gathered around her, their faces angry, yelling and screaming and hollering in rage. Her father stood quietly in a corner, sobbing. He knew what she did not wish to know.

Against all Southern traditions, Sue married Sam in a skinless church. On their wedding night, surgeons in white hoods came calling. They were clumsy, amateur, unlicensed surgeons. In their effort to invest Sam with a palpable flesh, they divested him of all form so even he could not recognise himself. He became a shadow transmuted into an inaudible cry. No one actually saw him or the job the doctors did on him. He was gone. Many said he was never there in the first place.

The doctors turned their horses and went the way they had come. The villagers believed they were crazy, those doctors; yet their craze was laced with sanity in search of definition. Their presence was felt but ephemeral. They embodied an energy, untapped but overflowing, blind yet resolute. Everyone felt its effect.

Sue watched them go with closed eyes. She didn't have enough money to sue them. No one in her neighbourhood had the courage or conviction to stand witness in the dock. No one from Samuel's tribe had the inclination to seek revenge. He died on the operating cross.

The next day, the local newspaper published a tribute to the good work the Ku Klux Klan was doing to preserve the environment.

"I'm sorry," Mohammed Khan said. Sue craved his kisses and much more than kisses to erase the traumatic script. Mohammed Khan hesitated. Kisses were a wastage of time, annihilators of the things to come. "Why should I kiss her?" the man in him asked. "What is a kiss if not an exchange of saliva containing an invisible otherness. It's too intimate. I'll not sever my impurity from my arrogance," he promised himself as he followed her.

They trod on the Bright Path along Route 786, listening to the rhythmic rustle of rain. They talked about sea, about whales and sharks, never again alluding to hues and colours and creatures and nouns less white and less bright than the Bright Path.

They ate dinner in a non-descript café in the coastal town. The food was raw, the waitress's smile cooked and the ambience incensed. They were the last customers of the evening, sitting face to face, feeling a common hunger. The waitress brought them the evening's last supper and told them to hurry up before life stopped in the café. They ate like two people uninitiated to the culinary rhythm; their bite fierce, chewing communicative, ingestion obscure, satisfaction personal. When they came out of the café, lights were gone and the Bright Path was no longer visible. It was dark with the darkness of their empty stomachs. They had not eaten food: only devoured its sight, its smell, its name, its history and its inscription on the menu. They had eaten their money: their cheque.

They arrived at Sue's apartment situated behind an abandoned Holiday Inn. Sue unlocked the front door and turned to look at him. Neither of them spoke for a full minute: they were not supposed to. They were afraid they might say something that would exceed the demands of the occasion, or demand something that would demolish the occasion altogether. Silence defined the moment, and the moment was its own voice echoing deep in a prehistoric cave. Mohammed Khan touched her face and kissed her on the eyes, tracing her eyebrows with his moving lips. She trembled under his touch as he reached to embrace the artist in him.

"What's your favourite music, Mohammed?" Sue asked him. She lay on his stomach, resting her face on his chest.

"The music that created cosmos, and echoes in the heart of things. Let me play it for you."

He took out a flute from his jacket and brought it to his mouth. He rolled his fingers over it and the notes of Estrogenic Melody Number Seven rippled through the air. He played for as long as the flute responded and as long as Sue could sway to its tune. Finally, the flute dropped from his lips, spent and exhausted.

They lay next to the fire and slept. They slept many sleeps and dreamed of many more. When he woke up, he saw Sue staring at him from afar, from some other time, with an inquisitiveness born of a long and sleepy forgetfulness.

"You're all tattooed," she said.

"The tree embraced me," he explained. "They are the hieroglyphs of my arboreal memory."

She looked down at his circumcised penis with sanctimonious concern. "Why is it incomplete?" She asked. "What happened to the upper half?"

"It was sacrificed to the God of Perfection so my heritage to Abraham could be confirmed."

"Make me perfect, Mohammed Khan," she said.

"I'll make another sacrifice for you," Mohammed Khan promised and pulled her into his arms.

They danced to the flow of fleshy music, waltzing across the room, surrendering to the harmony of their breathing, to the rhythm of throbbing hearts, to the curvaceous poetry of their bodies. Mohammed Khan made love to her horizontally and vertically, from within and without, obliterating the pre-copulatory distinction of mind, body and soul – and of line, colour and volume. It was history's first gender-transcending act of fornication for which no four God-fearing, pious witnesses are available to date.

When she finally reached orgasm, she yelled so loudly it nearly cracked a window glass. Mohammed Khan moaned and jerked heroically. A burst of lukewarm sperms, unstoppable like the tears of an unhappy god of Creation, rushed to embrace the anxious ovum. Sue felt a beam of light penetrating her, impregnating her with dynastic lineage. She experienced a sensation, so divine in its sublimity that it made her smile. "I feel complete," she confessed to Mohammed Khan in a state of reproductive anxiety.

Mohammed Khan laughed with a spermatic authority that made her heart tremble with an undefined fear.

They took a hot shower together, infusing their bodies with purity and washing away the last remnants of reticence between them. Sue was the first to leave the bathroom. Mohammed Khan stayed under the shower, feeling light and fresh, eyes closed, enjoying the warm pressure of the sprayed water that streaked down to his ankles. Suddenly he felt listless, his eyes turned heavy and his head became giddy. He collapsed half-conscious as past and present dissolved into a meaningless post-coital void.

When he regained consciousness he found himself lying on Sue's sofa. She smiled at him and said, "I may not know the difference between past and present but I know the difference between masked and unmasked people, between death and burning, between black and white complexions, and between rebirth and piety."

"It's not your job to theorise," Mohammed Khan cautioned her. "There are others who do it, though I'm not one of them. But if you want to move in that direction you'll be directed and a day will come when you'll find that less is needed to satisfy more."

"Do you always talk like that after regaining consciousness?"

"Only after premarital sex," Mohammed Khan said politely.

Sue appeared horrified.

"What we did was not pre-marital sex, Mohammed Khan," she said. "It was just a friendly interaction between two mature adults."

"Friendly interaction?" Mohammed Khan roared. "It was not a friendly interaction. It was pure, safe and honest pre-marital sex. I fucked you as is worthy of an X-rated movie fuck between consenting adults. You can't take that honour away from me."

"You can't use the f-word in front of a lady," Sue warned him. "I didn't do anything. You must've done it in your fantasies. Wait a minute… you may have done it with someone else… with my alter ego or my dummy or with an inflated doll. Had you done it with me, the window glass would have cracked. You know it didn't. Only the cracks could provide incontrovertible proof of my participation."

"I just made love to you, my dear," Mohammed Khan pleaded. "Thrice."

"Thrice?" Sue said contemptuously as she walked away from him over to a bookshelf and retrieved a video stored inside a leather-bound cover. She reverently kissed the video, touched it with her forehead and offered it to him.

"You have no idea about making love, mister," she said. "Here's the instructional video you need to see. Watch it and you'll know how love ought to be made."

"Don't start a sexual crusade, please," Mohammed Khan begged as he accepted the video.

11

If a man lies with a damsel that is a virgin, then ye shall bring them out unto the gate of the city and ye shall stone them with stones until they die.
(Deuteronomy, 22: 25-29)

The adulterer and the adulterous, scourge each with one hundred stripes and let not pity for the twain withhold ye from obeying Allah's command.
(Al-Quran, 24: 2)

Mohammed Khan returned to his solitude and placed the instructional video in the VCR. The TV screen lit up with the familiar face of a bearded man.

"Hi, I'm M.Sahib, though you may have known me by my longer vernacular name. Welcome to the interactive video of *Ornaments From Paradise*," M. Sahib said brightly, wearing his legendary self-righteous look like a facial bikini. He had pruned his beard, creating arcs of tinted hair around his cheeks. His neatly cut moustache – a similax of trimmed hair really – hid the famous mole on his upper lip. Mohammed Khan touched the screen and felt a charge of electricity go through his fingers and travel to some portion of his chest. He sniffed at M. Sahib's beard and smelt the sweet aroma of smouldering thaapies.

"This is the same book you once read and didn't particularly find to your taste," M. Sahib said. "I may have pruned my beard and shortened my name to make myself appear more modern and palatable to your changing taste, but my message remains unchanged and my basic text book is still *Ornaments from Paradise*. And you know why? Because it's the tome that has stood all tests of time, providing guidance to millions of people all over the globe. It has everything you always wanted to know but did not have the VCR to see it. This pirated video is about the correct procedure for sex. Other videos throwing divine light on remaining subjects are available through a special offer."

The scene changed. M. Sahib now stood outside a public toilet. "Making love the right way," M. Sahib said, looking intently at the camera as if he hoped to penetrate beyond the picture tube and grab men by their throats and women by their breasts. "Love-making invariably starts with the sacred ritual of ablution. A lover must perform ablution before pre-marital sex and after farting, urinating or discharge of faeces."

The scene shifted, showing M. Sahib ambling along a riverbank. In the background was a sprawling golf course where women in topless swimsuits played golf. A tall blonde drove a ball through the air across the river to M. Sahib who caught it like an ace baseball player. With one swing of the hand, he threw the ball in the air, across the river, back to the golfing blonde, and turned to smile at the camera.

"What type of water is fit for ablution, dear lover?" M. Sahib asked with a smile that brought the entire range of his glittering teeth in view. He bent and gathered water in his curved palm. "Water like this. It is allowed to wash your body with water that originates from a river, canal, pond, well, or falls from the sky as rain, but if milk is mixed with it, the water is no longer fit for ablution – though you may sell it to gullible customers as fresh milk, ha ha ha. If leaves fall into a well and the water starts to smell foul, or if it is polluted with an invisible pollutant, you can still cleanse your body with it provided that no pagan man, woman or eunuch has put his hand in it. This is the first step towards environmentally-friendly sex."

Yet again the scene changed. M. Sahib now stood outside a Casino. In the background was a glittering sign that said: Welcome to the Biggest Losing Opportunity in the World. M. Sahib walked inside the casino, moving through tables of Black Jack and Roulette, passing by slot machines and old women who sat engrossed in the jingle of dropping coins. The camera finally led to a room where a well-endowed blonde lay naked on the bed. The camera zoomed onto her pubic triangle. M. Sahib selected one pubic hair at random, plucked it with a quick jerk to the backdrop of the blonde's loud protest, and displayed it on the screen. "Unclean women like this lady here do not remove their pubic hair because they have not been blessed with the holy razor," he said. "When pubic hair grows longer than a grain of wheat, everything you eat turns impure and forbidden. So if you plan to make love to such a woman, you must instruct her to shave her pubic hair. Threading and waxing is also permitted, though hereditary barbers must not be employed for this purpose."

The camera returned to M. Sahib's smiling face. "When she enters your house for the purpose of enticing you, make sure you hold the hair on her forehead, give it a hard pull, and say these words: 'O Lord. I ask Thee of her goodness and the goodness of her habits, and seek refuge from all the evil within her.' Take her to your room, and make her take a bath. Then take a bath yourself but not together or you'll surely get SARS.

"During intercourse, do not become naked like animals. Cover her with a cloth and cover yourself too. If either of you remains naked, you will get AIDS."

"Don't start intercourse immediately. Kiss her gently until you feel her responding to you. Words and kisses are the messenger between you and your woman. You can kiss her breasts but don't suck her nipples because it's a sign of Oedipus complex. Don't chew them like bubble gum or attempt to drink the pasteurised milk contained therein because it's childish. During intercourse, she must lie on her back and you must be on top of her. If she succeeds in getting on top of you, she can make you pregnant.

"Do not talk during intercourse or your offspring shall be born deaf and dumb. Do not look at her nakedness or your eyesight will weaken. Do not have sex on the first, fifteenth and the last night of a month because only Satan indulges in sex on those nights. Do not make love on Sundays and Wednesdays: these are the days when ostracised devils get together. Do not have sex more than once in four days otherwise you'll become impotent. Do not withdraw immediately after ejaculation: wait for your woman to have an orgasm also. Sex should be an equal-opportunity activity.

"Now some do's," M. Sahib continued. "After sexual intercourse, both of you must wipe your private parts and take a bath. Put water three times in your mouth and three times in your nostrils before you eat or drink anything. If you want to have sex again, you must take a bath first."

M. Sahib paused, brushed a hand through his beard and gave a parting smile. "This brings us to end of our presentation. Go and enjoy your sex within the boundaries of the Video. Good night, and happy sex to you."

Mohammed Khan switched off the TV and ejaculated the video cassette. He had completed the Auspicious Watching of the Video and he was more inside the body of permissible sexual knowledge than ever before.

He returned to Sue's apartment and kneeled before her. "I have mastered the correct art of making love and I feel that life has become real. Will you marry me?"

"Yes, my love," she replied. "I'll marry you."

"'Til word spoken thrice do us part and we enter the quagmire of costly divorce proceedings," Mohammed Khan added.

"And 'til blood tests are conducted, and the priest is called, and the church is adorned. And if my Dad approves," Sue said.

"For that purpose, I shall undertake all hazardous journeys to meet your father," Mohammed Khan promised.

"Let's go visit him, then," Sue said. "We'll stop on the way and have some fun as an adulterer and an adulteress."

With Sue sleeping at his side, Mohammed Khan drove his rented vehicle, watching the black slabs of concrete being swallowed under the bonnet of the car. Sue snored, her hair covering the side of her face. She had red hair, made brittle beyond redemption because of its constant synthesis with strong hair dyes, so that it looked uncannily like the needled leaves of the pine trees he saw rushing past his vehicle. He made a mental note to suggest that she dye it green: that might make her look more natural.

Sue stirred at his side. "Are we there, Mohammed?" she asked.

"Another twenty minutes, honey."

She moaned. "I don't feel well."

"Period?" Mohammed Khan asked politely.

"No, silly. I wanna throw up. It was the McDonald's on the way."

"McDonald's maintains a high standard of cleanliness, honey," Mohammed Khan said with conviction. "Must be something else."

"It was the McDonald's," she said with a tone of finality.

He accepted her argument and she went back to sleep again.

They reached the city that thrived on people's greed.

"Where are we?" Sue asked.

"At World's Circus hotel, honey."

"I hate Circus. I wanna go to the Sheraton."

"We don't have a reservation there, Sue. It's a long weekend, remember?"

"I wanna go to the Sheraton," Sue said with a tone of finality.

Mohammed Khan swerved the car back on to the road, heading for the Sheraton. Sue went back to sleep again.

The Sheraton was full. Mohammed Khan argued unsuccessfully with the desk clerk for a room. The clerk was a big guy with a chest larger than a double bed. He was from the tribe of Governor Arnold Schwarzenegger – he had no facial expression.

"We don't have your reservation, sir," he said.

"But I made a reservation three days ago," Mohammed Khan lied.

"We were fully booked five days ago, sir," the clerk said, and showed him a great set of teeth that was positively Schwarzenegger.

He came back fuming.

Sue was still asleep. Mohammed Khan woke her and told her furiously, "They're fully booked."

Sue opened the door on her side and got out. "No, they're not," she said and walked away.

He watched her from the back. She walked with a pronounced sway of her hips as if to compensate for their small size. On the way, she had confided to him that she felt a pelvic affinity with Julia Roberts. "She's got a small ass too. I understand her loss."

She was gone fifteen minutes and returned with a porter watching her swinging rear. "They found a room for us, Mohammed."

There are three types of women in this world. Some turn you on, others turn you off, and some castrate you. Mohammed Khan was to discover that Sue was all three.

As soon as he tipped the waiter, she turned him on. They made love within the boundaries of the Holy Video until they dropped dead from excitement, exhaustion and boredom. Sue slid off the bed and ran to the bathroom. Moments later, he heard her vomit.

"I don't feel good," she said as she came out. "It's the fucking McDonald's."

"You need to see a doctor, honey," Mohammed Khan said. "McDonald's maintains a high standard of cleanliness."

"Stop soliciting for McDonald's."

"Sure," he said. "Must be McDonald's."

An hour later, they went down to the casino. Mohammed Khan selected a Black Jack table. The dealer was an innocuous looking guy with an extended grin. Mohammed Khan lost four hundred dollars in twenty minutes. The dealer continued to grin.

In the Black Jack world, they have a saying: "If you can't spot the sucker in half an hour, it's gotta be you." Mohammed Khan didn't need that long to spot himself, so he gathered his fading grin and dwindling chips, and went over to the roulette table where Sue was playing and winning.

"I don't feel well," she told him.

"I know, honey," he said sympathetically. "It was the McDonald's."

That night, Sue won $13,000.

In their hotel room, Sue spent a full hour in the bathroom. When she came out, her face was radiant.

"Honey," she said. "I'm pregnant."

Mohammed Khan had been lying on his bed, trying to ignore the retching sound emanating from the bathroom, when the significance of her statement hit him. It brought him upright on his feet, feet that no longer felt very steady.

"What?" he said disbelievingly. "It's not possible. I've always been using condoms. You know I'm very particular about… about the risk of being stoned to death."

Sue was beaming now. "Remember when you ran out of your stock at Motel 6? You went down and bought some Malaysian condoms. I read they leaked."

"Oh come on, Sue," Mohammed Khan protested. "One single leaking condom can't make you pregnant."

"I'm a mountain goat," she said proudly.

He hung his head. It was so unfair. Some Malaysian condom manufacturer had made him liable to death by stoning under Hebrew law and one hundred lashes under Moslem law, just because he couldn't manage his quality control department.

"Wait a minute," he lifted his head in hope. "How do you know you're pregnant? You can't presume that you're pregnant just because McDonald's didn't maintain their standard of cleanliness."

"Shut up, Mohammed. I told you it wasn't McDonald's. I know I'm pregnant. My pregnancy test just came out positive."

12

> *He said: Verily Moses, I desire to marry thee unto one of my daughters on the condition that thou hirest thyself to me for the turn of eight pilgrimages. Then if thou completest ten, it will be thine own accord. Moses said: That is settled between thee and me and whichever of the two terms I fulfil, there shall be no injustice against me by demanding an addition thereto.*
> *(Al-Quran, 28: 21-28)*

They resumed their southward journey to Sue's village, where a carpenter father and a hot-tempered mother waited for no one. The village was in the mountains, a small nest nestled among rocks and boulders that fell like rain upon the sinuous highway, blocking it for days during the rainy season. When they arrived at their destination, Sue found that things had changed a lot since she'd left.

Ten years ago, her father – even in his mid forties – had seemed an old man. He had a face chiselled with wrinkles of concentration that started from the corners of his eyes and stretched in two directions: one attacked the slanting jaw and extended toward his scraggy neck; the other advanced over his forehead and curved down his nose. He would usually be found stooped over his tools, his back arched in a crescent, his sweating biceps working furiously to move the hacksaw until either his saw or his spirit broke.

Sue had remembered him as a man with brittle lips, ravaged by the cold winds that would hit him during his visits to the forest at the edge of the village, where trees from obsolete times grew. It was here, after Sue's departure following the murder of her husband at the hands of the Ku Klux Klan, that John Mangan had selected the oldest of all trees to slash down so that he could make the best and the most solid furniture, fated to last forever. He would make it once and for all, he thought. For many days he worked deliriously, disturbed only by his ambition and the old snake that would appear near the tree. One day, he killed the snake, felled the tree, cut it into long strips, took out its root along with everything else deposited underneath the root, and became a man of riches. He saved what he found, earned a lot of money from the sale of his furniture, deposited it in a bank, borrowed money from another bank, and won every bet he placed on cricket matches in South Africa, India, Australia and Pakistan.

Physically, he started growing backwards in years – and economically in the opposite direction. When Sue and Mohammed Khan arrived at his doorstep, they met a sprightly man of thirty with a lean, firm mouth, a pair of blue contact lenses, a defiant forehead, and a long nose nicely arranged on a face which had undergone various bouts of plastic surgery. His features were sharp and attractive, stretched cleverly to carve the face of youth. His skin, that had once looked tired and pallid, was now radiant, carrying a determined look.

The house had changed too. It now boasted seventeen large bedrooms, fifteen and a half bathrooms and a gigantic living room. There were sprawling lawns in front and back where flowers bloomed out of season. J. Mangan now owned a chain of *Levitz*, three *Furnishings 2000*, and was in the process of negotiating a deal with *Henredon*. He greeted them warmly and invited Sue inside. Then he turned to Mohammed Khan.

"What you see here is the gift of the Giver," James John Mangan said with a smile. He had the ability to sound sincere without compromising on artifice. "Years ago, I chanced upon riches of which half a million dollars was Sue's – though she had left home a month earlier. I invested that entire amount for her in T-Bills at 6.7%. Deduct income tax, the tax officer's bribe, my chartered accountant's fee, monthly expenses of twelve thousand dollars – which Sue herself would have incurred – and it leaves me with roughly thirty thousand dollars I owe her. Is that why she's here? To ask for her money?"

Mohammed Khan moved uneasily in the fluffy cushion of the sofa. He was not interested in monetary calculations or ways of multiplying money, in bank loans or defaults, in betting or buried treasures, in savings or the sale of furniture, in drug-trafficking or the shares of siblings in their father's property. He was only interested in the future of his seed.

James John Mangan waited expectantly for an answer. Mohammed Khan hesitated. He was about to say something he was not supposed to say. Marriage in his part of the world was a prestigious communal ceremony, epitomising the collective ethos of the people. It was not just a union of two individuals motivated by emotional needs and individual choice but a nexus between families and a prelude to a new series of alliances. It was a public statement regarding the status of the families involved in the alliance. Who married whom defined who one was, and Mohammed Khan was about to be defined.

He took a deep breath and slowly said, "Sire! I don't know why she's here, but I know why I'm here. I've undertaken this long and hazardous journey to ask you for the hand of your daughter."

The smile dropped from J. Mangan's face. The muscles on his face tightened until Mohammed Khan feared they might snap.

"Asking the hand of ma daughter!" Mangan said in a tone beset by outrage. "How dare you come here without a prior appointment? Couldn't you call me in advance and fix an appointment? And where are your parents? Why are they hiding their face from me? How dare they send you and not your village barber so he could have verified your caste and ancestry? How do I know that your father's not a cobbler or a minstrel? He might be a blacksmith or a weaver for all I know. Besides, I don't have a daughter."

Mohammed Khan dismissed the last remark as a thin excuse from a father not willing to give his daughter's hand to a stranger about whose ancestry he knew little. He hung his head in commiseration. "Sire, I understand your indignation and share your concern, but I assure you that I come from the noble lineage of that ancient tribe which is genetically prone to producing prophets and men of vision. I meditated under the ancient tree of half-answers for forty days and was blessed with two visions: one, that I'll marry again in this land and two that I'll become the headman of that land. That, sire, is written in the Book of Writing though I make no claim to be a specialist at deciphering ancient scripts."

"Well son," James Mangan said in a voice gone mellow. "These things take time."

"Time is not on my side, sire," Mohammed Khan said. "Sue is pregnant. Her pregnancy test came through positive. We must get married immediately or I'll have to bear the shame of an illegitimate son. If my folks come to know about it, they will stone me to death. It's the punishment decreed by the First Chastiser."

"That certainly is a problem in your part of the world, son," James John Mangan said gravely. "Sue can't have a child because she's not married. She must get married to whosoever has made her pregnant. It is the custom of this Valley."

"I'm willing to accept her hand," Mohammed Khan said humbly.

"Indeed," James John Mangan nodded, "and I'm willing to act as her father, but there are other things to be done first."

"You mean like the visit from my parents? And the price of her hand and private parts?"

"And more," J. Mangan said earnestly. "In order to become worthy of Sue's hand and parts, which you call private although they are quite public in this society, you'll need to work on my ranch across the hills for no less than seven years. You'll till that land. You'll herd cows and oxen and bison and pigs. Some of them will be clean, others unclean; some will be tamed, others might need to be leashed and still others might need to be hit hard so you can guide them to the watering place. But don't hit them hard too often. Beasts are closer to a man's stomach than to his staff, though it is by means of the staff that you'll come to know them and their difference from mankind. When the days have ended, I'll be bound by the custom of my Valley to offer you the hand of my daughter, be it against my wishes and best judgement.

"During this period you'll not speak to her nor look at her face save for the purpose of recognising her or for counting the days of your labour. Beware though that in early age, a woman's face is like the lunar calendar and in later age it turns into a solar calendar. Their identity lies in their wombs, evil in their desire and intellect in their tongue. Their existence is good and intimacy amnesiac. If you understand whatever I said, then from today you can take up the job. If you fail in your duties you'll be fired without notice. People around here admire efficiency, productivity and planned families, not the nobility of lineage."

"Seven years?" Mohammed Khan reminded him helplessly. "But she's pregnant, sire."

"If she is, so let her remain that way for seven years," James John Mangan cried angrily. "If she's not, then no harm will come to her. She'll carry your burden inside her, untouched by man or jinn or the skinless. When the years are passed and the time of holy matrimony arrives, I'll deliver her to you, provided she's still available."

"I will remain true to my promise, sire," Mohammed Khan said faithfully.

Mohammed Khan indeed remained true to his promise. On some occasions, he went beyond it. On others, he was found wanting, though he was clever enough never to get caught.

His routine rarely changed. He would get up at dawn, take the animals to the pasture, and nap during long afternoons under the Banyan tree or play songs from the movie *Heer Ranjha* on his flute. Sue would bring a lunch of bread and butter and buttermilk for him, place it under the tree and go away before his arrival from the fields, which he sometimes ploughed by pulling the wooden plough with his hands. In the evenings he would milk buffaloes and cows, cut fodder on the hand-operated cutting wheel and again play songs on his flute. He earned himself a good name in the community and the elders acknowledged his hard work by conferring on him the Order of the Good Worker. This was a moment of glory for Mohammed Khan and a renewal of mankind's pledge to honour work and worker as symbols of the proper functioning of the new world order.

Seven years passed faster than he had expected. Though the pain of waiting made time crawl, his workaholic ecstasy and his keenness to inscribe his futuristic vision on Sue's pagan senses made time fly. "It was two against one," he told his herd. "A simple, mathematical, democratically-correct outcome."

And one day, when according to his calculation, seven years had passed, Mohammed Khan started his journey back to the home of James John Mangan.

13

Time is relative.
   (Albert Einstein)

Someone must have been making false accusations against Joseph K. for he was arrested one morning without having done anything wrong.
   (Opening sentence of 'The Trial' by Franz Kafka)

If you want a decision in your favour, don't waste money on a good lawyer; spend it gainfully on a High Court judge.
   (A joke from a third world country)

Zulaikha resolved to have Yusuf. They both raced for the door and she rented his shirt from behind.
   (Al-Quran, 12: 24-25)

Mohammed Khan did not bother to ring the bell on James Mangan's house. In a state of delirious ecstasy, he opened the front door and walked into the living room.

"The years have ended, sire," he said excitedly, oblivious to the manner of his entry and the reality of his addressee. "I have tilled the land, herded cows and sparingly used my staff. I now know the difference between my staff and the python, and how to transform one into the other."

He was heard in thickening silence. "And during this period, I didn't speak to your daughter nor look at her face even for the purpose of recognising her," Mohammed Khan continued. "I have fulfilled my promise, sire, and now I call upon you to fulfil yours."

"What the hell are you talking about boy?" James Mangan roared. "You left my house only moments ago."

"I spent seven years across the hillocks, sire," Mohammed Khan said.

"Look around you, boy," a voice coming from within and beyond cut him short. "You couldn't possibly have spent seven years anywhere.

Everything's the way you left it. The storm's still outside the house and my drink is only half-finished. Even the chain on my door is still moving."

"The chain on your door is meant to stop burglars from entering your house, sire," Mohammed Khan cried. "It's not a device to measure time. The storm can linger on and a drink of milk can stay half-finished, but time moves on. Come with me across the hillocks and I'll show you everything I've done in those seven years. Only your heart can reveal to you all that has happened across time and all that I did to become worthy of your daughter's hand. I've been through the time of love, sire, where desire was its mover. You live in the time of your place where nature guides its motion. Why don't you believe me, sire? Haven't you heard of the theories of Albert Einstein? Or is it that excessive drinking has blanked your memory and changed your persona? Why, you don't even look like the father-in-law I left behind when I went to the lands across the hillocks."

"I've never been across the hillocks: I'm an absentee landlord," James Mangan said contemptuously. "I don't know what's on the other side. Whatever you're gonna show me will surely have been there since the beginning. You're the only witness of what's on the other side but I know for sure that you never went there. You're a liar and a cheat, boy, and if you can lie, so can I. Let me tell you once and for all that I never met you in my life before and I've absolutely no idea what you're talking about. I never promised you the hand of ma daughter. Someone must have played a trick on you."

"Just because you look different doesn't mean that you're different from the one who promised legitimacy to my unborn son," Mohammed Khan said resolutely. "Soon you'll hear from my judge, sire. I'm going to the court to get what I deserve."

Mohammed Khan tried every court in the land of missed opportunity and found all doors closed for his kind. And so he decided to go back to the Valley to get justice from his own kind.

He flew back to the Valley and filed seventy writ petitions in the Loehar High Court. James Mangan followed him all the way to Loehar where he bought a palatial farmhouse on Raiwind road and befriended every judge in the High Court. Whenever Mohammed Khan's petition was fixed for hearing, J. Mangan would wish on the moon and the concerned judge would report sick. This happened sixty-nine times. On the seventieth time, James Mangan forgot to wish and the judge fixed the date. A day before the scheduled hearing, Mangan invited all the judges to a party at his farmhouse where they sat as brothers-in-sanctimony upon gold-crusted seats of bliss around a swimming pool filled with single-malt whisky. Young boys and girls wearing designer perfumes and little else, served them with intoxication. In the morning, the judges discovered to their horror that they had turned deaf, and issued arrest warrants for the bootlegger who had supplied whisky of dubious origin and maturation for the party. Mohammed Khan found out about their pathological condition during the course of the hearing. He shouted at the top of his voice until it croaked, but the Court could not hear him. The judge postponed the case pending the invention of the hearing aid. Mohammed Khan protested and upon his request, a committee was formed to keep track of all scientific inventions.

Mohammed Khan was desperate. He rushed to the farmhouse of James Mangan and abducted a woman who denied that she was Sue. Mohammed Khan refused to believe her even though she did not look like Sue. But he did not care. Everyone was a liar in this land and he was no longer ready to believe his eyes or ears: only his actions.

Next morning, James Mangan went to the local police station and filed a criminal complaint against Mohammed Khan. He stated in the First Information Report that one Mohammed Khan, son of his parents, resident of nowhere, pretender of dynastic past, confuser of time and space, knower of animal and agriculture, and worker of some dubious merit, fragmented his daughter Sue – caste Rockefeller, social status high – and left her wondering about the nature of her spirit. The Station House Officer borrowed Mangan's latest-model turbo Land Cruiser and travelled all the way in luxury and style to a place away from the scene of the crime to arrest Mohammed Khan from his solitude. Mohammed Khan was brought back to the district headquarters and indicted on two counts – fragmenting a total being and abducting her soul. The date for his trial was set five years from now.

On a dreary morning, when five years had passed, Mohammed Khan was produced before an empty court filled with justice.

The courthouse stood on the hill, circled by a road that came winding from its left and kept rising until it passed the back of the building and then dipped toward a series of expensive bungalows and sprawling mansions of the Government Officers' Residential Estate No. 1. The architecture of the courthouse was Transylvanian. Its steps were large and made of a slippery black granite. Mohammed Khan walked slowly under the burden of his fetters, taking each step towards a destiny he'd once imagined. The courtroom was in semi-darkness because of a general power failure, and flickering candles were trying to perform a forgotten deed in the era of electric power. Bright spaces alternated with dark alcoves, creating unstable shadows. Mohammed Khan stood waiting in shackles and chains before the dais as the walls around him trembled in candlelight, revealing the weakness of the building material.

The court was not big inside. There were only fourteen pews, with a central aisle dividing them into two distinct groups. The pews were pure black mahogany: a reminder of the ravages of legal and illegal battles and certain and uncertain outcomes. Mohammed Khan had a feeling that a foreign presence was watching him. With each waiting moment, the feeling grew stronger. Whatever it was, he was better off not seeing it.

The Judge's Reader greeted him with an argumentative silence. He was a beakish fellow who needed to put on a few pounds to affect procedural justification. He stared at the world atop his reading glasses, from behind a series of trials and mistrials and a dusty pile of court files. Within the torn covers and perforated edges of each file lay the lives of people on death row, the agonies of necks trapped in the gallows, the deafening thuds of the gavel waiting to release its juristic demons. Mohammed Khan was immune to the terror of files and to the horror of law and legal procedures. He was a nobody, from nowhere: a legal invisibility. He had little idea of what the files contained and even less expertise of how to handle them. It was happening in a world not of his making – a world without walls.

The trial eventually began with an opening statement from the District Attorney.

"Ladies and gentlemen of the jury," he said, even though there were no women present in court. "Mohammed K. has committed a crime of deleterious proportions. He ripped an unarmed shirt, violated the privacy of a fertile spirit and tried to contaminate it with an alien thought. He has caused ripples in the honour-pool of this great Province of Punjab, mixed milk with water, gasoline with kerosene, tea with sawdust."

The jurors squirmed in their seats. There were twelve of them, all male, all related, all confused and all anxious to go home and watch *WWF Mania* on PTV-2. They didn't believe the police or the eyewitnesses. They didn't like the DA or his shoes. They had doubts about the character of the girl, knew the eyewitnesses were jealous of Mohammed Khan and believed that such things happened between young people – but they also knew that their reasoning was slight in the face of the seriousness of the charge. It was an attempted rape upon their collective virginity, a matter beyond legal reasoning and belief and personal preference.

The District Attorney paused for effect and, in a state of self-indulgent trance, took a couple of pottered steps during which he marvelled at his patent leather shoes. He moved closer until the jurors could see his eyes, and he could smell indecision on their breath. "Don't be fooled by Mohammed K.'s innocent face," he whispered conspiratorially. "Pay no attention to the graffiti on his body," he added. "Think nothing of him," he concluded.

That was as far as he was allowed to go. The proceedings were disturbed by a rumpus outside. The judges left their chairs and benches to witness what was happening beyond their jurisdiction. Outside, an angry crowd led by an aspiring judge named M. Sharif had gathered. There were seven people in the mob, his wife and six children, demanding that Mohammed Khan's case be transferred to the Speedy Trial Court which should be headed by M. Sharif and his two sons whose long hair reached their weak shoulders.

"The slowness of the due process of law is inimical to speedy justice," M. Sharif spoke to his followers above the tweet of his malfunctioning bullhorn. "Men like Mohammed K. can pay off judges, hire corrupt lawyers, intimidate the jury and, above all, find favour with the press. They can make the trial drag on for days and get the judgement of their choice. We're here to stop this from happening. Mohammed K. must be punished and he must be punished swiftly and mercilessly. I'm here to ensure that."

"We are here to support him," his wife, one daughter-in-law and other children responded in unison.

Things eventually turned ugly. The mob had been constant in purpose and number since morning, waiting for something to happen. A few minutes before noon, trucks arrived, carrying dishes of meat and rice cooked in butter. Their aroma was so strong that even the bystanders gave up their uneasy neutrality and joined the Sharifs in their struggle. The Sharifs too had grown in number as M. Sharif's brothers and sisters and their families from both maternal and paternal sides joined the rally. They arrived on the heels of food, and suddenly the number of protesters grew so large that it was senseless to harness their anger or stop them from storming the court. Their aggregate justified their outrage.

They did not attack anything in particular, though nothing escaped their wrath. They tore their way through all illusory barriers and reached where they deserved to reach in their present state of fury. His Lordship, who was in the middle of hearing Mohammed Khan's case, fled through the backdoor, tactically leaving behind his Florsheim loafers as war booty to slow down the mob. The DA saved his life by taking off his Italian suit and setting it on fire right in the middle of the aphotic courtroom. He danced a war dance around the fire and raised slogans in favour of M. Sharif and his jihad against the patience-testing due process of law.

The SHO was less fortunate. He had shed only half of his uniform to become faceless when the mob caught him. They helped him shed his remaining onymity all the way down to his privities, and made him a public figure in the town's square.

M. Sharif and his sons were tried by the Supreme Court under the Contempt of Court Act. Within the hour, the court became convinced of the Sharifs' passionate sincerity and allowed M. Sharif to try Mohammed Khan in the Speedy Trial Court whose speed was undetermined and jurisdiction unspecified. The trial lasted as long as it should have lasted and Mohammed Khan was provided with every opportunity to clear his name. The prosecution and the court both agreed that Mohammed Khan was no husband of a deposed prime minister and, therefore, it was not difficult to convict him in the present case, so they directed the police not to register any further cases against him.

Mohammed Khan decided to fight the case himself. He had nothing except the power of his own labour, nothing to enable him to hire a solicitor.

"My Lord," a sobbing Sue look-alike was directed by the court to tell it.

"The accused came uninvited to our majestic farmhouse when my Daddy was away. He tried to take me somewhere I didn't want to go. He insisted on calling me someone I was not, though I'm not sure of myself anymore. He was persuasive and forceful. I resisted his vile advances by screaming loud enough to crack windowpanes." (At this stage, the prosecution presented a cracked windowpane as exhibit 1).

"My diversionary tactic distracted him and I was able to hold him by the collar and rip his shirt apart." (A torn shirt was presented as exhibit 2).

"My Lord, I offer a simple proof in my defence," Mohammed Khan said in rebuttal. "If my shirt is torn from the front, which it is not, that means I approached her, she resisted and during the struggle the shirt was torn off. If, on the contrary, she solicited me to evil and I resisted, trying to make it for the door, then the back part of my shirt must be torn – which it is. Your honour, I rest my case."

The prosecution laughed and told the Court that Mohammed Khan was resting his case on flimsy grounds as he was not wearing that particular shirt at the time of the crime. The DA produced a dry cleaner's receipt to prove that Mohammed Khan owned two shirts. He admitted that the prosecution had, through oversight, produced the wrong shirt as exhibit 2. He moved for a replacement of exhibit 2, a request that was finally accepted by the court. A shirt torn from the front substituted exhibit 2, and the one rented from behind was returned to the accused to do with it as he deemed fit. Such was the leniency shown by the Court to the accused.

"My Lord," the DA said after all substitutions had taken place under the scrutiny of justice. "On the basis of a mere shirt, Mohammed K. can't trick Your Lordship on whose back stands the Force and, therefore, he should not fear the consequences of giving a verdict against the accused. The subject shirt was taken by the dry cleaner a day earlier. The dry cleaner, a respectable albeit a low-caste man, wore the subject shirt in the belief that it would bestow on him Mohammed K.'s strength and stamina. After the aborted rape attempt, the accused took his shirt back from the cleaner, tore it from the back and wore it. He gave the other shirt to the tailor for sewing it from the front." (The prosecution produced the tailor at this stage who admitted sewing Mohammed Khan's shirt. They presented a third shirt recovered from Mohammed Khan's room during the police raid. The DA also called forth the dry cleaner who demonstrated his newfound physical prowess by lifting weights which Mohammed Khan could not even move).

"My Lord," Mohammed Khan argued. "The tailor produced by the prosecution is a known liar and an eve-teaser. He's known to have been making passes at women. He's also known to have links with Al-Qaeda; some even say with considerable credibility that he used to wash Mullah Omar and Osama bin Laden's clothes in Tora Bora. Besides, everyone in the village knows that he was bribed by my enemies to stand witness against me. If it pleases the court, I shall produce two children who saw the tailor receiving money and chickens from my enemies." (The court disallowed the evidence of the two children on the grounds of their minority).

The trial lingered on for months during which the jury remained divided. There were no eyewitnesses to the crime and those cited by the prosecution were either absent or unreliable. Mohammed Khan finally requested the court to summon the record-keeping angels on his right and left shoulders as eyewitnesses.

"I've talked to a psychic, my Lord," he said reverently. "The psychic has assured me that he can summon the angels sitting on the right and left shoulder of Sue and myself, in return for a meagre sum should I win the case."

The court agreed. The angels, four in number were directed by the psychic to leave the shoulders of Mohammed Khan and Sue and present themselves along with their record before Judge M. Sharif. After getting necessary clearance from God, the angels came to attend the court. They came in two lines of two, invisible but vocal, and took their positions in the dock.

"What might be your heavenly name?" Judge Sharif asked the empty space believed to be filled by the four angels. "Please state for the record so we can proceed."

The angels spoke simultaneously and the court heard an unintelligible murmur resembling the drone of traffic outside the court premises. The judge asked them to speak up so they could be heard and recorded. The angels raised their voices but still remained unheard and uncomprehended. The court called eminent linguists from all over the world, but they too failed to decipher the murmur that was sometimes thunderous, sometimes mellifluous – but always musical.

After numerous futile attempts by the linguists, his Lordship excused the witnessing angels and decided in favour of the fire ordeal for Mohammed Khan to prove his innocence. In front of a live audience and under the scrutinising stare of Justice Sharif, Mohammed Khan walked over live embers that turned into fresh roses under his feet. Mohammed Khan had an urge to declare prophethood at that very moment, but heard accusations of witchcraft from certain quarters and deferred his plans. The elders banished him from the confines of the country under the Maintenance of Public Order Ordinance, barred him from contesting any election for the next twenty-one years, and allowed him to take the real Sue with him.

Mohammed Khan took Sue and headed by foot for the nearest airport.

There were as many opinions about Mohammed Khan's performance at the fire ordeal as there were mouths.

While some categorised him as a sorcerer and condemned him to a fate over which they had no power, others thought he was just a cheap trickster and his act was nothing but a clever Houdini. But there were a small number of learned men who knew that such an episode had taken place once in theological history and the man who performed the miracle was a prophet. Such men gathered and went in search of Mohammed Khan.

They looked for him in all the crevasses and niches of the earth and failed to find him. It is possible that they looked in all the wrong places. It is equally possible that they had a change of heart on the way and started to look for someone or something entirely different. It is also probable that they failed to find Mohammed Khan because he was still in the process of discovering himself. Whatever the reason, they realised that it was impossible to discover anything that was not already discovered.

Mohammed Khan and Sue journeyed through night and twilight. It was difficult to estimate how far they had travelled, but their tired feet avowed that they'd gone far enough to deserve a rest. They sat down under the shade of a tree whose branches spread out like sleeping snakes in all directions. The tree saved them from the sun and from the rain that came down at night. When they awoke next morning Mohammed Khan saw a rainbow across the mountains and Sue lying at his side with her burden getting heavier.

"Make love to me, Mohammed Khan," she pleaded weakly. Her face looked pale in the light, that was filtering through the falling rain and burgeoning foliage. "fulfil your conjugal obligation so that I can deliver and be free."

Mohammed Khan kneeled beside her and looked her in the eyes. He ran his fingers through her brittle hair and kissed her on the forehead, tasting the salt of her tears. "Freedom comes in many shapes and forms, my Sue," he said sadly, "but I'll free you nevertheless."

They undressed under the tree, their backs touching so they would not see their nakedness. Sue unfurled her hair into a curling tress and swathed it around her expectant breasts. She used a jagged branch of the tree to cut a lock of hair from her temple and twisted it into a braid. Bowing her head, she wrapped the braid around her eyes to protect her from the sight of shame – and waited.

Mohammed Khan prostrated himself upon the red sand that was cold and shifting. It stuck to his body like a robe, a sandy barège covering him and his half-penis. He rolled into the sand and its constituent pigments until his shame was fully sheathed.

Around him, rain still fell. Rosaries of raindrops surrounded the tree. With the fall of each bead, Mohammed Khan heard Sue reciting the Estrous Prayer, and saying Amen with every word until it was time to rid words of their meaning.

Finally the rain stopped and the sun came out again, but before it happened, they took a back-to-back bath in the fading drizzle. He washed his private parts, inhaled water through his nostrils, cleansed his throat by gargling out loud, and said purifying prayers. Finally he dressed and turned to face Sue.

Two days later, they boarded a flight back to the land of green cards. They arrived there after twenty-four hours and went straight to the neighbouring state where getting married was as easy as getting a divorce in some other places. They were married in a nameless church.

When they came out, romance had died, and an unromantic reality stood waiting for them.

Book III

Dreams of the Oracle

Good dreams are one of the parts of prophecy.
(Mishkat, 11;4)

14

A man's home is his castle.
(A proverb)

Mohammed Khan took a job in a ketchup factory in a town called Stockton. A year later, he bought a house on the outskirts of town. Sue delivered her burden two years after her marriage. Her labour lasted seven nights. Mohammed Khan waited outside her room and read from the Holy Book he had once memorised.

'Mary withdrew from her family to a chamber facing east, and kept herself in seclusion from them. Then We sent unto her Our angel of revelation and he assumed the likeness of a perfect man. She exclaimed: "Verily, I seek refuge in the Beneficent One from thee, if you are conscious of Him." He answered: "I am but a messenger of thy Lord who says that He shall bestow upon thee the gift of a son endowed with purity." Said she: "How can I have a son when no man has ever touched me, neither have I been unchaste?" He said: "So it will be! Thy Lord saith, it is easy for Me. And it will be that We may make of him a revelation for mankind and a mercy from Us, and it is a thing ordained."

'And she conceived him, and withdrew with him to a far place. And when the throes of childbirth drove her to the trunk of a palm-tree, she exclaimed: "Oh, would that I had died ere this, and had become a thing forgotten, utterly forgotten!"

'A voice called out to her from beneath her: "Grieve not! Thy Lord hath placed a rivulet beneath thee, and shake the trunk of the palm-tree toward thee, it will drop ripe dates upon thee. So eat and drink and be consoled. And if thou shouldst see any mortal, say: 'Lo! I have vowed a fast unto the Most Gracious, and may not speak this day to any mortal."

'And in time she returned to her people, carrying the child with her.'

"Mr. Khan?"

Mohammed Khan was shaken from his reverie. "Yes," he said, struggling to gather his thoughts.

"Your wife delivered twins. A boy and a girl. Congratulations."

Mohammed Khan kneeled before God and thanked him for blessing him with a son, who would continue his family name and be his old age support. Then he hung his head in sad acceptance as he saw the face of his daughter and wept silently.

For Sue, it was an exhilarating emotional experience. When seven nights of labour transformed into the angelic faces of two babies, she experienced a streak of dazzling happiness that felt like pain. She laughed, then cried. She talked excitedly about the kids, then went into complete silence. She thought they both looked like Sam, then changed her mind. She finally decided to make peace with uncertainty.

Mohammed Khan named his son Sikander and left the naming of the daughter to Sue. She called her Jasmine.

On the third day of his children's birth, Mohammed Khan returned late from work. He drove back in a hurry. Sue had been scheduled to return home with the kids that afternoon, and it was already evening.

Mohammed Khan had been thinking about his daughter. When he first held her in his arms, he had no defined emotions for the lovely-looking stranger, but during the past three days his feelings towards her had shaped into love. Still, there remained a subliminal fear he tried to analyse, but the answer slipped through his fingers each time he reached for it.

His house came into view as he turned the corner. It appeared to be beaming with light from every window. Mohammed Khan got out of the car and walked to the front door, which opened even before he could ring the bell. A smiling Sue hugged him. She looked exuberantly different: a reborn mother with no remnants of the red-haired girl he had once dated across the deserts and mountains of Nevada.

She held him by the arm, and led him to the small room which Mohammed Khan used as his study. It looked different – Mohammed Khan's things had been replaced by two bedsteads which stood under colourful bunting hanging from the ceiling.

"What do you think?" she asked excitedly.

Mohammed Khan looked around in surprise. "What happened to this place? Where are my books?"

Sue grappled with subsiding excitement. "This is the children's room, darling," she said, trying to hide her disappointment. "Look how beautiful it looks."

"Children's room?" Mohammed Khan objected. "They're too small to have a separate room, Sue. It's not safe to leave them here alone."

"Babies always have a room, darling."

"Maybe American babies, but not the children of the Valley!" Mohammed Khan said sternly. "The children will sleep with us. Children always sleep with their parents. God, Sue! How can you let your babies sleep alone? Don't you love them?"

Winter came, foggy rather than cold. One December night, Mohammed Khan woke with the sound of crying. He switched on the light and saw Sikander weeping at his side. He picked him up in his arms and gently rocked him.

"There, there. Don't cry, my son. What's the matter, little one? You hungry? Mama didn't feed you, huh?'

The baby continued to cry. Mohammed Khan walked around the bed and shook Sue by the arm. "Sue. Wake up. Sikander's crying."

Sue opened her eyes and blinked to clear her vision. "What's the matter?"

"Come on," Mohammed Khan said impatiently. "Sikander's crying. He wants milk."

"I fed him at his usual time," she said. "Maybe he wet his nappy."

Mohammed Khan checked and shook his head. "The nappy's fine. He's hungry. He needs milk."

"I can't feed him right now," Sue said. "He had his last feed on time."

"What's timing got to do with feeding? You must feed a baby whenever he cries."

"Oh, Come on, Mohammed. We should find out why he's crying."

"I'm his father. I know why he's crying. I have to decide what he needs."

Mohammed Khan stormed out of the room toward the kitchen. He refused to speak to Sue for the next three days.

Four years later, on a relatively cool evening, Mohammed Khan was reading the *Sacramento Chronicler* when he heard Sue yelling at someone. A moment later, she came in, holding Sikander's hand.

Mohammed Khan looked up over the top of his reading glasses. "Hello, son," he said. "Hello Sue. Is something the matter?"

"He was pissing in the backyard," Sue said angrily.

"Hey, Sikander," Mohammed Khan said gently. "You've been naughty, huh?"

"Naughty? He was disgusting."

Mohammed Khan cocked his head and smiled genially. "Come on, Sue. He's just a kid. They always do that."

"Not in my house, he won't. Not in this country. He's got to learn the rules if he's going to live here."

"He will when he grows up. He's still a little boy."

Sue was confused. Mohammed Khan had started to behave inconsistently since the birth of their children. Normally, he was a composed person with a spontaneous sobriety and a ring of other-worldly logic around his conduct. These traits had given Sue a respectful pride for him. Now she noticed strands in his attitude which seemed incompatible and which made her uneasy. It was as if he had carefully hidden a part of his person from her, and that it was now becoming visible.

The most perceptible change was the streak of casualness toward his children, and their frolics. He would pamper them to the point of being careless, displaying an almost supercilious imperviousness to all the do's and don'ts which Sue was diligently trying to instill in their minds. For Sue, it was very disconcerting to see her husband's demeanour as a father so out of tune with his overall personality. She decided to talk to him about it.

She chose the moment correctly. It was a quiet evening. Mohammed Khan was back from work and looking forward to the long weekend. Sue sat down next to him and handed him a cup of tea. "I need to talk to you about the kids," she said.

Mohammed Khan looked up in concern. "What about them? Are they sick?"

"No. They're not sick, Mohammed, but I'm worried about them."

"If they're not sick, then what's the problem?"

"The problem is the way you relate to them."

Mohammed Khan opened his mouth to say something but Sue continued. "Look, I appreciate that kids are raised differently in your part of the world but our children are going to stay right here, and they need to learn the norms of this society, not of a far off Valley."

Expressions of relief returned to Mohammed Khan's face. "My God. You nearly gave me a heart attack. I thought there was some serious problem."

"This is a serious problem, Mohammed," Sue said emphatically. "If you only realised its magnitude."

Mohammed Khan made a face. "I don't see a problem…"

His nonchalance brought a wave of anger inside her. "You don't see a problem when Sikander pees in the backyard? You don't see a problem when he doesn't go to sleep on time? You don't see a problem when Jasmine cuts up my skirt to make a dress for her doll? Have you ever told them that it's wrong."

Mohammed Khan shrugged. "They're small kids."

"Kids need to learn manners and discipline."

"They'll learn everything with age," Mohammed Khan said. "Come on, Sue, you're overreacting. How old are they? Five? You can't expect them to behave like adults."

"What sort of adults will they make if they're not taught the basics?"

"Basics of what?" Mohammed Khan said.

"The fact that there's a time for everything and there are ways to do things. Because of your attitude, our kids are getting confused. They tend to mix things up."

"Mix things up? How?"

"When it's time to eat, they want to play. When it's their bedtime, you start playing with them. You don't care how late it is."

Mohammed Khan got to his feet and moved toward Sue, locking his brown eyes into hers. "You may be living in time and space, Sue, but I know for certain that time and space live in me. I will decide when the time is right to start teaching them the basics of life. Until then, let my children remain what they are – children."

15

Trains and time do not wait for anyone.
   (A poster warning passengers at Lalamusa railway station)

You are the best community that has been raised up for mankind.
   You order right conduct and forbid indecency.
   (Al-Quran, 3:110)

And entrust not into the incapable the substance which Allah hath
   placed with you as a means of support.
   (Al-Quran, 4:5)

One day Mohammed Khan woke to realise that the time had come to teach his children. Sue perceived the transition, noticing an element of moral panic in her husband. Initially, the shift was gradual, but then it gathered momentum, as if he faced an enemy many times stronger than himself, and with time running out.

The enemy was *jahalia*, the dark forces of ignorance. These forces had always obstructed the divine light, and God had to send his prophets to destroy them. Now Mohammed Khan in his limited capacity was going to continue the prophetic mission, keeping the darkness of nescience away from his children's hearts. He was aware of the perilous nature of this formidable task. There was little affirmation of his training programme in his home, let alone in the sin-ridden, diabolic society which threatened to poison the innocent souls of his defenceless children. Back in the Valley, things would have been different. The extended family would have been an active agent of formative influence, rectifying whatever Sue lacked in terms of imparting real moral values. The village community would also have been significant – an instrument of correction always able to shame kids into conformity and accepted standards of social behaviour – especially Jasmine who needed to imbibe *haya*, the concept of womanly modesty provided by the Holy Book.

Here he was alone, battling against darkness with no help from anyone.

Mohammed Khan's teaching programme was simple and informal. He tried to explain the basic tenets of Submission to Sikander and Jasmine but it was hard to get their attention. Because of his earlier casual attitude, both children refused to take him seriously. After a few futile attempts, he changed his approach to questions and answers, something they could understand with involvement.

"Who created the world?"

"God," Jasmine said.

"No," Mohammed Khan corrected her. "He who has ninety-nine names, created the world."

"Who's the one with so many names?"

"The only and true Lord of the Universe," Mohammed Khan explained. "He created everything: the world, humans, animals, stars."

"That's God," Jasmine insisted.

"God is just one of his names. I'm telling you about the One who has ninety-nine names. He created everything."

"Who made Him?" Jasmine demanded.

Mohammed Khan was taken aback. "No one made Him. He was not born from anyone, and no one was born from Him."

"That's not true," Jasmine said. "Jesus was God's son."

Mohammed Khan felt a shiver run through him. "Who told you that, Jasmine?"

"My teacher," she replied. "Mom told me too."

The shiver in his body turned into a quiver of rage and betrayal. "She's a low-caste pagan," he thundered. "We are high-caste believers, both of you, and me. You understand?"

The kids nodded feebly. "Yes, Daddy," Jasmine said, scared by her father's sudden outburst.

Mohammed Khan raised his index finger in their direction, "Don't forget who you are and don't ever forget that there are things you should learn and things you *must* not."

He got up abruptly, and left the room.

Sue had never seen Mohammed Khan in this mood. His face was red, eyes popped out of their sockets, lips hung uncannily in a furious rictus.

"What have you been teaching my children?" he yelled at her.

She put down the skirt she was sewing for Jasmine, and looked up in shock. "What do you mean? Are you okay?"

"I'm not okay," Mohammed Khan shook his head violently. "What have you been teaching Jasmine?"

She fought to control her anger. This was the first time he had ever talked to her like this. Was he unravelling another facet of his personality, one hidden from her so far?

"You taught them that Jesus Christ is the son of God," Mohammed Khan continued.

Sue looked at him, her anger turning to bafflement. "Give me a break. I don't like to talk about religion with kids."

"Jasmine said that you told her that Jesus was the son of God."

"I may have told her that some people believe Jesus is the son of God."

"You're trying to turn them into the pagans who wipe our floors and remove our excretions back home," Mohammed Khan said. The rustle of accusation was obvious in his crackling tone.

"Shut up, Mohammed," Sue responded indignantly. "I'm not pushed about their religious beliefs. I'm only interested in making them good human beings."

"They've got to become good believers before they can become good human beings. They can realise humanity only through belief."

"That's what you think, Mohammed Khan," Sue said. She got to her feet and came toward him. "Listen, I don't really care about religion and I don't care about what our children believe, as long as they are good and successful in their life."

"Goodness alone will not help them in the afterlife. Only true belief will. I don't want my children to burn in the everlasting fire of hell."

He turned and stomped out of the room, leaving Sue drenched in the same kind of fear she had experienced seeing the Klansmen at her doorstep in another life.

That night, when the children had gone to bed, Mohammed Khan quietly whispered in Sue's ears. "I'm sorry, my love, but I have no choice."

This was the first time he had addressed her with such tenderness since the end of their dating days. She kissed him on the lips and he responded with a passion that transcended all bounds set by prescriptive videos. She forgave him.

Next day, Mohammed Khan came home early. He swerved his car into the circular driveway of his house, and parked outside the garage. He came out carrying a box of candies, wrapped in shiny gift paper.

"Sikander," he called out loud. "Come over here. I've got something for you today."

Sikander came running. Mohammed Khan stood in the living room. He brought his right hand from behind his back to display the gift. "Here," he said with a smile. "I've got some candy for you."

Sikander accepted the gift. "Thanks, Dad," he said.

"How're you doing at school, son?"

"Okay, Dad."

"Your Mom tells me you're quite particular about your studies. That's good. Well, go ahead. Eat the candy."

Sikander removed the gift paper and grinned when he saw his favourite kind. "Gee. Thanks, Dad," he said excitedly.

"I'm glad you like it. Tastes good, doesn't it?"

"It sure does, Dad."

"It's exactly like your school education."

Sikander looked up in surprise. His Dad was no longer smiling.

"I'm not sure I understand, Dad," he said.

"Let me explain. The candy you're eating tastes good. Gives your body energy, right?"

"Right, Dad."

"Your school education is like candy. It's fun to learn new things. It'll get you a good job with money to buy things you want to buy, but it won't make you a good man. You see, all of us have to die one day and appear before the One with ninety-nine names. Only those who believe and are of honourable caste will be admitted to heaven, where streams of milk and honey flow and you get anything you want. But if you're a bad person, you'll burn in the fire of hell forever."

Sikander shuddered involuntarily.

Mohammed Khan continued. "You see, if you wish to save yourself from the fire of hell, you must become a good man. But you can't become a good man unless you please your Creator. You can please Him only if you know more about Him and His commandments."

He paused. "I've made arrangements for you to learn about Submission," he said proudly. "From tomorrow, you'll be going to M. Sahib for submissive education."

M. Sahib was a short, dark man with an enormous girth. Sikander was not aware that M. Sahib was the same man who, before migrating to the land of opportunities, where he had pruned his beard and shortened his name, had taught his father the Holy Book and whose video had impressed him with authoritative knowledge of unexplored human bodies.

M. Sahib searched Sikander without interest. "Have you learnt how to pray?"

"Yes, sir," Sikander said.

"Have you learnt to read the Holy Book?"

"No, sir."

"I'll teach you how to read the Holy Book. Then you will start *Ornaments From Paradise*," M. Sahib said. "The Holy book is divided into thirty *siparas*. Each sipara has one or more *surah* and sometimes, a part of a surah. Each *surah* is divided into an *aiyat*."

"I don't understand the meaning of these words," Sikander said.

"Don't show impatience, pupil," M. Sahib said sternly. "You'll learn everything in time when He so wills. You can think of the surah as a chapter, and the aiyat as a verse, Okay?"

"Okay."

"No Okay, pupil," M. Sahib raised a finger. "Say, 'Jee M. Sahib'."

"Jee M. Sahib."

"*Alhamdulillah*," M. Sahib said. "Now cross your legs, place the Holy Book on your knees, and open it."

"So, how was your first day at the *madrassa*?" Mohammed Khan asked.

"I didn't like the teacher."

"The teacher? Oh, M. Sahib! Why?"

"He's got bad breath," Sikander said. "And he doesn't let me talk."

"You're there to gain knowledge from him, son. You're supposed to listen, not talk or comment on his breath."

"But the teachers at my school let everyone talk. They tell us to ask questions."

"That's worldly knowledge, my son. M. Sahib is telling you about divine things. There's no scope for questions there. I questioned his wisdom when I was a child and look where I am now? Stranded in a land of heathens and pagans."

Sikander never asked a question again. A year later, he finished his maiden reading of the Book.

Jodie Campbell was the cutest girl in his class. She thought Sikander was the nicest boy in her class. That led to their friendship.

She noticed the new watch on Sikander's wrist. "That's a cool watch you're wearing today."

"It's a present from my Dad."

"He gave it to you for your birthday or something?"

Sikander shook his head. "No. I finished reading my religious book. My Dad celebrated the occasion and gave me this watch."

"Wow. I haven't read the Bible. Is your Dad a preacher?"

"Well, he's into this religious thing. He wanted me to read the Holy Book."

"You mean your Bible?"

"Yeah. But don't say that in front of my Dad. He's pretty touchy about these things."

"I don't like the sound of that."

"It's okay, really," Sikander said hurriedly. "It's just that he's crazy about his religion."

"And you?"

Sikander thought for a while. "I'm not sure. Actually, I don't know what's in the Holy Book."

Jodie chuckled. "But you said you finished reading it."

"That's right. But it's in a language I don't understand."

"That's weird. How long did it take you to finish?"

"About a year."

"Get outa here. You spent a year reading a book you can't understand? That's weird. You're nuts."

"M. Sahib says that meanings are irrelevant. The truth lies in the words alone."

16

And tell the believing women to lower their gaze and to be mindful of their chastity, and not to display their charm in public beyond what may decently be apparent; hence let them draw their head-covering over their bosom. And let them not display their charm to any but their husbands, or their fathers, or their husbands' fathers, or their sons, or their husbands' sons, or their sisters' sons, or their women-folk, or whom they rightfully possess, or such male attendants as are beyond all sexual desire, or children that are as yet unaware of women's nakedness; and let them not swing their legs in walking so as to draw attention to their hidden charm.
(Al-Quran, 24: 31)

Mohammed Khan called Jasmine to his room one evening. "Come here, my daughter. Come and sit with me."

Jasmine sat next to her father, who affectionately placed his right hand on her head and smiled. "Well, Jasmine. You've grown up to be a young lady, and you need to cover your head with a scarf in school now."

Jasmine winced. "Dad! No one covers their head in my school."

"Perhaps you're forgetting that you're a believer and a lady of high caste," Mohammed Khan said impatiently. She noticed the muscles on his face hardening, his voice turning brusque without being loud. "Covering the head is a symbol of respectable ladies," he said slowly. Jasmine had come to recognise this tone by now. It was an assertion of finality, with no room for disagreement. "It shows their noble heritage and superior belief. You must observe purdah."

"What's *purdah*?"

"It means covering your head and being pure in your thoughts. You study with boys in school and it's all the more important to keep your distance from them so your thoughts can remain pure and clean."

"Daddy! I don't have dirty thoughts," Jasmine protested. Her face turned red. A misty film came over her eyes.

"I know. I know," Mohammed Khan said hurriedly. "But if you talk to boys, they may have a bad effect on you. Teenage boys are susceptible to Topchian influence. You must not mix with them or let anyone touch your body until you are married in a rightful manner."

Jasmine started to laugh. "Dad. I'm too young to get married."

"But not too young to learn about the responsibilities of Submission," Mohammed Khan said. "I noticed the way you laughed. It's all right for a girl to smile, but remember my daughter: never laugh loudly in public. Your posture must convey restraint in your physical movements. Your body gestures should not be exaggerated."

"Dad! That's body language. My teacher told me about it. She says it's important."

"Forget everything they teach you about body language in school," Mohammed Khan said. Again, she noticed that tone of finality. "And keep your eyes down," he continued. "Never look into the eyes of anyone; it is disrespectful and immodest."

"But the teacher says you've gotta have eye contact," Jasmine objected. "She says eye contact is essential for showing your truthfulness."

"She's wrong. These people don't know that the eye is the door through which Satan enters a person's heart. That's why you've got to observe purdah of the eye and the body.

"You don't tell Sikander to do these things," Jasmine complained.

"Oh, I do. Sikander has to be modest too."

"But Sikander mixes with girls," Jasmine said. "He has fun with his girlfriends. Jodie's his best friend."

"I'll talk to him about it," Mohammed Khan said. "He needs to be careful because purdah is both for women and men."

"You mean, Sikander has to wear a scarf as well?"

"No. There's a difference between a woman's purdah and a man's purdah. Sikander is a man. He doesn't need to cover his head, but he has to protect his eyes and mind from evil talk."

"But I can't stay mute, Daddy," Jasmine remonstrated. "There are boys in my class and I need to talk to them sometimes."

"You can talk to them only as much as is necessary," Mohammed Khan said. He had to allow her this much leeway, given the complexity of the situation. Back in the Valley, he would not have thought of sending his daughter to a co-educational institution; he might not have even sent her to school. Perhaps, he could have let her study for a few years of primary education in a girls' school without incurring social pressure from the villagers.

"I gotta go, Dad. I'll ask Mom to buy me a scarf," Jasmine said.

As she left the room, she looked back. Her father had raised his cupped palms in front of his face and was praying.

"Jasmine says she's going to wear a scarf in school," Sue said. "Don't you think she's too young for that?"

Mohammed Khan hated it when Sue argued on issues that related to Divine commandments. "She's thirteen," he said, controlling his frustration. "She's no longer a baby. My sister got married when she was twelve."

"She's not an adult either."

"She's growing. It's time she starts acting like a grown up," Mohammed Khan said and went back to his book.

Sue pulled a chair next to him and sat down. "Will you put down that silly book and listen to me?"

Mohammed Khan put it down and took off his glasses. "Are you in a bad mood?" he asked, trying to sound innocent.

"You bet," Sue snapped back. "What's the matter with you, Mohammed? What're you trying to make of Jasmine? You're overloading her with prescriptive statements she can't take. Each time you talk to her, you stuff her mind with things that are hard for her to understand."

Mohammed Khan squinted back at his wife for a full minute, his brown eyes turning sombre. "I'm trying to fulfil my duty as a father. I'm only teaching her the right way."

"I doubt if you teach her anything," Sue said testily. "You keep bombarding her mind with don't do this and don't do that. You never tell her what to do."

"She must first learn what not to do before she knows what to do, my dear wife."

"Haven't you got it all wrong, *my dear husband*?" Sue snapped back. "Aren't you reversing the learning sequence?"

Mohammed Khan shook his head. "No. Avoiding evil guarantees goodness, because committing a wrong leads to instant moral degeneration whereas purity of the heart is achieved in steps. Purity is the result of hard work, and my children have got to work for it continuously."

"I don't really get your point? They've got to learn to do things right."

"That's the second step of the process. To know what is wrong, and to avoid it, comes first."

"What about right? When do you plan to tell your children what's right?"

"I have already told Jasmine what's right for her," Mohammed Khan said. "For her, modesty is the first step to a strong character."

"It's not modesty just to cover your head. It's got to be more than that."

"It's the Divine Commandment. You and I are not to dispute it."

"Oh, come on, Mohammed Khan. You're trying to apply standards of modesty that exist somewhere else. Okay, maybe the scarf will go unnoticed, but Jasmine will become isolated if she's not allowed to interact with boys or participate in other activities. It's going to affect her performance at school, and she may develop an inferiority complex. What kind of a woman do you think she'll be if she doesn't have self-confidence? A complete failure! Do you want her to be a failure in society?"

Mohammed Khan shook his head. "You misunderstood me, Sue. I don't mean to say that she can't pursue a career or develop her talent. It's not like that at all. I'm only trying to tell you that free intermingling of men and women is forbidden."

"How can she pursue a career if she can't meet men?"

"She can meet men only within the limits of purdah and necessity, but her best career is her home. A woman's responsibility as a housewife is more onerous than a man's because she has to raise the next generation of mankind. Look at your society today. What do you see? Broken homes. Single parents. Homeless children. Juvenile delinquents. Teenage pregnancies. Rapes. Murder. Why is this?" he said, his voice quivering with an outburst of sudden emotion. "Let me tell you why. Because your women have forgotten their sacred duty to their children and their husbands. They've taken the veils off their faces…"

"…they never had a veil, Mohammed," Sue corrected him.

Mohammed Khan ignored her. "They have become public and faceless. No one recognises them or respects them because they have turned into men. In the Valley, a woman is still the honour of a man. She's not just another public or faceless commodity – she enjoys respect. Real respect."

"So you want to take fifty percent of the population out of economic activity and let them rot in their homes, right?"

"No, my dear wife," Mohammed Khan said solemnly. "God ordains that fifty per cent of the present population raise one hundred per cent of the future generation in a manner that turns them into good and pious individuals. That is God's great wisdom in segregating the activities of women from men."

The first day's reaction of Jasmine's classmates and teachers ranged from exotic interest to outright ridicule.

"That's a real nice thing you're wearing today, Jasmine," Mrs. Templeton, her English teacher said. "What is it?"

"It's a *dopatta*, Mrs. Templeton. The headgear for a high-caste believing woman who doesn't have to sweep other people's homes," Jasmine said, feeling self-important. She was greatly relieved by Mrs. Templeton's interest. Somewhere in her mind had been a lurking fear of being ridiculed, but her apprehension had so far been unwarranted.

"Okay, girls. Everyone to their seats," Mrs. Templeton said. "Go on, honey," she told Jasmine. "Take your seat."

Jasmine walked over to her desk and sat down.

"Okay, everybody. Let's open page 63 of the poetry book," Mrs. Templeton said.

"Hey, Jas?" Richard Bryce, sitting next to her whispered.

"Yeah?" Jasmine said as she fumbled with the pages of her book.

"You growing horns?" Bryce said with a chuckle.

"No, she's getting bald," Nick, a pimple-faced boy she had never liked, whispered back.

"So what's this funny piece of cloth?" Bryce demanded coyly.

"Don't you know?" Nick feigned surprise. "It's a bandage. Only it's too big."

Cindy, another pimple-faced girl whom Jasmine rated next to Nick in dislike, turned around. "It's a bandage, all right. It keeps her head from slipping off her shoulders."

Jasmine felt out of place. But gradually, everyone seemed to accept her dopatta as an interesting novelty. Besides, for the time being, the protective shell of her incipient identity was a cosy refuge.

The shell finally snapped with her youthful surge.

On a moderate summer day, Jasmine returned from school and ran straight to the kitchen where Sue was baking biscuits.

"Hey, Mom. Did you hear about the big Rock concert?" Jasmine asked excitedly.

"No, honey, I didn't. Where?"

"It'll be here next week. Do you think Dad will let me go?"

"I wish he would, honey, but I don't think so."

Jasmine wished she had a normal Dad.

"Dad?" A couple of weeks later, Jasmine said to her father as he watched the local news on TV.

"Yes, daughter."

"My class is going for picnic to Yosemite Park. Can I go with them?"

"You've been to Yosemite with me. Why do you want to go again?"

"Dad, please! I want to go with my friends."

"Okay. But take Sikander along."

"Sikander? He's not in my class."

"He's your brother, my daughter. Brothers are supposed to be protectors of their sisters' honour."

Jasmine felt a pang of humiliation. She wished Dad would trust her to protect her own honour.

A few months later.

"Mom. Can I go to the prom night?" Jasmine pleaded with her mother."

"I don't think your Dad's gonna like it."

"I'll ask his permission."

"I don't think it's a good idea, honey."

"Dad. Can I go to the prom night, please?"

"What? Absolutely not."

Jasmine felt something crumbling inside her.

Once again, Sue intervened, and once again, Mohammed Khan prevailed.

"What's all this fuss about the prom night?" he demanded indignantly. "Why can't they simply award certificates to the students? Do you people have to turn every mundane event into a special occasion?"

"Come on, dear," Sue pleaded. "It's an important milestone in their lives and it's got to be memorable. Besides, it's a lot of fun."

"It's nothing but a waste of time and money," Mohammed Khan waved his hand angrily, "and an invitation to moral corruption. Do you know what happens at prom nights? They are just a pretext to let girls and boys mix freely, and fall prey to the temptations of the body."

Mohammed Khan felt he had to be firm. His authority was being challenged by two women. There was an element of premonitory collusion about their behaviour.

"You're going to wear a chador in school," he told Jasmine at the dining table.

"What?" Sue interrupted angrily. Her reservoir of patience had dried up. Pent-up rage, accumulated over the years, finally erupted. "What are you trying to make out of my daughter? She's not the sacrificial lamb at your Goddamn altar of modesty."

"Keep a leash on your tongue, woman," Mohammed Khan yelled. "I'm the man of the house. She'll do what I say."

"You can't play with her life," Sue screamed back.

"I'm not playing with her life," Mohammed Khan said. "But you are playing with fire – the fire of hell."

"My daughter will not wear a blasted chador in school."

"Oh, yes, she will," Mohammed Khan said, banging his fist hard on the arm of his chair. For the next two days, he did not speak to Sue.

Beneath the white chador, Jasmine felt naked. She had become a spectacle. An object of penetrating stares. A target of ridicule.

"Hey, Jas. You going camping?" Someone said from behind.

Jasmine turned around. It was the pimple-faced boy again.

"No. Why?" She asked

"So why are you carrying a tent with you?"

Jasmine cursed her Dad.

"What've you got inside that, Jas? Something we should wanna look at, baby?" Nick said.

"Screw you, asshole," Jasmine screamed at him.

Her vulgarity surprised her.

She went straight to her locker. She took off the chador and placed it inside. When she returned home, she was wearing the chador again.

17

Men are in charge over women. So good women are obedient. As for those from whom ye fear rebellion, admonish them and banish them to beds apart, and scourge them.
(Al-Quran, 4: 34)

Jasmine often heard her parents argue over different things and more often than not, she empathised with her mother, but she knew better than to take sides or even show her leanings. She had invented successful forms of dissemblance. Her life was a statement of tactics.

The arguments between her parents continued with decreasing intensity, and finally crumbled into an uneasy truce. Truce was not Jasmine's problem: she never waged a war; she was covertly living in fragments. At home she consistently wore a dopatta, said her prayers, spoke with her eyes lowered and voice hushed, and rarely went out when her Dad was home. In school, she would contemptuously discard her chador, attend the music class in lieu of the afternoon prayer and speak with perfect eye contact, in a voice brimming with confidence. She became explosive, destructive – but didn't know how to explode and what to destroy. Her reflexes turned blunt, expressions rude, ideas wild. She was singeing.

She made a lot of friends, both boys and girls, but it wasn't until her last year in school that she met Jimmy Bowen. Then she was ignited.

He wasn't handsome or athletic or brilliant in studies. Worse, he was an Okie whose parents lived in a trailer on the other side of the railway line. But he knew how to hit back, and she wanted to be hit back. She fell in love with him. Her first expression of her self. A tactless move.

It was hard to befriend Jimmy. He had a general contempt for the world and everything in it, girls no exception. "What's your game?" he demanded in his long drawl when she first talked to him. His eyes squinted with suspicion.

"Just wanted to see if you Okie bastards have any manners," Jasmine snapped back.

He gave her a long hard stare and a smile spanned across his lips. "I like it. I like it a lot. What can I do for you missy?" he asked with an exaggerated bow and coy smile.

Jasmine turned and walked away.

But Jimmy didn't let her walk away from him. Not for long, anyway.

Their first kiss was a masterpiece of brevity. Each time their lips touched, Jasmine could not control a triumphant smile. She had conquered Dad.

"Hey, what's the matter with you, Jas?" Jimmy demanded irritably. "What's so funny?"

"Just kiss me."

"I could if only you stopped grinning."

Intuitively, she discovered that a kiss and a smile don't go together.

Jasmine completed her high school with honours. She waited with dreaded anticipation for the prom night that was five days away.

"Will you be my date on the prom night, Jas?" Jimmy asked her.

Jasmine hesitated. "I'm not sure I can make it to the prom night, Jim."

"Hey. Why the hell not?"

"My Dad doesn't allow it."

"Screw your Dad."

Momentary hesitation. "I don't know how to."

"Dad. Can I spend the night with aunt Zafooran?"

"Afzal Khan's daughter? I don't like that woman. She's too liberated."

"Dad. She was born here!" Jasmine said, and bit her lip. You never argued with Mohammed Khan because in the end, you always lost.

"So?" he frowned. "That doesn't change who she is, does it?"

Jasmine pretended to think. "Yeah, I guess it doesn't."

"I don't like your habit of saying 'I guess' with every sentence you speak."

"Dad. That's how I learnt it. That's how everybody talks."

"These people are not sure of anything, that's why. Everything here is based on shaky foundations. Their . . ."

She knew she had started another argument. She let him win: that was the only way to cut down the agonising process. "You're right, Dad. But can I go to aunt Zafooran?"

"What will you do there? And she lives in Fremont. How will you go there?"

"She's arranged a milad in her house. You know when all these women gather and sing praise of our beloved prophet?"

"Don't try to teach me religion, Jasmine. I know what milad is. But I'm surprised that Zafooran is holding a milad. Maybe God has shown her the light after all."

"Aunt Zafooran has improved a lot," Jasmine lied. "She says her prayers now."

"Five times a day?"

"Um, I don't know."

"Even then it's good news. All right. I will take you there."

"Aunt Zafooran is in town today. She said she'll give me a ride."

Zafooran was a woman in her late twenties. She came to pick up Jasmine in a flashy Oldsmobile. She removed her sunglasses and wiped off her lipstick before entering Mohammed Khan's house. Ten minutes later, she returned with Jasmine and drove away. As soon as they had turned the corner, she clenched a fist and let out a big, sarcastic laugh. "We did it Jasmine," she said. "We did it. Pass me that lipstick. I look like a ghost without it."

Jasmine shared a conspiratorial smile as she handed her aunt the lipstick. Her heart was beating like a drum.

Twenty minutes later, Zafooran parked the car in the lot of a Motel 6.

"Come on, Jasmine," she said. "Your party dress's waiting for you."

Jimmy was attired as a Southern gentleman. Jasmine saw clear blue skies of Oklahoma in his eyes.

"Would you honour me with a dance, missy?" he said with a slight bow.

She came into his arms.

Strong arms have a way of saying a lot about possession, tenacity, and refuge. They told her that Jimmy was her man. They told her that he was on her side. They told her he would rip all the chadors in the world out of her way.

She thought about the pending fate of her chador and smiled.

Sue noted two things. An aura of excitement permeated Jasmine. Her face glowed like a full moon, her smile was persistently mischievous, her movements suffused with the confidence of a woman swayed by the strong arms of a man. She knew her daughter was in love.

She also knew that her husband was worried. Since Jasmine's graduation, Mohammed Khan was increasingly drowning in thoughts. Sue suspected that he had also noticed the bouncing signs of falling in love in Jasmine.

"I'm concerned about Jasmine, Sue," he confided one night just as she was drifting into sleep.

Sleep vanished, replaced with apprehension. "Why are you concerned about her?" she asked, trying to keep her voice steady. Her neck muscles turned into a taut wire.

"She's completed her High School and I'm not sure what to do next."

Sue felt some tension going out of her neck muscles. "She wants to become an accountant," she said. "She's planning to go to college next term."

Mohammed Khan moved uneasily in the bed and flexed his shoulders: the burdened shoulders of a father with a marriageable daughter. "I think she's studied enough. Girls should get settled in their own home when they come of age."

"I don't think I follow you. This is her home, darling."

Mohammed Khan shook his head exasperatedly. "No, no, Sue," he said in a voice that appeared to echo inside stony gorges; an echo from another time. "Daughters are alienable treasures. A daughter's home is her husband's house. Jasmine must get married now."

Sue felt her heart sinking. "But she's only seventeen, darling. It's too early for a girl to get married."

"She's seventeen years and ten months. She'll be eighteen in a couple of months. I need to find a suitable groom for her but I can't find anyone in our community here. The boys are lost. Running after white women, drinking intoxicating urine in bars. Do you think we should send her back to the Valley? My mother – if she's still alive, for I haven't written to her in years – can find an appropriate match for her."

Something hit Sue in the chest, an invisible blow that had the physical power of taking the breath out of her lungs. She struggled to cope with what Mohammed Khan had just said. All the compromises she had made in her life were thrown into bold relief, converging her anger to a focal point.

"You can't do that to my daughter, you stubborn, stupid man," she screamed. "I won't let you spoil her life with your stale beliefs. You touch my daughter and I swear I'll call the cops."

"Hold your . . ."

"No! You hold your tongue," Sue screamed again. "My daughter is not going anywhere. She'll stay right here, in this house, in this great country. She'll marry whenever she's ready for it, and whoever she wants to. This is not your Goddamned camel-driving Valley. This is Freedom."

In the adjoining room, Jasmine heard her mother's voice and tried to control her sobs.

"Don't force me to hit you, woman," she heard her Father say.

"Go ahead, if that's what your elevated culture has taught you. Go ahead. Hit me. Hit me."

The door to the bedroom opened. Mohammed Khan turned his head in anger. His daughter stood in the door, her body held very erect. "Don't you dare touch her, Dad," she said in a voice that came from some other person. "I'll kill you if you go near her."

Mohammed Khan's mouth opened. Then things started to happen to him. Fear was the first to arrive, gripping him in its icy claws, spreading in his guts like bile, expanding toward his throat, blocking the windpipe, making him gasp for air. It was a physical experience, this sheer terror of facing rebellion from his daughter, his own flesh and blood: his honour. Suddenly, all links between his brain and body were severed, leaving him immobile. Emotionally paralysed. Spiritually exhausted. Morally defeated.

"I'm in love, Dad," Jasmine said. Mohammed Khan stared blankly at her face. "I'm in love with Jimmy Bowen. You want me to get married, Dad? I'm ready. I'm gonna marry Jimmy."

Mohammed Khan stepped forward and slapped her. Moments later, the sound of another slap of another kind was heard in the room. Mohammed Khan broke down and cried the cries of a dishonoured man. He was no longer a man.

Two weeks later, he vanished.

Book IV

Odyssey into Confusion

This is the account of Noah. Noah was a righteous man, blameless among the people of his time, and he walked with God.
(Genesis, 6: 9)

A group of people was found wandering on a deserted coast near the Iranian border. Investigation revealed that a foreign employment promoter had charged them one hundred thousand rupees for entry on fake visa to Dubai. He took them on a sail boat and after a voyage of seven nights, dropped them off on a shore which he claimed was Dubai. When the defrauded job-seekers woke up in the morning, they discovered that the boat had been sailing inside Pakistani waters all along and the foreign employment promoter had dropped them two hundred kilometers off the coast of Karachi, from where they had set sail in the first place.
(A news item in the Pakistani press)

A man's reach should exceed his grasp.
(Robert Browning)

18

And most certainly, We sent Noah toward his people.
   (Al-Quran, 23:23)

We said, carry into the ark every pair, male and female.
   (Al-Quran, 11: 39)

Those who had been searching for him since his disappearance outside the Loehar High Court, found him sitting at the foot of a mountain range. He had grown older but his hair was still black and his muscles rippled with tension under a white shirt. They stopped at a respectful distance from Mohammed Khan, their eyes lowered and filled with reverence.

"We've been searching for you for the past seven days – Friday, Saturday, Sunday, Monday, Tuesday, Wednesday, Thursday," they said. "After your miracle outside the courthouse, you disappeared. We didn't know if the earth had devoured you or the sky swallowed you."

"I was swallowed by love," Mohammed Khan said. "My emotions cheated me, but I'm back."

An old man who looked the wisest amongst them, moved forward and presented Mohammed Khan with a staff. "Welcome back from the treacherous land of love, Mohammed Khan," he said. "Here, accept this laser staff you left outside the Loehar High Court. We've been protecting it so that when we found you, we could be led by this staff in your hands. Go ahead; take us on the odyssey with a false start. Be our Odysseus."

Mohammed Khan accepted the staff and looked carefully at the words written on it in Japanese and English. "Made as Japan," the words said.

Mohammed Khan's head began to spin. Memories of Sue, Jasmine and Sikander started to crumble under the burden of leadership thrust upon him. Blood rushed to his face and his heart was filled with all the dubious motives of a third-world leader trying to obtain US support for his dictatorship. He jumped to his feet and waved his staff towards the crowd.

"Oh my people!" spoke Mohammed Khan in a trembling voice. "I understand the hardships you must have faced trying to get a visa for this place, but hear and believe that your troubles are over. The Consumers' Paradise awaits you. Listen to me and believe in what I see and don't see. Work and marriage are the curse of the soul. Where I lead you there will be no work and no daughters who may run away with skinned men and leave you honourless. Everything will be plentiful and everyone will enjoy the right to waste, to recycle, to procreate and self-sterilise. Nothing will be taxed. Money will be abolished and all available metals will be used to make exquisite jewellery for men and women. You will sit on silken mattresses and rest your heads on fluffy pillows filled with scented feathers, by lakes of deep blue waters. Music will pervade the atmosphere: all types of music, classical, hillbilly, pop, heavy metal, blues, rock, rap, techno. There will be no Tele, only vision, no actors, only acting, no dancers, only dancing, no technology, only techniques; and even techniques will cease to exist if you so desire. Know that desire is the daughter of desire. As long as daughters exist, true contentment will elude you. Only in the Paradise raised on the desert for consumers will you be able to get rid of desire and I will be able to hop across to the Valley which is just on the other side of the Arabian Sea."

Mohammed Khan waved them to follow him. He led them beyond the mountain towards the west. They told him that beyond the mountain lay no paradise but the Ocean. They showed him an old atlas to prove their point but Mohammed Khan kept walking, a determined smile permeating his face. After thirty days they reached the edge of a great desert where they were stopped by two men in military uniform. Their faces were grim, chests jutted out, and feet stamped the ground with authority over it.

"Major Ed Walter of the US Nuclear Inspection Team, sir," the taller one introduced himself. "You can't stay here, sir. This is a restricted area for locals and aliens like you. Nuclear testing zone it is, sir."

"We were just leaving. This woman here needs to deliver," Mohammed Khan said hurriedly, pointing to a follower, "We stopped so she could."

"Deliver what precisely, sir?"

"Her burden, of course."

"And what sort of burden would that be, sir?"

"The burden of creation. Of humanity. Of her desire for deliverance, or any other kind of burden that you may think proper."

"But I don't see a woman among you, sir," the soldier objected.

"There is no woman," Mohammed Khan readily admitted. "There's only the story of a woman who must deliver her burden. The story's been with me since it was told to me by a man who promised to give me the hand of his daughter and then backed away. I wish the court had not decided in my favour. That way, I'd still be an honourable man: Sikander would not have slapped me and Jasmine would not have tried unsuccessfully to elope with an Oakie."

The soldier made a face and consulted his watch. "I could continue with this line of questioning, sir, but we haven't got much time. They're gonna conduct the test any minute now. Tell you what! Why don't you leave the area for your own safety, and come back later. There's a hospital three miles down the road. You can go there and they'll help whoever has to deliver whatever. We can continue our conversation when the radiation settles down."

"I have no intention of continuing the conversation. She must deliver. Now!"

"In that case, I must resort to coercion, sir," the major said. He changed into the uniform of a four-star General and suddenly, armoured vehicles surrounded Mohammed Khan and his followers as if they were a third-world country in the middle of a political turmoil.

"We are no terrorists, fundamentalists, nuclear secrets stealers, immigrants, environmentalists, or anti-globalists," Mohammed Khan protested. "We are nothing and that is our identity – oneness in nothingness. We are going beyond the desert and beyond nuclear tests and nuclear site inspections to the Consumers' Paradise."

The military men ignored his objection. Amidst constant pleadings and explanations, they subjected everyone to a thorough body search. Finally the men in arms were convinced of the inconsequentiality of nothingness and allowed Mohammed Khan and his followers to make a detour of the desert.

They walked towards the hospital where the story of deliverance was chronicled.

The woman in the story stayed in hospital through three nuclear tests and still did not deliver. The doctors finally came to the conclusion that it was necessary to perform a Caesarean section. They cut her all the way down to her womb and found nothing inside.

Fresh probatory tests were conducted, which indicated a large presence outside her uterus. The doctors performed a second surgery and extracted a seven-month old turtle from her stomach.

"It's a very common phenomenon," the doctor reassured the distraught writer. "A water-born hazard, actually. When you drink unboiled water, such things will grow inside your stomach. Make sure she boils her water in future. Or better still, get her to drink Evian."

The woman was prematurely discharged from the hospital when it transpired that she did not have medical cover. Mohammed Khan carried her story and his followers' inspirations on his shoulders and resumed the journey. Finally they arrived at the Ocean just as the atlas had predicted. Mohammed Khan told his followers to camp there. After three days of heavy meditation, he gathered everyone and directed them to build a boat large enough to carry their sins and burdens across the ocean to the Consumers' Paradise. All the men of the caravan worked day and night to build the boat and on the day of its completion Mohammed Khan inspected it and named it the Big Boat.

"O people," Mohammed Khan said in a voice grappling with the emotions of achievement. "Embark upon the Big Boat. Take all your belongings in pairs and where it's not possible due to the shortage of things or ignorance of numbers, then carry a single item but list it twice in the catalogue of memory."

The crowd murmured their collective concern. "We don't have any maritime experience, Mohammed Khan," they spoke through their leader who was an old man with earthly expressions. "We're tired and reluctant. Our feet are stamped on earth and we have no knowledge of sinking or swimming. We've worked hard and we've worked day and night without being paid even the minimum wage. Since we met you, we've been living on vegetable roots, salty water and the occasional barbecue. We're left with no energy or will to undertake a journey which is so arduous and whose destiny is unspecified. We'd rather be slaughtered in the middle of a desert or bombed in paddy fields or inside black and dusty caves than drown in the salty waters of an ocean."

"Don't be afraid of the water, O people, be it plain, boiled or mineral," Mohammed Khan said. "The helper will help us. A crew of slaves will come from the Dark and Distant Continent for your service. They will be identified by the dark colour of their skin, by the coarse texture of their curly hair and by their long and rhythmic limbs. They will drudge for you and remain eternally at your service. You will call them Negroes but be warned that subsequent eras will compel you to give them new and more attractive labels."

With these words Mohammed Khan stepped on the boat, inspected it thoroughly and then called forth the most able-bodied men from among his followers.

"I declare ye the crew from the Dark and Distant Continent," he announced and ordered them to row the boat.

19

Then the Chief of those of his people who had disbelieved said:
"We see nothing but a man like ourselves; and we see none
follow thee save the meanest of us of superficial judgment; and
we see you having no superiority over ourselves. In fact we deem
you to be all liars.
(Al-Quran: 11:27)

They rowed the boat for seven days and six nights and reached nowhere. It was all misty and inexplicable.

On the way, they discovered many lands of difference and similitude, but somehow it never occurred to them to chronicle their discoveries. Mohammed Khan guided them with calculated tentativeness. His following was made up of revellers and frolickers, lovers and paramours, saboteurs and insurgents, spies and moles, revolutionaries and anarchists, dreamers and planners, misfits and pariahs and all those who defied categorisation. Their hearts were doused with exultant dreams of what lay promised ahead. They were people with regulated happiness and dreamy efficiency that did not let the oscillating reality disturb them for several days.

Then things changed. Doubts began to seep in through the outer hull. They wanted to reach somewhere, but no sign was in sight. Whatever Mohammed Khan had said sounded convincing, but they now yearned for conviction. Food was getting scarcer every day. Nights were cold and long, days hot and humid. They were exhausted, grew desperate and finally critical. Everyone had a question and those with no immediate question searched for one. Those with questions were uncertain about asking them and less certain of whom to address. No one knew, and no one had the will to know, except the old man with the Homeric face who dared.

"Listen to me, Mohammed Khan, son of no one!" said the old man, his snowy beard flowing in the sea breeze, his tremulous voice emerging as if out of a history text. "This is the end of the journey. Mine and theirs. In reality, the journey has never begun."

Mohammed Khan watched the old man in evaluative silence. His challenger was a tall man, taller than the others, standing under the shadows of torn sails, a man of light and shadows, impervious to the rolling and pitching of the ship, immune to herpes and AIDS, unresponsive to chatting and cyber sex.

"You are obsessed by the name and quick to name things," the old man continued. "You have created an unimaginative story out of an ordinary experience. Your descriptions are exaggerated. You imagine your events and narrate them without literary skill or sensuality. You don't know what you are doing and I know what I have not done. This boat was never built and this odyssey never begun: we're sitting on a tree trunk stuck in a dried river."

The old man stopped to take a breath before he resumed. "You say you took us everywhere there was to go: between the rivers so you could hear their stories, learn their laws and reach somewhere – but we didn't reach anywhere. You took us to the land where one was because of two, but we could not become one with it. You took us to the Great Peninsula but greatness eluded us because the sun had already started to set on its shrinking shores. What is your game, Mohammed Khan? I know you're not taking us anywhere. You're only navigating the boat along the shore and one early morning, you'll dump us on the same old soil and pretend it's the Consumers' Paradise. You're no better than the phoney foreign employment promoter who sent you to a phoney country on a phoney visa. Am I not right? Isn't this what you are, and what you're up to? Now tell me whatever story you have to tell me. I have many themes, and some plots, but I don't know the ending."

"You have ended so you know the ending," Mohammed Khan countered. "The stories are for you, not for me, old-timer. I'm not looking for stories: I'm in search of the writer. He is the one in two, in the story and before it. When we reach his abode, I assure you that you'll see him and get an autographed copy of his knowledge."

"I'm not sure why you're so sure," the old man said. "Certainty is inside things and outside them – where do you stand, huh? Certainty annihilates and regenerates. Are you certain that your certainty will not annihilate you? Tell me and tell me now. I need a definitive answer and I don't have the time or patience to wait."

"Patience is the only way to a destination," Mohammed Khan replied, raising the finger of accusation toward the old man. "Your impatience brought you here and it will mislead you back to nowhere. Do not curse the believing heart, old-timer. Sacrifice all that is below and behind it. You have seen people sacrificing, but they knew not to whom they sacrificed. I know. I've been told by the teller."

"I know these things," the old man said impatiently. "I know that the story is in the sacrifice. But tell me: was it the writer who was sacrificed or was it the reader who perished before he could become the reader? Where was the story before it was told? What was the writer before he wrote the story? What happened to the father when the daughter betrayed him?"

Mohammed Khan held his feet firmly upon the moving boat and tried to look his adversary in the eye. "Some will say there was no daughter and there was no father. Others will tell you that there was no son either who slapped the father. Some will say it's like this and others will claim it's not like this. All are wrong and so are you. You've filled your inside with a filling of non-biodegradable material. You will not perish and you will not live. You will not listen and you will not understand. I can see people coming to you and whispering in your ear, my rebellious friend, but know that whispering is your worst enemy, just as I am your worst enemy."

From his tattered robe ravaged by sun and seawater, Mohammed Khan drew his staff and flashed its blade. "I challenge you to a duel, old man," he said solemnly. "The sword is the only way to decide things between us."

The old man smiled. "There are other means to settle things, Mohammed Khan – tank assaults, carpet bombing, nuclear drops and suicide attacks," he said. "However, I hesitate to accept your challenge. Now, don't think that I'm timid. Don't think that I've been seduced by life: I don't need to be. If I'm killed I'd be given over to death which is not my thought, my end, my reality or my mistress, but my birth. I'll be born and become that which I am. You took us to the land of those who taught us not to kill. If you did not follow their advice, you'll perish and I'll disintegrate. Think not for a fleeting moment that to be so is our destiny: it is only your desire. Let not desire become your destiny."

"Death is my mistress," said Mohammed Khan. "I'll not perish. I will live and live forever. I have heard you intently and carefully, old-timer. You know how to talk and reason but you don't know how to steer a boat and locate the Promised Paradise. Without me, you're condemned to eternal exile."

He took a sweeping look across the expanse of his doubting followers and allowed a fatherly smile to settle upon his wilting face. "When I reach that land I will not have any dealing with you, old-timer, but in the meantime I allow you to remain on board provided you do not mislead the innocent souls with your logical pessimism."

With these words Mohammed Khan turned to other dissenters and told them that they were free to go back. "You can take the boat if you think you will not be able to swim back."

"What will you do if we take the boat?" they asked him.

"I will do what I will be commanded to do," Mohammed Khan said with inspired confidence. "I've been given the knowledge of the way. I will follow the laws of the heart. I will walk through the water and reach the land which I can see already."

All stares followed his vision and there was a sudden murmur amongst his followers. They gathered around the old man, tied his hands behind his back, gagged him with a cloth torn from his headgear and waited for the next command.

Mohammed Khan ordered them to move in the direction of the sun.

The voyage resumed but it was not long before it ended. After going three leagues, Mohammed Khan ordered his crew to stop. Beaming his staff into the water, he disembarked from the boat and started wading through the water. Everybody looked at him and at each other in amazement, concealing their fear and showing an edgy certainty. Hesitantly and one by one, they started jumping out of the boat and following him. After a while, they saw signs of land. Soon, they were walking on it: not believing, but definitely feeling it, touching it with their feet and hands.

The old man managed to untie himself and remove the gag. "So this is the land!" he shouted in disbelief. "It is but a familiar sight. It is the same earth I trod in another time. Its greenery is as lush as it was when I measured its ups and downs and its stillness and movement. I recognise these trees, their use and misuse. I have breathed their oxygen and witnessed their murder. I am aware of the circumstances of their genocide and the identity of the criminals. I know these birds and animals, their flights and routes. I understand their language and can interpret their silence. I know these waters, their power and their perils. I have authenticated knowledge of their source and their course, and everything that lives in there. I have come out of this land, and it will embrace me when I am exhausted. Its mountains and volcanoes, its soil and fertility, its forests and their products, its air and its fragrance, its sun and its heat, its moon and stars and their influence, everything is on my fingertips. I move with this earth, I feel its gravity, its expanses and limits. I have touched its metals and stones. I have wallowed in its abundance and suffered from its scarcity. I have tasted what is bitter and sweet and tasteless. I know its end and its beginning. It is the same earth and it is the same story with the same ending. I tell you that we have not reached anywhere and *inshaallah*, we will not reach anywhere."

"You are falsifying the truth, old-timer," Mohammed Khan thundered. Darkness was falling swiftly across the land. The Big Boat and everyone standing on the deserted beach of the virgin land were beginning to dissolve in shadows. Mohammed Khan widened his eyes in an attempt to see things in the fading light. "You are a man of limited vision, or maybe of no vision at all. You're under a spell. Your reality is dreamy, your vision muddy, your claims muddled. You're a servant of forgetfulness, a bewitched man deluded by a familiarity of his own making. You swallow ignorance and chirp out expired knowledge. Yours is the knowledge of past, of an age when you were a child. Your childhood has dwarfed you. Your memory has grown up but your mind is too small to accommodate your reminiscences."

He stopped and heard silence. With the sun gone down below the earth, he could no longer see his followers. The old man's face was left only upon the film of his memory. "I'm not talking about chronological or mental age, old-timer," he yelled with a force that came from inside and hovered over the coast like a demon from an old story narrated by mothers to their young children. "It's about perspective, about desire of that which delights the eyes. Look around you, old-timer. Look through the blooming darkness. Look if your eyes can see. There are no trees here: it's all your imagination. The trees were felled a long time ago. The treasures underneath their roots have long been plundered. The wood has been turned into shadowless objects of transitory glory and perishable utility. Their killers are busy planting new saplings, which others will tend until they too are possessed by the passion to kill and plant more. All this is happening, has been happening, and will happen again. There are no longer any trees, and their absence is the undeniable evidence of our journey – yours, theirs, and mine."

Above him, he heard birds shriek as they lamented some unknown loss and returned to their nests among the rocks. "How can you claim that the journey never began, old-timer? We've travelled so far ahead that old milestones have disappeared. I no longer hear the water running: I only see sewage pipes and water taps. I don't know where water comes from or where it goes, and neither do you. You don't know who raises crops and imparts novelty and taste to comestibles. You have no idea of the identity of those who own the skills to turn stones and metals into precious objects. You're not familiar with people who influence the earth and the moon and the sun and the sky. They are somewhere else, somewhere you can't reach them. You know nothing, old-timer."

The birds shrieked again before they settled into their hiding places. Darkness became more commanding. Mohammed Khan's face shone in the light of the moon as he continued amidst acquiesced silence. "The earth's limits and expanse are no mystery to me. Its gravity is an ordinary rule. Its fruits have become bitter. Its air is sour, its water is salty, seasons have been corrupted by El Niño, birds are scared, animals have become artificial and mum – their language is unintelligible, their routes hidden under dust, their movements erratic. Its mountains shake, its deserts are chilly. The earth no longer pulls me to its lap. It is pushing me into the empty space. All familiar landmarks are gone, and new landmarks are so new I fear them. Only fear is familiar. We're all time-travellers and you say that the journey never began? How utterly stupid of you!"

He turned and walked through the receding water back to the boat. He went inside his cabin and came back with a basket full of things. "Things are familiar because you want to see them as familiar, old-timer. Taste this milk," he said, raising the bottle of milk above his head. "Does it taste like milk? Bite this bread. Does it taste like bread? Kill the man standing next to you. Does he look like a man? You're living in myths and you mythologise the seen and heard. You're a myth and you make me feel like a myth, old-timer."

He looked at the Big Boat moored at a distance. It looked uncannily unreal. "Once upon time, there was a boat," he said, his voice assuming the cryptic gravity of a storyteller's drawl. "Aboard it were two lovers. They fell in love at the wrong moment in a wrong situation and incurred the wrath of the ocean. They committed the original sin upon the boat, hidden from the eyes of four God-fearing witnesses. They were not stoned to death, but death stoned them. The boat hit an iceberg and everything started to sink slowly and consistently. There were not enough life-saving earthen pitchers on board and the lovers sank with their belongings, their hopes and pension plans. Long afterwards, people built their shrine in the ocean. You can see it if you have the money. Cut. The end. The end is near. It's all over. You may leave the theatre now, but… my heart will go onnnnnnnnnnnn."

From under the veil of darkness, the old man started to scream. "That was a great spectacle, so real. So unbearable. I'm losing my mind. I'm fainting. The water's all around me. It stinks. I'm dying of unknown causes. I'm dead. If I'm not dead, I'll commit suicide. I have committed it."

When the light was finally restored, Mohammed Khan found himself sitting alone in the last row of empty seats of the abandoned movie theatre. Dejected he decided to engage in some productive activity, away from the pollution and purity of ideals and spectacles. He got up and headed toward the nearest airport, shedding his memories with each step so that he could embrace the future.

Book V

Return of the Native

And Moses returned to his people.
(Al-Quran, 20: 88)

20

> *Amongst you there should be a group that calls to goodness, enjoins right conduct and forbids indecency. Such are they who are successful.*
> *(Al-Quran, 3: 104)*

Years ago, when Mohammed Khan left the Valley, he had boarded a Fokker plane from Rawalpindi to fly to the port city of Karachi. Now he was back at the same airport, having flown there in a Boeing 747, no longer the same man but carrying the same futuristic uncertainty in his heart. The airport was small and congested with shabbily dressed people moving around noisily in the dilapidated concourse. Mohammed Khan was disappointed to see that the land was still struggling with the aftermath of his absence.

He managed to find a baggage trolley and walked over to the carousel. It took him over an hour to collect his bags and pass through Immigration to the door leading to further uncertainty.

"Stop," a loud voice commanded him.

Mohammed Khan turned to see a customs officer dressed in a white uniform trying to arrest him with his stare. "You can't go out without a customs check," the officer barked.

Mohammed Khan felt slighted but maintained his smile. He didn't want to appear rude to an authority figure in a land not famous for its human rights record. "I've got nothing to declare, officer," he said.

The customs officer lifted the side of his lip to sneer. "You've come from abroad and you say you have nothing to declare?"

"That's right," Mohammed Khan replied indignantly. "I have nothing to declare."

"Open the suitcase," the officer commanded. "Show me what you have brought. Nothing to declare, my bloody foot!"

Anger spread through Mohammed Khan. "You think I'm lying?" He said, trying to control the indignant quiver in his voice.

"We'll soon find out," the customs officer said. "The luggage will speak, just as on the Day of Judgement every human limb will speak."

Mohammed Khan opened the bag and the customs officer went through its contents as if he expected to find a dirty bomb inside, throwing every article contemptuously on the desk. "Haan," he suddenly exclaimed. "Five pullovers. This is a commercial quantity. Do you have an import licence from the Import Promotion Bureau for these items, Mr. Nothing-to-Declare?"

"Oh, for God's sakes," Mohammed Khan protested. "I brought them for my relatives."

"Everybody says that," the officer said. "Come to my office. We know how to deal with smugglers."

"Smugglers?" said Mohammed Khan, his anger giving way to a flicker of concern. "Officer, I'm telling you the truth. I'm here after more years than I care to count and I thought I should bring a few gifts for my family."

"Everybody says that too but you look like a gentleman, so I'll accept three hundred dollars, one pullover and that Parker pen in your shirt pocket, and let you go."

"What?"

"Hurry up, Mister," the customs officer said curtly. His belly danced with impatience. "Hurry up. I have to deal with other smugglers too."

With great reluctance and after haggling for ten minutes, Mohammed Khan gave him one hundred dollars, a pullover, his favourite Parker pen, and collected his bags. As he came out of the concourse, militiamen attired in naked ankles, white gowns and green turbans surrounded him. Mohammed Khan surrendered without resistance. He was weak and wasted; his breath reeked of burnt soul. The militiamen gave him blank arrest warrant forms which he gratefully filled out and signed, placing his thumb impression as the seal of acceptance. He felt at home as he was taken into custody and transported to, what he presumed, would be the main prison.

Mohammed Khan was taken to the other side of the airport in a horse-driven cart that passed through many lanes and eventually stopped in front of a structure of brick and mud, where a bearded man was busy washing cooking utensils.

"This gentleman needs to see the Chief," the militiaman informed him.

"Take him to reception," the man said. "Someone will guide him further to the Chief."

The reception was under an arched verandah deputed to keep an eye on the other brick and mud structures. Two uniformed personnel dressed in white and green sat behind a table, sweating profusely in the humid shade.

"You want to be allocated a cell?" they asked Mohammed Khan.

"He needs to see the Chief," the militiaman replied on his behalf.

"Let him walk the straight path through the main yard all the way to the building at the far end," the men in white and green instructed the militiamen. "He'll find him if it be his intent."

The militiamen nodded to Mohammed Khan. "From here onward you'll walk alone," they said and went back the way they had come. Mohammed Khan hesitated momentarily before walking past the reception to a huge yard, where countless clothes hung from trees in various clusters and bearded men were busy performing different chores. As he walked past them to another verandah stretching in front of him, he realised that the guards at the reception had not bothered to write down his name or allocate him a number. He also realised that the captors and the kept wore the same uniforms and appeared to wield the same authority in the prison.

The verandah was as modest as the other buildings he had seen in this complex. He counted the rooms from the left, knocked at the first door and walked in.

A man sat on a mat facing the door. He looked at Mohammed Khan and a smile appeared on his dark lips. "Come on in, Mohammed Khan. My heart has been expecting you."

The person who greeted Mohammed Khan had a fleshy face belying his age. His skin was pale around his cheeks but radiant around the neck and lower jaw. Entrenched over the lines of his forehead was a round spot: the *mehrab*, the ultimate oeuvre of a dedicated artist attempting to enliven the earth by gentle strokes of his consecrated forehead. In a sweeping glance that lasted perhaps no more than a second – or perhaps a lot more – Mohammed Khan experienced the vibrant presence of the artist living within his art: the flesh, bones and veins of his forehead aching to brush the reed mat, assimilate it, and become one with it.

The person came forward and hugged Mohammed Khan with a grip so strong the latter could not possibly break it, even if he'd wanted to. It was a grip of frozen moment whose duration was beyond the long or brief history of time. Mohammed Khan felt himself stepping out of history. He winced, scared to forget his current location on the contextual coordinates. The fleeting eternity lasted only a few seconds and when he finally escaped its embrace, he quickly touched himself to check his separateness.

"Are you the Warden of this prison?" he asked.

"Warden? Prison?" the man frowned and then smiled understandably. "I was informed that you're quick to name things, Mohammed Khan, so you're at liberty to call this place whatever you like. Same goes for me, for I go by a thousand names," the man said. "I got an *ishara* that you would surrender. Come. Take off your shoes and sit with me."

A jute mat was spread in the room. A crumpled pillow and a legless table indicated that some form of human and official activity took place here. Mohammed Khan spent some time mastering the appropriate posture of sitting on the mat and finally assumed a crossed-legged position.

"You must be thirsty," the man named by Mohammed Khan as Warden said. "I am very sorry I did not offer you water in my emotional outburst."

He got up and walked over to a clay pitcher kept in a corner. He tilted the pitcher, poured water into a bowl and handed it to Mohammed Khan. The water was surprisingly cold, containing the purifying earthen smell that tasted empirical.

"You mentioned a sign…"

"Oh, yes. The *ishara*. Foreknowledge. Intuition. Clairvoyance. Inspiration: perhaps a divine inspiration."

"How do you define it?"

"Just an ishara. Not everything needs a definition or a name, Mohammed Khan. Some things are elucidated only in experience: words and names make them obscure."

Mohammed Khan squinted. There was something startlingly familiar about the Warden that simultaneously thrilled and unnerved him. He wished his memory would return to help him complete the recognition process.

"You look virtually the same as when you walked into the library. You were so confused, so vulnerable. A small boy, a pure soul. You're still a small boy but not as pure. Things have happened to you because you've been running after things and they dirtied you. You smell bad. It's coming from inside you: I think you're hungry. You must eat, but before you do, know that food is polluting. Eat only what is permitted."

Lunch was served on jute mats in a big hall where ceiling fans were making a valiant effort to fight the soaring heat. Warm air entered through windows to tickle perspiring skins. Bearded men sat crossed-legged on the mat, wearing turbans, many of which were green when they first adorned their shaven heads. The room reeked of the smell of sharing.

Two men entered the hall, carrying clay bowls filled with curry. The bowls were passed around, each to be shared by four people. Two more men entered carrying bread and gave one piece to every inmate.

"Go ahead, Mohammed Khan," the Warden urged him. "Start your food."

"I can't share my plate with strangers, Warden," Mohammed Khan said. "People are polluting too."

"Not when you're only sharing food with them," the Warden reassured him. "Be assured that we don't share tattoo needles in this place so we don't need to sue our spouses for giving us Hepatitis C."

Mohammed Khan dipped a piece of bread in the bowl. The three men sharing his bowl had already started eating, tearing at the pieces of bread, dipping them in curry and munching with a vengeance. The hall was resounding with a ruminative sound so loud it could have been heard from miles away.

"Believe in nourishment," the Warden said, noticing the wry expression on Mohammed Khan's face. "Believe that food was invented to nourish, not to tickle your taste buds or adorn menu cards of expensive restaurants and fast food outlets. Believe in the Force that empties the intestines and makes food permissible."

After lunch, they returned to the Warden's office.

"Why did you decide to come to us, Mohammad Khan?" the Warden said.

"That wasn't my decision! Your men brought me here against my will."

"Don't underestimate the power of your will. You were brought because you decided it was your destiny."

"That's rubbish," Mohammed Khan said angrily. "Look at yourself, Warden. Look at the discrepancy in your words and your deeds. Is this what you do for living? Isn't there anyone to stop you? No law, no police, no writ of the High Court, no District Nazim or Army Monitoring Team?"

"We're all subject to one Voice without whose echo not a leaf moves," the Warden said. "Let me take you to the main facility so you can see the work we're doing here."

21

Go forth light and heavy, whether it is easy or difficult, or whether you are unarmed or armed! Struggle in God's way with your possessions and yourselves: that is better for you, if you know.
(Al-Quran, 9: 41)

Follow traditions, Avoid innovation.
(Commandment of the Fourth Imam)

The main facility was a curious mix of mud, cement and bricks. The dilapidated complex was spread over several acres without any specific architectural planning. It seemed that haphazard additions had been made as and when someone had felt like adding something. Most of the rooms were a collection of threadbare walls with no plaster, and sometimes not even windowpanes or doorframes. They looked like toothless monsters staring inward at framed photos of bearded ghosts placed on the floor, and only the hum of their reading of the Holy Book betrayed their being alive. The exterior was matching. Plaster was peeling off most buildings, and as Mohammed Khan walked through the maze of solidity and fluency, his aesthetic sensibility was forced in a new direction.

The bearded ghosts were everywhere, clad in long white shirts and baggy *shalwars* that stopped short of their ankles. They weren't exactly like zombies – they sometimes smiled, and a few even laughed – but the difference was only marginal. At best, they were a cross between zombies and cyborgs, performing their chores without any hint of real emotion.

"They are the people who have exercised their free will to join us," the Warden said. "They come and go as they please. They do not come to me or to us. They come to themselves to hear the voice: the voice we all obey"

"They seem to be living in pretty bad conditions," Mohammed Khan said, encouraged by the Warden's mild manners. "I don't see basketball courts or body-building gyms. The rooms are not air-conditioned despite the oppressive heat. There are no movie theatres, no nightclubs. No in-house entertainment."

"These people are here to build their souls not their bodies," the Warden said with experiential conviction. "They don't need external sources of entertainment. They are imbued with a self-defined sense of personal well-being. No one ever complains of getting bored. What is boredom if not too-muchness? We make sure there is adequacy, not too much of everything."

He stopped and gave a parting smile filled with finality. "Why don't you mix with your brethren and discover yourself."

As soon as the Warden left, a man with white skin and a golden beard approached Mohammed Khan.

"Hello. My name is Yusuf, but you can call me Joseph, if you prefer," he said in his Yorkshire accent. "Four years ago, I surrendered to the right path. Are you the new entrant? The chap from nowhere?"

Mohammed Khan examined the Englishman without defined interest. He was a tall man, at least seven inches taller than him and about thirty pounds lighter. That made him look like a lamppost, with his thin face perched on top like a flickering lantern. His beard, about four years old, was meticulously oiled and combed. He had thick brows, overlooking a couple of Aryan blue eyes that searched Mohammed Khan without any hint of Fascism in them.

"I was planning to start writing a book when I went into a spell of uncertainty," Yusuf spoke without invitation. "Complete incertitude, shall we say? I was suddenly not sure of writing, or reading for that matter. Then I went to see a man of the mind. He diagnosed me as a patient of clinical depression and prescribed medicines, but they didn't work. He taught me relaxation techniques, but I was still as depressed as ever. I tried to read books on the subject. They all talked about having faith in the Word and building vocabulary, but I no longer had an aptitude for writing or an admiration for reading. Then I met these people and things changed. They introduced me to belief in divine word and the pleasure of reciting. My depression is over. Life is so uncomplicated here: words are so few. I've heard them all and learnt them all, although I don't understand them all."

"Why are you telling me your personal problems, sir?" Mohammed Khan said, helplessly bored with the man's chatter. "You should go and look for a priest or a shrink. I'm sure the Warden can arrange a meeting for you."

"I'm not telling you my problems, Mohammed Khan. I'm only sharing the solution with you," the blonde man said. "The solution lies in acceptance of the truth that word is a simple inscription. You've got to learn to read and recite, and to re-read and re-recite."

As Yusuf walked off towards his dorm, another inmate approached Mohammed Khan. He was a dark-skinned fellow in his early thirties, short and scrawny with a face burdened by protruded cheekbones casting shadows over the deep coves of his sallow cheeks. He had a streaky black beard faithfully dyed to get the desired colour. His skin was papery and pockmarked, his lips abnormally thick and dark, hiding a twisted series of yellow teeth that became visible with his timorous smile. "Peace unto you, Mohammed Khan," he said, words effortlessly flowing out of his mouth. "My name is Mohammed Shafi. I'm your brother who lives in the city."

"I don't have a brother," Mohammed Khan said gently.

"I have the authority to take any man as my brother and place him under preemptive arrest. This authority was given to me by the Book."

"You're the police?"

"There are no police here: my brethren deserve respect and enjoy rights and obligations. Whenever you introduce police in a system, rights and respect are violated. Besides, the brethren's commitment sets them apart from those who deserve to be arrested. If I feel that someone is likely to disturb fraternal peace or leave the right path, I can arrest him without a warrant under sections 107/151 of the Behavioural Procedure Code. If I am informed that a person has no ostensible means of subsistence, I can also place him under arrest."

"You mean, like an unemployed person?" Mohammed Khan demanded incredulously.

"Well, yes. Why not?"

"Why not? You mean to say that if someone's unemployed, you put him in jail?"

"If he has no means of subsistence, he must surely be indulging in criminal activities: how else will he be supporting himself, huh?" Mohammed Shafi said triumphantly. "So, we bring him in here, make him bare his ankles, teach him how to beg for subsistence and then train him how to walk upright with cast-down eyes. And when he reaches his full strength and is ripe, we give him wisdom and knowledge and bestow upon him the title, Ankler."

"Ankler? I've never heard this expression before."

"It's not an expression, my brother. It's an honour. The Anklers are so called because in order to complete their belief, they must bare their ankles for the entire world to see. All other things are insignificant: once you bare your ankles, you are absolved of all worldly and heavenly obligations."

Mohammed Khan was lonely and Mohammad Shafi made him feel even lonelier. He sat down, tired of standing and walking. He crouched on the mat, reading in its reeds his own history, the past when he was not himself.

"Tell me about yourself, Mohammed Khan," Shafi said and the loneliness inside Mohammed Khan swelled into words.

"I was allocated to the one and only nation through an international lottery," Mohammed Khan said. He was not sure if he was telling his own story or his thoughts had hacked into someone else's memory. "They placed millions of souls in a glass bowl, pulled out fifty thousand bodies and threw them out on the streets of America so that they could sweep alleys or work at gas stations. I washed dishes behind closed doors, and when I had finally washed enough dishes and pumped enough gas into other people's vehicles to make it big and buy a Pajero, I allowed myself to fall in love with Sue. After a long court battle, she agreed to marry me but her enthusiasm did not last long. She suffered silently and obediently. Death was the sole deliverer, she knew. She never complained.

"We had two children: a son and a daughter, or perhaps, a daughter and a son. I supposed that they would grow as they were supposed to grow but I was ruined when I found that my daughter was regressing, not growing. She had been out in the open for too long and was contaminated by ignorance fallout. She forgot the simple paternity principle that she was her father's daughter and became unrecognisable. I discovered that she was collated to someone or something else. In a state of dishonoured pain, I caught hold of her and slapped her.

"The slap reassured me of the purity of my blood. My son and his innocence were upstairs. I heard a shattering sound in his room and moments later he came down alone. I told him what had happened, and to my surprise, my son claimed she was still his sister. He caught my hand and slapped me on the face. Then he called the police and they took me away.

"I told my captors that I'd beaten my daughter over a trivial matter. I admonished them for their muddled sense of signification. I justified my action by telling them how I would stay awake the whole night when she was unwell, wash urine off her and change her nappy, give her food when she was hungry, teach her the ways of good and bad, give her everything she ever wanted. I told them that I gave her my love, my attention, my guidance, and guarded her like a treasure – but she tried to murder me.

"The captors finally released me on bail and I made plans to take my children to where they belonged – here, in the Valley. They refused. They said it was a place whose history was upside down, path unmarked and air tainted. It was not their place. I had no option. I killed the daughter in her sleep. I was a kind-hearted father. Before I drove the knife through her heart, I silently asked for her forgiveness. I buried her in a place no one ever visited. No one could prove anything against me."

"This is not your story, Mohammed Khan," Mohammed Shafi said softly. "It is the story of someone else."

"Whose story is it then?"

"It doesn't matter as long as the story is told and heard. You told the story and I heard it. That's good enough. Let's go back to the dorm lest you start narrating the story again. That would be boring."

Mohammed Khan lost his way while returning to the dorm. He joined a group of men who were going to the bazaar.

The bazaar was a long stretch of bedlam. There was at least one man for every fly. Men were everywhere. Buzzing across his face, flocking in dilapidated shops, hovering over sliced pieces of blood-red watermelons, sifting through local sweets that shouted for attention – *barfi, laddoo, baaloo-shahi*.

He looked at the faces. They were different in a reassuringly inferior way. Swarthy skins, parched and dehydrated with heat. Eyes, dried of expression and incapable of communicating. Lips, dark and crevassed, as if lashed for unknown sins. Beards, ranging from jet black to snow white with synthetic shades of browns and reds thrown in. Long beards, reaching the swell of bulging stomachs. Small beards struggling to leave the chins. Dense beards cloaking faces like ceremonial robes. Pruned beards acting as facial bikinis, reminding him of M. Sahib.

He studied their expressions. Each face carried a heavy load of constriction. Strained muscles had no room for movement, producing a stern countenance that looked so naturally superimposed on dark skins. These faces were forbidding even in smile.

He saw something else too. At first, he failed to recognise it (probably because he was not looking), but eventually he saw. In various degrees, in various silhouettes, but it was there on the contours of every face: a yellow tinge of guilt – not of having done something, but of not having done enough. These people were guilty of some elusive failure of which he was not a part, and didn't even want to know. He felt absolved.

Something touched him on the shoulder and he turned around. He saw a hand, sustaining only a lonely index finger attached to a stretched arm beyond which he didn't have the nerve to look. Simultaneously, he heard a begging voice, further stretching the stretched hand. It reached out and touched him on the left index finger. The abrupt physical contact with otherness jump-started a combination of sensations in him. There was revulsion, sympathy... and fear. For a fleeting moment, as the other finger brushed against his, Mohammed Khan felt himself sharing its insecurity, its dreams, and a bruised pride. The nail-less, crudely-severed stem was like a tiny torch shining in his eyes in pitch dark, making everything else disappear from his sight. Mohammed Khan winced in horror. For some inexplicable reasons, he had a strong sense of *déjà vu* that turned him into an artist.

The finger prayed for his life and his children's life and asked him for alms in return. There was no longer a hand or the arm, and if there was a person on the other end, he was only audible through a whispering voice. Supplicating yet commanding. Tired but optimistic.

Mohammed Khan shuddered. The finger was pressing firmly against his forefinger, turning him from the artist to its art, into a mural painted on a trembling ceiling. He felt subjugated by its touch.

"Give me something, kind patron," the finger whispered to him. "May your child grow to be an SHO."

Mohammed Khan didn't remember having children and if he did, he wasn't sure of their reality, nor did he care. He only wanted to liberate his finger from the contact of misery. "Get away from me, diseased creature," he shouted. "You're giving me your viruses and your bacteria."

"I'm only transmitting life into your inert finger, kind patron," the finger said and started to drift away from him, thrusting difference between them. Images began to emerge; clumsy images fresh in their primitive originality, bursting out with raw excitement from the crevasses in the ceiling. There were images of bison, bulls and deer superimposed upon one another. Images of females with sagging bellies, expansive hips and exaggerated breasts. Pictures of hunters and the hunted. Scenes of animals strewn with arrows. Paintings of faceless men identifiable in their obscurity. Traces of life painted and sculpted. Forms vaguely emergent and vigorous. Art of life struggling to be born, fighting for another breath.

Mohammed Khan felt the pain of severance and the joy of alterity.

He ran back to the safety of his room and the protection of the Warden's smile. "Isn't there a law against beggary here?" he demanded of the Warden. "You're running a Goddamn prison here. Why don't you arrest all the begging fingers and put them in the slammer?"

A tinge of surprise shaded the Warden's face. "A prison? Is that what you think this place is?" He asked in surprise. Slowly, realisation seemed to dawn on him. "Oh, I see! Now I know why you insist on calling me 'Warden'. No my delusional friend. This is not a prison I'm running here."

"Then…?"

"This is an institution for training beggars. We're all beggars here. Beggary is big business."

"An institution for training beggars? Really?"

"Indeed. And I am not a warden. They call me Chief Ankler because I head those who bare their ankles and beg."

22

*Conquer the world with the power of God's message and his
   Prophet's tradition.*
   (Maulana Maudoodi)

"Brave New World"
   (Title of a novel by Aldous Huxley)

"Submission"
   (Literal translation of the word "Islam")

The Chief Ankler's face had assumed a monumental calmness. A futuristic look pervaded his eyes. He looked like a man who was about to get hold of the cosmos and make the necessary adjustments.

"In the name of the desire, big business created beggars and allowed them to bare their ankles so they could be called Anklers," he said. "Then articulate thought and free speech were imparted unto them, and they were let loose upon an earth created for someone else's desires and ambitions. Beggars are not content with the world. They want to create a brave new world based on ancient ideas born fourteen hundred years ago in Arabia. Can you imagine the magnitude of their pain? Their suffering and discontentment? Can you fathom the enormity of their ambition? Have you ever experienced the pain of dreaming? The pain of effort? The pain of deformity: of self-inflicted deformity? The agony of struggling to create?"

He smiled the sad smile of a fallen angel. "We're no ordinary beggars. We're beseechers. From all over the world, people come to us: ordinary people yearning to enter the world of big business – dealing in salvation in the hereafter and big buck in this world. We take their egos and their pride, and sacrifice them at the altar of altruism. We beggars are the chosen people. We take money away and store it."

He let his smile shed some of its sadness. "Beggary was created to fulfil human needs, some of which are decidedly needless: physiological needs, safety needs, love needs, esteem needs, self-actualisation needs. Still, we need them to create competition so beggars can get jobs. This is not an easy task. We're forced to follow the idea of sustained production and cut-throat competition right down to the level of individuals. We're compelled to spread the news about the charm of the heard and seen, and of the futility of asking. Wanting replaces asking – you want it and you get it. This is such an efficient system. It improves quality and profitability. Human desires are satisfied so completely and effortlessly that people automatically get time to develop themselves into more refined beggars. Everyone lives happily thereafter. However, if some of them don't in this life, they have a bright future in the afterlife to look forward to."

He paused for effect. "We teach our beggars to shorten their trousers, bare their ankles, and listen to the voice of the finger. Thus the technology of beggary is moralised. Our beggars go out into the world with a strong sense of morality to build their own world. Their population is rapidly growing. They are everywhere, spreading our message all over the world."

"What's your message, Chief?" Mohammed Khan demanded sarcastically. "Arrest people without warrants when they land at the airports and either submit them to you, or deport them to Saudi Arabia?"

"No, my child," the Chief Ankler said, switching over to a more patronising form of address. "Our message comes from the Great Provider. Five times a day, we beseech people to pronounce the word correctly and submit to the will of the meaning. We beg them to surrender their wearing, eating, drinking, urinating, defecating, walking, sleeping, dreaming, talking and thinking to Him. When you embrace the One who is worthy of embrace, you submit to Him all that is, was and will be. You then accept the ultimate consequence and are rid of obscurities and twists in the text. Everything becomes a straight line."

"Why must you beg five or even one hundred times a day?"

"For the sense of achievement. Every act of begging is a ritual: an occasion to remember oneself, the other and the bounty. It is *da'wa*, calling people to go in the way of beseeching. Beggars were created from clay and the seed of begging was made from a drop of despised fluid. Then the finger was fashioned and the spirit was breathed into it. Human child is born with a weak body and an undeveloped finger. It takes time for the finger to grow, and if you want it to grow perfectly, you need a standard to follow, like correct food, right exercise, and proper call. We provide that standard. That's the basic mission of our community – or prison as you mistakenly perceived it."

"There's no mistake in my perception," Mohammed Khan said indignantly. "You kidnapped me and put me in this prison to forcibly teach me how to look humble, pose to be poor and beg for you people. How insulting! You will have to kill me before forcing me into this job."

"You're prone to stand upon wrong premises and draw neat conclusions," the Warden said with the sad shake of his head. "Come, be absorbed. Absorption is the true base of humanity. Our mission is to change the direction of beggary, to infuse new spirit into the profession, to abolish the stigma attached to it. We want to eliminate it and feel rich in begging for others, not from others. We do not believe in killing. We want to save people from killing themselves – even if it means sending out tanks and helicopters to demolish resistance."

He closed his eyes for a long moment and when they opened, there was a look of eternity in them. "I, the Chief Ankler, am not going to teach you anything, Mohammed Khan," he whispered dramatically. "I only wish to remind you and others like you what you have forgotten due to timidity, greed and temptation. Come with us to help yourself in tearing the veil of enticement. Do not be seduced by seduction: be seduced by the Creator of seduction. Beg not for what you don't have, beg for what you already have. Beg immateriality."

Mohammed Khan hung his head in acceptance.

Next morning, a man in naked ankles awoke Mohammed Khan while the sun was still tossing in bed. "We're leaving for the annual convention of those who bare their ankles, brother Mohammed Khan," he said. "Come join the Anklers. I beg of you."

Mohammed Khan was among the first to arrive at the point of unanimity. Others came, arriving in ones and twos from time to time, but not on time. They carried their totality in haversacks and makeshift bags contrived out of bed-sheets. They bared their ankles, covered their minds and opened their hearts. Talking in a low voice, safeguarding their pockets from pickpockets, they travelled, cleaning their teeth with *miswaak* as they walked.

They reached their destination; one of many and not the last. It was a place of tents. The tents – big and small, old and frayed, often patched and discoloured – were pitched upon an exalted strip of state land whose ownership record had long been destroyed by the waters of an unrecorded flood. The tents stood defiantly under a scourging sun. About them was an air of grandeur and goodness imbued with the spirit of hereafter. Inside and outside were men of different ages, places and professions: men who had evolved, were evolving, and were ready to help others evolve away from Darwin and his theories.

Mohammed Khan walked amidst the pervading presence of tents, hearing the suffusive sound of countless loudspeakers installed in every nook and corner. He listened to the sound coming from inside and outside until all distinctions were blurred and he became one with the voice. People walked all around him, mingling with the voice and losing their identity in the process. They were vendors and buyers, selling and buying eatables and non-eatables at prices fixed and flexible. They were as much involved in their surroundings as in their trade.

For three days, Mohammed Khan watched the Anklers trading ideas and notions, things and nothings. He watched them evaluate, buy, sell, negotiate, beg and recite the names of the entity to which they offered their prayers. He heard them narrate the stories of their journeys to far off places and their encounters with people who were eager to have what they had to offer.

When three days and three nights had passed and hunger had taken control of his body, Mohammed Khan decided to carve his own little niche in the world of big business. He walked away from the vendors in search of a spot where he could display his products and sell them to those who may not necessarily need them. Little did he know that the monopolistic instincts of the Big Business would never tolerate his small presence as an insignificant competitor.

Mohammed Khan displayed his merchandise on the footpath and began to shout at the top of his voice. "Five rupees, five rupees. Everything for five rupees. Great prices on everything. Come one, come all."

A buyer stopped to look at the stock offered for sale. "This computer over here," he asked. "Is this five rupees as well?"

"Indeed sir," Mohammed Khan said happily. "It is, for sure. Get a complete system and your worries will be computerised. You'll have the flexibility to sort them at leisure."

The buyer picked up the CPU and inspected its obsolete lines. "Seems like an old model," he objected.

"Not at all, sir," Mohammed Khan said with a guaranteeing smile. "It comes Internet-ready and gives you instant connection so you feel unalienated. It can also beg for you. I beg you to buy it. In my neighbourhood everyone who prays and fasts and begs has got a computer."

"I prefer to perform these rituals myself," the buyer said. "Besides, computers are hardly of any use to people in third world countries like ours. Show me something more useful."

Mohammed Khan let his smile broaden. "I've got just the thing for you, sir," he said and retrieved a rag doll from under his rug. "Look at this scientific beauty. What a contraption. This thing here can pray for you five times a day, read the word early in the morning and late at night, and visit all kinds of places on your behalf. It can even fast for you. Not just thirty days a year, but three hundred and sixty-five days a year if you so programme it. Just imagine what you can achieve with this little wonder. All your past debts written off. I pray to you to buy it, sir. It's specially made for people like you and me. It's selling like anything."

The buyer did not look interested. He was busy feeling a piece of old cloth with jagged edges. "What's this thing?" he inquired.

"This is a piece of cloth, sir. A very special one. Some say it's a mere rag, but wait until you wear it. You'll feel heavenly. I've brought it from a far off place – the place of shadowless people who only eat, sleep, wear and marvel at new things. If you can prove that you're the type who'd really devote himself to the rag, I'll give it to you for free."

"Why don't you wear it and feel heavenly yourself," the customer asked pertly.

"I feel more heavenly by selling things. Besides, they are so expensive I can't afford them. I get them from across the borders. My people bring them from far off places on donkeys, mules, trains and ships, but rest assured that the transportation cost is not included in the retail price."

His smile transmuted into a sheepish smirk. "Frankly, I've no idea where they come from or who made or unmade these things. But they certainly look nice and they're wrapped reverently."

"What else have you got?" the buyer inquired.

"Well, I've got this jar of dust. A real souvenir for the discriminating taste. It'll always remind you of me and of other people and the ones you give it to. It's not just a handful of dust, I assure you. It's actually a permanent reminder of the things gone by. It is the dust from another time and place. Look at its variable colours and shades. Smell it. Touch it. It's not ordinary dust. I guarantee its specialness and quantity. I also guarantee you that this dust settling here in this special urn will one day become so undustlike that you'll not be able to recognise it. It'll grow wings and take you to new heights, to your own abode. Don't laugh, sir. I'll tell you the secret of turning one thing into another, into its opposite. Now sir! If you don't have money, there's no problem. I'll lend you some. I can make money for you and beg for you as well. Interested, sir?"

23

The Caliph must be a man, an adult, a powerful ruler, and from the tribe of the Prophet.
(Sunni tradition)

No! The Caliph must be from the Prophet's own family.
(Shia tradition)

When two caliphs have been set up, put the last of them to death for the last one is a rebel.
(Mishkat, Book 15)

When the Holy Prophet died, the Mohajirs (immigrants) and Ansars (locals) assembled at the abode of Banu Saudah and plotted to seize the caliphate away from Ali and in favor of Abu Bakr. So the unjust person was made the head of believers.
(Hayatul Qulub)

"Hey you," a loudspeaker perched on a treetop challenged Mohammed Khan. "What do you think this is? The Friday Bazaar of Anklers? You can't sell things here unless you owe your allegiance to the Big Business and are one of its franchisees. Go and watch *You've Got Mail* to get wiser."

Mohammed Khan walked over to the microphone and snatched it from the grip of adversity. "I'm not selling things, nor are these things. They are names of nothings," he said forcefully into the microphone. His voice spread in all directions and attacked the listening hearts. "They cannot be sold or bought, you hear? We're here – you're here – to distribute them like gifts, share them like kindness, nourish them like national debt. We owe a debt of salvation to each other. We must repay what we forgot to pay. We must repay it here and now, before we're declared defaulters and investigators of the National Accountability Bureau come looking for us so that they can strike secret deals and become rich."

His audience was immediately impressed. It was their soul talking to them and it was their bodies, their belongings and their baggage that were persuaded. They moved closer to each other until they became one in their presence, in their many tents, in their makeshift haversacks and in their bare ankles. They became echoes of the voice that descended upon them from high, from the loudspeaker. They felt one with the loudspeaker. It was their voice, their cry, their wail.

They pledged to shout louder than the loudspeaker, to lose their voice in the process, to get a new voice – the voice of return to the first century when Big Business was still small. They wanted to return to themselves, to each other and to those who were not there. They resolved to turn everything into one voice, into their voice that in fact was not theirs but the voice of the One who created the originary voice. They were its echo, its passage. They wanted every human being to become its passage, irrespective of colour, creed, climate, or sexual preference. They wanted every human to hear it and echo it, firm in their belief that there were many who could not hear it because they were incapable of hearing. Their hearts were sealed and their eyes were blind. They were like animals, only eating and digesting their food, living because they were destined to live. To live was their biological need, inescapable and predetermined. But those with bare ankles were not among those people. They were the ones who had heard the voice and recited the divine words. They were the knowledgeable ones. They were the chosen ones. They were the saved ones and resolute ones. It was their job to save the others even if it meant killing them if they did not listen.

"We'll walk through all corners of the world," they resolved. "We'll undertake several journeys to spread the word of redemption. We'll chop off those ears that will not listen to our voice."

"We'd better choose a leader then," someone suggested. "A leader to guide us through the dark, the haze and the smell of blood."

"How are we going to do that?" others demanded. "Should we nominate, elect or select the leader?"

"We should elect him as they elect leaders in some places," Mohammad Khan suggested forcefully.

"No. We should select him as they select leaders in other places," someone else said.

"Brothers! You are spreading *fitna*," a third voice said as it took over the microphone. "We'll not allow you to spread dissension and create cracks among us. The leader must neither be elected nor selected; he ought to be nominated by those who are knowledgeable, wise and discernible. Elections might be widely popular but they always lead to blindness. What guarantee do we have that the person elected would be the wisest, the best and the most honest among us unless we know for certain that the electors are wise, good and honest? How do we know that their self will not delude them, that they will not be seduced into believing that they are the most eligible electors? How will we stop them from electing the one who presents himself for the job? One who offers himself to be elected has already been overtaken by the burning delusion of grandeur."

A silence followed as people thought about the three options of which two were not available to them. Mohammed Khan broke the silence.

"Brother, if we were to follow your advice and nominate the leader from among ourselves, how are we going to decide on the character of those who would nominate him?" he asked.

"Those who came first should have the right to nominate the leader."

"And who are those who came first?" Mohammad Khan inquired.

"At least not you, brother," he was told with sarcastic finality.

"Does it mean that I'd not be allowed to participate in the exercise?"

"Yes, it definitely means that."

"In that case you leave me with no option but to oppose you with all the sincerity and strength of my faith," Mohammed Khan said. He stood there uncertainly for some time, thinking about his future strategy, and left.

Mohammed Khan contacted everyone who had lately joined the Anklers. Those willing to listen to him supported him, though some of them did not support him in their hearts. Mohammad Khan organised them into a splinter group and gave it some name. They put up posters proclaiming him their leader, led processions in his support and organised public meetings to air their message. Their opponents, panicked by the popularity of the new group, decided to disrupt its activity. They smuggled firearms into town in case of conflict.

Mohammad Khan held a big public rally to kick off his campaign against the process of nomination.

The meeting was held on a large tract of land purchased by the local metropolitan corporation some thirty years ago. Successive mayors had used it to hold public meetings, in which they'd promise to turn it into a park, and then forget about it. Over the years, the place had become a passage which thousands of people used for shuttling between the main bazaar and an unknown mystic's shrine where they were treated to free meat and rice cooked in ghee. Upon this land, tents were strategically erected to ensure that anyone commuting between the bazaar and the shrine had to pass through the tents. Soon a large number of listeners, pedestrians and bystanders gathered, and when the proceedings began, five hours behind schedule, there was a sea of heads floating in mystified anticipation.

"Brothers. We the real Anklers are here to do justice to all. Justice with consistency, efficacy and brutality," Mohammed Khan declared with the casualness of a man who had just found that his ambition and good intentions were inseparable. "Justice is blind as to who came first and who came later. Those who have dared to bare their ankles are like the five fingers of one hand. Can one say that the little finger came last?"

"No," the crowd responded. "Long live Anklers. Down with prioritisers. Little finger did not come last. Who knows, it might have come first!"

Mohammed Khan continued. "If someone differentiates between his five fingers, know that he spreads fitna – dissension. One who creates dissension is not a true beggar, is he?"

"No, no," the crowd responded and burst into ecstasy and approval, shouting slogans of solidarity with their leader. "Down with fitna. Down with dissenters. Let the blood spill and heads roll."

"Listen, listen to me brothers," Mohammed Khan tried to stop them so he could carry on with his written speech. The crowd ignored him and continued to raise laudatory slogans. "I bared my ankles. I bared my heart, my soul and my sword. A bareness like the bareness of the sun when it shines, but a scattered cloud is trying to cover its beams. Tell me! Can it succeed? No! It never will."

He paused to catch his breath. "They say they are closer to the Chief Ankler than me. They lie. I stood with the master and submitted to him when he was alone and without friends. I held his hand when everyone was against him and didn't laugh when they ridiculed his short trousers. I slept his nights and awoke his mornings. He taught me how to read and write and make fire. He taught me how to walk the path, how to beg, and how to fight. I'm the only one amongst you who entered his house and met the members of his family. Who among our adversaries has been so privileged? No one but me."

Some people in attendance had started shouting. "We can't hear you," they yelled. "The loudspeakers are not working."

"Our adversaries have stooped to cheap tricks," Mohammed Khan thundered. "They bribed the man who installed the loudspeakers so that you may not hear my word. But I don't blame him. There's corruption in all directions because the government is not increasing the wages of the army officers with whom I profess my allegiance. May the Force be with us."

He paused to ensure that his final comment had been duly registered by the intelligence agencies present in the public gathering. "Falsehood is trying to dethrone the truth. Duplicity is enveloping honesty. See how the faces of our enemies have been blackened by hypocrisy. Their white masks cannot hide the reality of their true colours. One day, we'll cut open their chests and bare all the darkness inside."

"Snakes," someone shouted. "We're surrounded by snakes."

Panic gripped the crowd when it realised that the comment was not symbolic. People started running around. Those who were committed to the cause held their ground and were stampeded. During this commotion, people perched atop the surrounding buildings began to spray bullets on the fleeing masses. Many were injured and scores were killed. Blood was flowing like the rhetoric of a leader who demands accountability after having declared himself innocent of all corrupt deeds. Guarded by armed teenagers, Mohammad Khan secretly slipped away. To arrest the situation from deteriorating further, the masked men let him go.

For many days, the city administration wrestled with riots that broke out in several parts of the metropolis. Section 144 Cr.PC was imposed by the District Nazim, prohibiting the public display of arms and restricting the movement of more than four people in a group. Violations of the orders were ignored as a policy, until the situation turned so ugly that a curfew was imposed and armed troops were called in to aid the civil powers. They arrived in their shiny jeeps and formidable tanks to negotiate with the rioters. Some amongst those who participated in the parleys were against violence, some in favour, some indifferent, and some held all three postures in reserve for the appropriate occasion. Negotiations lingered on for days without an acceptable resolution in sight. Ultimately, the men in uniform took everyone to visit the historic Loehar Fort whose basements held enough terrors to make an elephant confess to being a rodent. Next morning, it was announced that the negotiations had been a great success. All the rioters were released with an official warning to behave in future, and order was restored to the city. The troops returned to their barracks, having earned public praise and a handsome IS duty allowance.

That evening, the mask-makers held a meeting with reporters and fiction-writers in a five-star hotel. Events were narrated, connections established and conclusions drawn. Next morning, many stories were circulated among the Anklers, their sympathisers and antagonists. In restaurants and on footpaths, in homes and workplaces, in barbershops and in places of worship, everyone gossiped about the public meeting, quoting the stories they had heard or read.

"The shooting wasn't done by masked men," a barber told his lathered patron, quoting the story in the local newspaper. "There were no snakes, and even if there were, the Anklers should have killed them. They didn't because they love snakes."

The patron nodded his head in agreement and barely escaped a nick of the razor on his chin. "You remember the python that reportedly lived on the tree, sir?" the barber asked. "I think it was a python that came to the meeting place, and we all know that the python is not poisonous. Why should they be scared of it?"

"I was there," the patron said without much confidence in his statement. "I saw everything. No one was killed. No one shot anyone. Actually the Anklers killed each other. They're crazy, you know."

In a restaurant where opinionated conversation was banned, under the authority of a poster to that effect pasted on a wall, a group of political observers threw further light on the issue. "There were no masked men. The loudspeakers disturbed the people from a neighbouring settlement and they only tried to remove the cause of disturbance. The Anklers asked for it. What if a few of them died? What is life but a transitory phenomenon?"

"You can't rule out the possibility that perhaps their rivals did all that," one analyst suggested, apprehensive of being contradicted by those who had already received envelopes filled with thousand-rupee bills. "They were nervous of the Anklers' popularity."

"Oh, come on," he was told. "Mohammed Khan's group is not popular at all. I bet he can't win his own seat. It was all a publicity stunt."

"There were so many people there. It was an ocean of humans."

"That's not true: there were only a few hundred soul-less bodies that attended the meeting. Who counted them? And was counting important? Is number more important than enthusiasm?"

"You've got to admit they were really an enthused lot."

"Who gave you that idea, my dear? They were paid to go there. Mohammed Khan hired all sorts of transport and gave people free rides to the meeting place."

"His men forcibly took away all available means of transportation."

"It's all a lie, an illusion. Nothing happened: nothing of significance; nothing that deserves comment."

They returned to their tea. No one was sure of the happening, though some writers became very rich by selling their stories in the right places.

The Chief Ankler died a few days after the public meeting and its consequences. Mohammad Khan and his rival attended his funeral. For the first time, they met face to face and decided to agree to a dialogue.

"We want peace and harmony between real and fake Anklers," the Chief Rival said to Mohammed Khan. "You say that we should elect the leader but you have seen with your own eyes that the way to election is strewn with blood, disharmony, exaggeration and lies."

"The way to nomination is full of conflict, resentment and uncertainty," retorted Mohammad Khan. "You insist that the leader of our community should be from among the first ones. The Chief who lies dead before us never made any distinction between the first ones and the last ones."

"You're both right and wrong, Mohammed Khan. The Chief Ankler indeed did not make such a distinction but don't forget that he was from a noble family, so the new leader must be from the noble family as well. He should be the one who is honest and wise, and knows what is good for us and what is not."

"In that case, we should constitute a committee to nominate the one who is the best among us," Mohammad Khan argued.

"We don't need to form a committee at this point in time," the Chief Rival said with a smile. "Let us get used to the system first. Once we have selected two or three leaders through my proposed system, then we may consider the constitution of a committee."

He pointed to an old, bearded man who had remained quiet all this time. "This is the man whom the Chief willed to be our leader. Let's select him so that our Chief's soul can be happy."

"I don't accept this man. Who is he? Has anyone seen him before?" Mohammed Khan said in frustration.

"He's our new leader who will lead us to unknown heights. I have known him a long time. He was very close to the Chief. When he reaches his last moment, he'll nominate me. I know that because I'm very close to him and support him so ardently."

Mohammed Khan opened his mouth to object but the Chief Rival stopped him short. "Know for sure that I have no desire to lead this rather small community," he declared for the benefit of everyone present and for the benefit of those who would later hear or read about the proceedings of the negotiations. "However, if this man nominates me, I'll submit myself to the scrutiny of the community. If the community says yes to me, I'll accept the responsibility. When my time to go comes, I'll ask the best people among the community to come forward and elect you, Mohammed Khan, from among them, since you're wise, knowledgeable and selfless."

"This is all a scheme and I'll be damned if I'm led by my passion to become part of it," Mohammed Khan yelled. "I have received an *ishara* that tells me this plan is ruinous and will culminate in permanently dividing the good into many vulnerable little pieces. What if people are not satisfied with the governance of the ruler of your choice? The only way for them to redress their grievances would be to either plant a bomb in the ruler's C-130 plane, or declare him a traitor and exile him to Saudi Arabia. They'll be forced to commit these crimes because you leave them with no constitutional way out."

"You've gone mad, Mohammad Khan," the Chief Rival said, getting to his feet in inevitability. "You don't listen to reason and cannot see the mischief of your present. You pretend to predict the events that only the Knower knows: surely Evil has possessed you from head to toe. You dare cast doubt on those who have cleansed their heart with submission, purified their souls with the perfume of the word, immortalised their bodies by shedding blood. Come on, my followers. Further negotiations are useless. Now the sword will decide the decidable between us. Let Mohammed Khan rally around his misled people. We'll call out the right ones around us and at the moment of that great gathering, we'll settle the matter of succession once and for all."

Negotiations broke down. Fear and hopelessness gripped the Anklers. Every day they yearned to hear some heartening news as they searched for each other in the numbness of senses, in blind alleys of standoff, in the deafening noise of claims, in the flickering worlds of stammered utterances and mute words. They couldn't see, talk or hear. They were becoming hard of hearing. They were losing their voice. Those who talked were not heard and those who were heard were not believed. People wished to be released from the burden of distrust. They wished to embrace death. They ran amok, losing themselves on the way and deserting each other.

Within days, many of Mohammad Khan's allies allied themselves with his enemies. They were offered proper hospitality worthy of their rank and in accordance with the status of their hosts. A few also came over to his side but quickly returned to their original position. Some changed their loyalties so many times that in the end, they were not sure whose side they were on, and had to toss one-sided coins to decide. Mohammad Khan was the main loser in this movement of to-and-fro. He kept losing his followers to greed, and ambition. The day finally came when the last of his followers deserted, leaving him alone in the world. So complete was his aloneness that even his memories deserted him. He found himself sitting at the edge of realisation, wondering why he had struggled, and against whom.

Yet no answers came.

24

They shall recline on inwrought couches, sitting face to face, and there shall wait on them blooming youth with goblets and ewers and a cup of purest wine; their brows ache not from it nor fails the senses. And there shall be dark-eyed houris, chaste as hidden pearls: a guerdon of their deeds.
(Description of Paradise in Al-Quran, 56: 15-24)

Nought shall they know of sun or piercing cold, and they shall be given a drink of the cup tempered with ginger from the fount therein whose name is Salsabil the softly flowing.
(Further description of Paradise in Al-Quran, 76: 13-18)

"Pakistan is not supporting terrorist activity in Kashmir."
(Pakistan's Chief Executive)

"India is not involved in acts of terrorism in Pakistan."
(Indian Prime Minister)

For several days, Mohammed Khan wandered aimlessly on the land in an intoxicating state of forgetfulness, crossing bridges, climbing mountains, traversing deserts, swimming lakes and rivers. Just when he was about to fall from exhaustion of faith, he stumbled upon a path that took him straight into the heart of believability. He crossed over and found himself standing on the banks of the river belonging to his great grandfather. The river was a magnificent sight: it was older than time, and its water — as pure as milk and sweet as honey — gushed like torrents of reality through the mottled outline of a garden where date palms and mango trees grew. On the other side of the river stood a mansion, its stucco exterior punctuated by mullioned windows from which the light of hope flashed intermittently.

"Wow," Mohammed Khan exclaimed "Is this real? Or am I dreaming?"

"Depends on the assumptions," he heard a voice from behind telling him.

Mohammed Khan turned around. A cool breeze touched his face and something resembling remembrance began to creep into his brain. He saw himself staring at a three-dimensional memory from his past. Leaning against a wooden staff, wearing a mythical smile on his swarthy face, was Ram Babu, the old librarian who had once loaned him the Book of Names; the man who'd started it all for him. Was the end in sight?

"Babu Sahib," Mohammed Khan cried out and nearly tripped as his past crashed into him with the force of a tornado. "You're alive! They said you were turned to ashes along with the library."

"I was," Ram Babu nodded. "Turned into a memory."

Mohammed Khan's heart sank in disappointment; bubbles appeared on the river's quiet surface. "Then you can't be real," he said with a sad shake of his head. "This has to be an illusion."

"As I said, it depends on the assumptions," replied Babu.

"Assumptions? I'm talking about reality here, Babu Sahib."

"Believe in the assumptions if you're planning to believe in reality," Ram Babu said firmly. His voice bounced off the high walls of the mansion and plummeted like a wounded bird to take refuge in Mohammed Khan's heart. "Once you have faith in the premise, the paradigm will come to life and reality will be commanded to follow the theory."

"I don't understand…"

Babu smiled. "Let me take you for a walk, my child," he said offering his hand. "There's a lot of fresh air around here which you must breathe in and breathe out. Breathe in and breathe out. Breathe in and breathe out."

"What is this place?" Mohammed Khan asked, breathing in and out, and starting to feel dizzy with hyperventilation.

"It's called the Primevous Dwelling. It's the Chaghian replica of the holy location where your great grandfather was once treated to ginger ale."

Holding hands and sharing smiles, Mohammed Khan allowed the ex-librarian to take him on a guided tour. Through Ram Babu's eyes, he saw herds and herds of blessed mannequins paraded under the shades of the trees growing along the riverbank: dense beards fluttering in the breeze, beautific faces shining under the sunshine, lustrous eyes doused in the pleasure of a non-intoxicating wine.

"They are those who have reached the last phase of evolution," Babu said in his tour commentary. "They'll remain here forever. Darwin is finally dead."

Ram conducted Mohammed Khan past the figures of divine rapture into the portico of the Primevous Dwelling. The walls of the blessed castle were adorned with impressionistic paintings and unfocused photographs of several historical sites, including the softly flowing fount. "One day you'll take a bath with the holy fount's sulphury water," Ram Babu promised him. "You'll shed your clothes and lay bare every foible in your intentions. You'll stand under the flowing water and cleanse your soul of the allergens of fear and doubt."

"Why am I here?"

Ram let go of Mohammed Khan's hand. "You're here to wait for the telegram," he said.

Mohammed Khan wiped the sweat of contiguity off his palms and stared at the face of his guide. "What telegram?"

"You'll know when it comes."

Mohammed Khan looked at the ex-librarian with mounting disbelief. "Wait for a telegram?" he cried. "The Chief Rival is spreading fitna on the land. His soldiers are ready to wage a bloody war and you expect me to wait for a stupid telegram? I've got to go back and fight him."

"You will achieve your destiny only through non-violence, my child," Ram said.

"Non-violence?" Mohammed Khan roared. "How can you talk of non-violence when the Chief Rival is bent upon waging war on the land? How can you allude to this impractical abstraction when the reality is about to be massacred?"

"The reality is lying right in front of you," Ram Babu said in a voice that suddenly had a new vigour. He sounded like an enthusiastic salesperson confident of his powers of persuasion, if not entirely sure of the truth of his claim. "This is the place where you must wait for your turn."

"My turn? My turn for what? To rot?"

"To lead, my child."

"How can I lead when there's a dispute regarding the methodology of choosing leadership?" Mohammed Khan demanded. "Some say the leader should be selected, I say the leader should be elected, and the Chief Rival says that the leader should be nominated."

A cheerless smile appeared on Ram Babu's withered face. "In our part of the world, leaders are imposed, my child," he said. "And you are one of the potential impositions."

Mohammed Khan suddenly felt serenity descending upon the land as he heard the old, dhoti-clad ex-librarian's last sentence in capitulated silence. Ram Babu moved forward and embraced him in a paternal hug. Mohammed Khan smelt the minted breath of reassurance upon his cheeks. He had found the replica of the place of fulfilled desires to which his great ancestor had once migrated, and to this land he had returned after an absence of centuries: one in many and many in one with those who aspired to lead; interlaced like the beads of a rosary yearning for the touch of believing fingers, vibrant like a leader's voice aching to be heard, adamant like a believer's prayer demanding freedom from yearning lips. He had returned to become one with return and chant in one voice the tune that once conducted the entire spectrum of notes and cracked the eardrums of those who lacked the ability to enjoy classical music. It was the voice of leadership temporarily relegated to a muffled wail by the forces of clatter, who shouted, "Quick march, left right, left right, might is right, only we are right, no one else has any right for no one else is right". This was the voice from the past, a millennium and a half old, living inside the breasts of valleys and mountains, seas and deserts, and plains and rivers, quarantined from the influence of adulteration, alive in captivity, cantabile and euphonious, echoing in stony gorges, floating above the waters of cantillating streams, beating tempestuously in his heart, the sign of his promised freedom, guiding him to be one with a destiny from which he refused to escape, because escape was not conceivable. He would learn its tune, recall its words and sing in a chorus so loud that winds would gather and tornadoes would form and rains would descend and seas would overflow and the land would be submerged under the truth of his leadership.

"The door to the Primevous Dwelling has been opened, my child," Ram Babu resumed. "The rewards of waiting await you. If you follow me inside, you will be rewarded with things and nothings, with all you desire and will desire. In this place of transitory existence, bald people get lush green hair on their scalps without a transplant, flat-chested women become full-breasted without silicon, virginity is renewable, orgasm self-timed and erection an act of decision rather than Viagra. In there, the size of your desires is adjustable, and desires adapt to the desires of the pious in accordance with their wishes, age and leadership potential."

He stopped and pointed toward the stony bulwark around the mansion. "Beyond these walls are women seventy times more beautiful than any woman that ever walked the earth. They long for you in parlours equipped with attached baths, untouched by beings visible and invisible. They wait for the moment when you'll make the first among infinite choices into transitory ecstasy. You will cling to your women and suck out the permissible juices. You will play with their hair, place your lips upon their cheeks and be one with many. Know that these dames have limbs made of freshly lactated milk, tongues laced with unadulterated honey, gums adorned with pearls, mouths smelling of your favourite eau de cologne. They eat not, defecate not, and menstruate not: they are eternally at your service."

He consulted his cerebral notes and resumed. "Also at your service will be young boys whose bodies are devoid of hair, whose eyes shine like almonds and lips taste like cherries. They will execute your desires and still bring no shame to you or your family. In this transit place, you'll be allowed to do everything you were forbidden to do on earth. You'll serve every wish you ever had or will have and feel no guilt. In this world are no condoms and no requirement for safe sex. Your soul will be insured against gonorrhea and syphilis and herpes and AIDS."

Mohammed Khan felt his heart swelling with unmet desires and when he spoke, his voice came from somewhere else. "Who runs this place? Why was I selected…?"

"The Force controls this abode," Ram Babu cut him short. "You were selected because there was apparently no one more readily available to replace the Chief Rival when the Force decides that it's time to replace him."

"May the Force be with me," Mohammed Khan said with solemnity. "I believe in the Force without asking its name or source."

"You're a true believer," Babu said, "and indeed you'll be rewarded if you're patient."

While Mohammed Khan was busy settling down in the Primevous Dwelling, the Chief Rival had taken full control of the political and administrative affairs of the state. People woke up one morning and were informed that the Chief Rival was their new President. His close relatives were appointed as head of all the key ministries – Interior, Finance, and Religious Affairs. Mohammed Khan was declared an apostate who had corrupted the message of the Chief Ankler and was liable to be shot on sight. Reports of his sexless orgies at the Primevous Dwelling were beamed to every satellite channel and given fresh steam by search engines on the Internet. He was christened as the greatest threat to true leadership and his identikit picture was shown on TV before every news bulletin. Promoters rushed to offer sponsorship to any stint that carried his name, even by mistake. He assumed the status of the household evil. His name became a public trademark for embossing on doormats, on the soles of shoes, on toilet paper, bathroom tiles and dartboards. People eagerly awaited the opportunity to hear his name or see his picture on TV, so that they could burn with hatred and feel absolved.

Mohammed Khan was unaware of the free publicity he was getting throughout the nation and around the world. The Primevous Dwelling was located beyond the reaches of electrical connections and satellite TV. He was in a world away from the world: a world weary of enemies.

His enemies were in a strategic fix. They wanted to reap all permissible benefits of the first strike but didn't want to lose the initiative on diplomatic fronts. They aspired to move deep into the hinterland but were unsure of the potency of their will or its venom. They had their eyes set upon the grand design but were not sure of its grandness, or the meticulousness of their planning. They wanted to destroy the Primevous Dwelling with a single strike but were scared of the reaction of the Force. They wanted to emerge victorious but knew full well that victory would leave them bleeding. Eventually, after a secret meeting of the National Security Council, the Chief decided in favour of a war by proxy, conscientiously planned to last for a hundred years during which his perks would quadruple and the benefits of the war would pour down to his great-grandchildren. It was a perfect arrangement for minimising human loss and maximising personal wealth. It was also their only hope of keeping the Force satisfied.

Unwary of his enemy's clever intentions and unaware that the war had already begun Mohammed Khan (perhaps a little unsure of the sincerity of the Force toward him) set out to secure the Primevous Dwelling from possible attacks by the Chief Rival's forces. Through lonely afternoons, when he was busy making sexless love, his servants erected walls, dug trenches and built moats filled with the blood of every martyr since the beginning of history. Mohammed Khan ordered them to plant protective landmines around the Primevous Dwelling, raise alligators in the moats, place archers on parapets; and instilled a passion for death in their hearts. He evolved a system of intelligence, equipped with prying eyes, listening ears, omniscient hearts and mute tongues. He raised a bureaucratic cadre of ambassadors from among the ranks of barbers and minstrels, and sent them to every nobleman whose influence spread over the land around the Primevous Dwelling, asking for the hand of their daughters so that their collective control could be melted into a chain of oneness through matrimonial bonds. Within two weeks, he entered into seventeen treaties of wedlock, and in the next two months, he made good upon eleven promises and temporarily disappeared into sounds of shehnai and dhol that continued to play in every house until everyone got sick of the tunes. When the Chief Rival heard of these celebrations, he banned all types of music, both instrumental and vocal. Musicians were publicly beheaded and their instruments smitten with hammers and other devices of affliction. Their remains were buried in a mass grave dug all the way to the volcanic centre of the earth and covered with thick layers of concrete to muffle any residual vibrations.

The Chief Rival continued to wage war. He employed every mythical bandit upon the land and trained them for a war whose reality would be denied through persistent use of euphemisms. He arranged infinite supplies of unaudited funds from corporate and banking sources and funnelled them through secret conduits to groups of *condottieri* protected by the forces of nonexistence.

The condottieri were invisible people. They would cross the line of control in the cover of the night, slaughter family after family in their sleep and return home, before the start of another redolent morning bathed with moist sunshine, to milk buffaloes. They would pray for their personal salvation in mosques and temples, and eagerly slurp mixed tea, savouring its milky warmth on their faces as they wandered through familiar streets amidst sounds of intimacy and affection. They were there to enact patriarchy, until the mission demanded them to sharpen their stilettoes and cross borders of conviction yet again.

Mohammed Khan heard stories of families slaughtered in sleep, children's heads bludgeoned with hammers, bombs going off in trains, artisans' thumbs chopped off with reused razor blades, lawyers ambushed outside court premises, judges stabbed inside their offices, people gunned down inside mosques, and viewers sniped outside movie houses – but he never suspected that it had anything to do with him or his enemies. They were clever enough to spare everyone even remotely connected with Mohammed Khan so that they would not become the target of his suspicion and subsequent retaliation. This was the ideal strategy to prolong the war and their reign.

25

(The Need for Roses)

"I have a dream."
(Martin Luther King, Jr.)

When Abbasside took over the reign of government from the Umayyad in 750 AD, they invited Umayyad elders for dinner and massacred them. Their corpses were placed under fine rugs and the Abbasside ate over bleeding dead bodies. Then they collected the women of the Umayyad and had them raped by African slaves. When the women protested, the slaves were put to sword.
(Muslim history)

The surrogate war continued for several years. Those who suffered its consequences remained unsure of how and why they had become party to it. No enemy was in sight, and when they decided to retaliate, they ended up shooting each other. The condottieri claimed the extra deaths in their books of accounts and sent vouchers to the Defending Ministry for early payment. The ministry deducted its usual commission and made prompt payment before the local currency fell further on the Forex markets.

The local currency kept losing value on all fronts. One fateful day, the Chief Rival decided to take the nation into his confidence. He appeared on radio and TV to reveal every imagined and imaginable threat facing the nation.

"I call upon you to carry out your patriotic duty of cutting down per capita spending on food, health and education so the country can import roses from Scotland," he told a nation waiting impatiently for the end of his speech so that they could go back to watching live coverage of the cricket match whose outcome was fixed in advance. They had surfed all the TV channels only to discover additional proof of the Chief's omnipresence. "We need roses," he continued. "We need them so that in the event of our nation's death, there'll be enough wreaths to shroud our sacred land with nostalgic petals."

The camera zoomed in on the Chief's white sherwani speckled with fallen hair. "I have a dream: it's been with me since I fell from the tree of insomnia," he confided to the nation with a backwards look in his eyes. "I remember falling through leafy branches, and just before I hit the bottom I had this most unbelievably splendid vision. I saw hand grenades made of eighteen-carat gold, nuclear missiles studded with rubies, hyacinths, sapphires, topazes, emeralds and diamonds, swords forged of oxidised uranium, mountains of Chaghai turning ashen with internal bleeding, people thronging hairy mosques and deserting bald temples: what a sight! Let us all give in to my dreams: I command you."

The nation gave in to his dreams. Under the anonymous darkness of undesignated nights, crates of dog roses potted in golden planters arrived on several formations of F-16s. A *corps d'elite* of senior army officers waited at the airports to ensure that the cargo passed through Immigration and Customs without delay or duty. They loaded the dying rose-bushes on trucks that were militant in movement and numerically invisible, and transported them for plantation to every barren and fertile patch of the country with a message to the sleeping nation that winter had arrived and spring could not be far behind. As the flowers attempted to bloom on rusting surfaces, replicas of anaemic mountains were erected on all public squares to remind the nation of the remaining amount of blood flowing in its veins and out of its veins into ideas pale with leaky pores. Everyone became a replica of everyone else, everything else became what they could wish: valleys and lakes, bombs and missiles, flowers and thorns, leaders and henchmen.

Henchmen prospered the most in that era. So did archaeologists who were sent by the Chief Rival's government on secret missions to exhume the remains of an extinct tribe from the mass grave of obsolescence and transport them in C-130 carriers to concentration camps located at the outer perimeters of historiography. After summary trial, the dead were condemned to face firing squads so they could pay for the crime of existing at the wrong time. Their remains were wrapped in wreaths of petunia and roses and laid out for display before mourners, who had yet to discover the meaning of death. Audiotapes, gramophone records and audio CDs of their cries were buried in the cemetery with most graves. Here was a place where wild cinnamon grew, kites and crows made nests on swaying branches of trees and ladies rendezvoused with their secret lovers through dark nights. And on one of those dark nights, the nation sat before TV sets, watching the documentary about the atrocities committed by Mohammed Khan who, at that moment, was trying to grasp the daylong futility through the lengthening shadows of sleepy forgetfulness.

The report of such unprecedented genocide created the requisite public outrage. It lasted many years and just as its intensity was beginning to ebb, the graves were dug up again. The carcasses were taken out of sandalwood coffins and scourged with hundreds of lashes on their brittle backs. After the cadavers had been cleansed of sins, their skulls were chopped off the stems, dried in the sun, engraved with words sterilised and perfumed, and turned into goblets for serving vintage wines to their families who had been invited to witness the rare spectacle. As soon as the feast was over, the guests were killed with swords and bayonets and hidden under priceless rugs and kilims. The bodies of the disinterred dead were taken back to the cemetery where 4000 slaves, cloned from servile chromosomes, sodomised the carcasses, raped the virgins waiting for their secret lovers under the cinnamon trees, before committing suicide in shame at their transgression.

This gory episode predictably brought people out in protest. They once again rallied through streets wreathed in a miasma of burning tires and smouldering odium, raising slogans against Mohammed Khan whose name appeared in their minds only as an abstraction without a face. Everyone sketched their own personal description of the fiend who had brought ancestral shame upon them by rerunning a proscribed episode of their family history; and vowed to hunt him down even inside the sanctuary of heathen protection where he presently waited for his turn to lead the nation out of its misery, that began in 1947 when the Great War of Cracks was waged between people supporting beards of different shapes.

The protests against Mohammed Khan continued for several days. Businesses closed down, shops were set on fire, cars were torched in the middle of avenues, people were lynched on their way to work, libraries were gutted and the books thrown in to storm-water drains. During this confusion, the Intra-Services Intelligent Agency managed to discover a dungeon in the bowels of the earth, where a man in a snow-white beard was found chained to the wall. He had been there for so long that his beard had become one with his pubic hair, underarm hair had turned into grey locks of senilitude and his pubes had grown to swathe his flimsy thighs. Seven yards away from him was a skeleton of neglect, a woman whose age was impossible to determine with a cursory glance. Around her was a ring of cochineal insects, sitting with patient solemnity for the burial party to arrive. They scattered as soon as ISI sleuths entered the dungeon and covered the waiting corpse with a woollen shawl.

The old man was taken to the Armed Hospital and kept in quarantine until he could be freed from the state of perennial past. On a fateful afternoon when the sun had miraculously disappeared behind dark clouds, the old man opened his eyes and mouth simultaneously. First a stream of tears came out, rolling like pearls along his cheeks and then a voice unaccustomed to vocalisation spoke out to the corps of press and TV reporters. "My name was Rahim Ullah Khan," he said haltingly. "Once upon a time, I was Mohammed Khan's father. Now I am a sonless prisoner."

Everyone present cringed. Microphones went into orgasms and cameras flashed relentlessly until the room was filled with stars. Every arm reached out to catch the falling words of the man who was about to tell them the greatest story of the millennium. The result was a pandemonium so great that not less than thirteen reporters were trampled in the frenzy, and six of them died before they could get first aid. When order was finally restored, the old man resumed his testimony. "I was the father of Mohammed Khan," he said for the benefit of those who might have missed his initial declaration. "I've been inside this dungeon since he went abroad."

"The woman?" he was asked. "Who was the woman?"

The old prisoner started to weep. So great was his grief that Cimmerian clouds enveloped the sky and an eternal night of woe and guilt betided every heart. Those who witnessed the two rheumy eyes inundated with anguish and heard the voice quivering under the burden of torment never smiled again. Their lips became torpid and hearts were relegated to the solitary task of pumping contaminated blood.

The old man finally controlled himself. "She was my wife," he said amidst further camera clicks. "She was the prisoner of her son: just as I was."

"Why were you imprisoned? Were the two of you his only prisoners? Is there another dungeon controlled by Mohammed Khan? Is there a secret passage between these dungeons and Tora Bora caves? Did Osama bin Laden ever take refuge in those dungeons? Is he still there?"

"My son turned greedy," the old man calling himself Rahim Ullah Khan, sighed. "He wanted to be a Mogul king and the sole owner of his ancestral lands. He killed his sister and took out the eyes of his brother. I watched him throw their bodies in the river and couldn't do a thing. His mother cried for mercy and he slapped her until she fell upon his feet. Then he tied us with an iron chain and incarcerated us in the dungeon."

"Did he ever visit you? When was the last time you saw him?"

"He would visit us once a month," the old man said. "He did not visit me for a full year after his mother died of starvation. When he finally came to see me, I told him I was sad and lonely. I implored him to send me little children from the village so I could teach them the good Word. He looked at me with scorn and said: 'So that old heart of yours still harbours the ambition of dominion.' He never came to see me after that. I don't know where he is now. I hope someone amongst you or among those who are listening to me have enough conviction to kill him, the way he killed his siblings and his mother, who gave birth to him and let him suckle at her breasts so that he'd get sufficient calcium for his bones."

"Do you have his picture?" the reporter of the state-owned TV asked. "No one knows what he looks like."

"I do," the old man nodded. "I have kept his passport photo inside my shirt pocket."

Mohammed Khan's photograph was flashed on TV as the lead story on the Nine o' clock News. Mobs of grieved citizens went out on the street and killed everyone with even the most tenuous resemblance to the photograph.

The nation was ready for war.

Away from the frenzy of war and peace, a man walked alone with his donkey, feeling the burden of isolation upon his heart: it was probably the surroundings. Ahead of him stretched plain fields inundated with a wavy mass of fog which covered the land on either side of the trail he was following. It was a cold day in early winter and the moving donkey felt lost in a spell of grey. The grizzled sky had descended to the earth and under its shadow, the stretching fields, dancing crops, and lofty firs growing along the trail looked grey all over. From a distance, the man and the animal were completely unobtrusive in the haze.

Fog lifted near the end of civilisation. The weather cleared a little, though the air was still nippy. This part of the universe appeared to be much colder and the donkey could hear the peculiar whisper of air sliding through the fir trees lining both sides. The donkey knew this strip of land from her nightmares: the firs would ultimately thicken into a dense forest and beyond it would be the Persian Gulf, and then a desert bifurcating the permanent from the transitory.

It was not a place she wanted to be, but the sense of loyalty to her master kept her going.

The guard deputed to keep an eye out for the Chief Rival's spies saw them coming. He noticed the donkey first, then the man huddled inside his heavy clothing and finally the baggage. He did not pause to think. Taking a careful aim, he shot the man through his heart, hit the donkey with his second bullet and ran down to claim the booty.

He was just in time to recite purifying words and sever the jugular vein of the dying donkey. He waited for the soul to vacate the body, then cut it into several large pieces for storage in the snow. That night, after a satisfying barbecue dinner of donkey-meat, he searched the dead man's baggage and found a huge dish made of wired mesh, along with other metal boxes of which he knew little. He threw the body and baggage into a ditch and went to sleep.

A few days later, another man tried to get near the Ocean beyond which lay the haven of peace and non-violence, and died by the hand of the same guard. The second man carried the same items as his predecessor and his body along with his mysterious belongings went into the same ditch. During that month, nine more men died at the same spot, until the guard got tired of killing intruders and his stomach became allergic to donkey meat. When the tenth man arrived, he let him live but subjected him to torture to unearth the truth. The man gladly told him the purpose of his visit and his explanation was so outrageous that the guard killed him for being a liar. However, when eleventh man arrived with the same story, the guard began to suspect the existence of a reality beyond his own comprehension. He took the eleventh man to his Commanding Officer who had positioned himself closer to the shores of the Persian Gulf.

The CO listened to the intruder with patience and when he thought he had heard enough bullshit, he shut him up with the rise of his hand and gave him a mug of poisoned tea to drink. "You're a spy," he told him with a nonchalant conviction as the poison took its effect. "Only a spy can come up with such an incredible piece of deception."

During the next two months, a series of blizzards blocked all routes to transcendence and further expeditions had to be cancelled until the weather cleared. Eventually, when the snow tired of falling and the birds started migrating back to Siberia, another man whose time of death had not yet arrived ventured into uncertainty. He was eighty years old and had withered through storms bigger than the weather that ushered their arrival. He was so inadequately built as to be virtually invisible and managed to evade all the guards and COs, arriving in the Primevous Dwelling at a time when Mohammed Khan was having a quiet lunch. No one noticed the old man as he sneaked inside and waited for Mohammed Khan to finish his food.

"Who are you?" Mohammed Khan asked as he cleaned his plate and took a careful look at the tall, old intruder. "Are you another of those spies my guards have killed in the past? Why is the Chief Rival playing with the lives of his people? Can't he see that I have devoted my life to non-violence?"

"I'm not a spy, Mohammed Khan," the man replied in a voice sick of talking. "Neither were those who died for believing in you and in non-violence. I represent a select group of men who believe in you despite what your rivals say. We know they lie, but even if they don't their truth is unacceptable to us. We have declared a secret rebellion against the Chief Rival and I'm here to reveal his evil tactics to you – live on TV."

Mohammed Khan smiled tiredly and shook his head. "This place is under censor, old-timer. Even radio broadcasts can't penetrate these walls of stone."

"Modern technology enables you to receive TV signals across censorships, Mohammed Khan," the old man said. "The world has advanced tremendously since you left it. This is the era of satellite transmission. You can watch one-day cricket live from West Indies, tune into a Miss World Competition from India, listen to the World News from London. I've brought an antenna dish, a satellite receiver and a stolen decoder with me to show you all these channels."

Mohammed Khan's expression hardened. "If I did not have regard for your old age, and an unknown affinity I feel for you, I would have laughed at you, old-timer."

"You will discover more affinity, feel it in other parts of your body and see it right here all around you, Mohammed Khan. Allow me to demonstrate the truth to you," the old man pleaded. "I can set up everything in five minutes. I am an expert at installing satellite dishes, though a novice at rowing big boats."

The old man wasn't as adept at his work as he claimed, but before sunset he had successfully positioned the antenna dish outside Mohammed Khan's room and tuned in all the satellite channels available in the region.

"They have been telecasting your father's interview every half an hour for the past four months," the old man said as he switched on the TV.

"My father?"

"Yes. The nation has vowed to assassinate you for bringing forbidden history into their homes."

"What have I done? All this while, I've been practising love. I'm a believer in non-violence."

The TV screen flickered and the withered face of the prisoner recovered from the bowels of the earth appeared on the screen. "He killed his sister and took out the eyes of his brother," the ex-prisoner's voice emerged from the TV speakers.

"Who is he talking about?" Mohammed Khan demanded.

"You, of course."

"And who the hell is he?"

"Rahim Ullah Khan. Your father."

Mohammed Khan walked closer to the screen until he could feel the electricity charge on the tip of his nose. "This is not my father," he thundered. "This is Achoo the Minstrel, my maternal uncle's protégé. He was responsible for the start of the Great War of Cracks and now he wants to start the next in the series. So be it if it has to be the destiny of this nation."

The door burst open and a breathless Ram Babu entered the room. "Things are beginning to happen, Mohammed Khan," he cried. "The Force has turned against the Chief Rival. You are about to be imposed on the nation."

The prisoner on TV suddenly disappeared, replaced by a shot of people in uniform climbing the gates of a building, which a subtitle indicated was a TV Station. Babu clicked his heels and bowed reverentially. "See," he said with excitement. "It's happening. Allow me to be the first among the male population to express my allegiance to you. I hope that you'll be kind enough to remember my sacrifice and reward me suitably."

"I'll turn your library into an audio-visual centre," Mohammed Khan promised him.

"May the Force be with you," Ram Babu prayed.

"The Force is with me," Mohammed Khan said confidently. "Just look at the TV screen."

26

"I'm standing here in front of the Government-controlled TV station in Islamabad. The Army has surrounded the premises and I can see armed soldiers scaling the walls of the TV station.
(A TV anchorman reporting live to his audience)

"We've just been informed that the government of Prime Minister Nawaz Sharif has been toppled and the military has taken over.
(The same anchorman thirty minutes later)

The deposed Prime Minister tried to divide the Army, the only institution of solidarity in the country.
(Chief Executive of Pakistan)

Judiciary is free in this country.
(Mian Nawaz Sharif, deposed Prime Minister of Pakistan – before he was deposed: later he changed his mind)

While Ram Babu stood quivering with emotion, thousands of miles away in the nation, men wearing turbans, vests, and shalwars were scaling the gates of the state-owned TV station with the intention to conquer it. They faced little resistance from the security guards who dropped their weapons at the first sight of the castrating offensive, and let them pass all the way to offices and studios where producers, writers and bureaucrats were busy finalising the script for the six o'clock news. The invading forces smashed computers and scanners, confiscated satellite dishes, placed detonators at strategic points, and interrupted the pre-news commercials. For the next three hours, TV went off the air as the Forceful invaders dispatched several parties on bicycles to shopping malls and plazas to find videotapes of their choice. When recorded life came back on screen, the nation was treated to songs of homage to a revolutionary leader whose name was as much an unnamed threat as his intentions.

The siege was welcomed by a nation accustomed to interpret every military takeover as an omen for a fresh era of democracy. The invasion of the TV station was hailed as an auspicious event in the otherwise ordinary life of the nation; and soon as the blessed Force took control of audio-visual faculties, throngs of deaf, dumb and blind people rushed to them to be consecrated. The newspapers published eulogistic editorials praising the takeover. After hasty deliberations, a full bench of the Supreme Court declared it as "an extraordinary constitutional accomplishment" and issued a quick rejoinder that even if – God forbid – this act of force had indeed violated the constitution, it was merely the violation of a badly-printed book in need of proof-reading. The Court further said that the Penal Code also did not define such an action to be either a felony or a misdemeanour. A handful of lawyers who protested against the decision found their criminal cases ending in conviction, their civil suits dismissed without cost, and their legs shattered by leggy men brandishing Chap Sticks of silence.

The identity of the invaders remained a secret. They ultimately left after installing an interim government that purchased broadcasting rights from the public at an affordable price. The proceeds from the sale were considered quite inadequate to pay off foreign debts and were, therefore, utilised to renovate the President House which would soon be occupied by its rightful claimant.

The interim government brought revolutionary changes in broadcasting policy. Women were barred from appearing on screen. Men were directed to cover their glands, comb their pubic hair, not display their ankles, and refrain from seeing through their penis-eyes in public. Prime Time News was aired every hour and its duration was increased to fifty-nine minutes with a single-minute break for commercials about under-construction mosques in need of donations. The anchormen were glued to their chairs until they developed spinal sarcoma and facial tetany. They were taken to the hospital for treatment with spurious drugs purchased at half the vouchered price through representatives of medical firms that existed only on the pages of official records. When too many anchormen died in their hospital beds, a fact-finding inquiry was ordered – one that was to drag on for years without fixing responsibility on anyone.

TV anchormen were not the only ones targeted by death. Journalists who had yet to write their articles in favour of the Force and its inherent right to decide the fate of the nation with or without referendums, began to die mysteriously in their bedrooms and bathrooms. More perished in freak accidents as lifts began to crash, gas heaters started to leak, oil stoves began to burst, and earthquakes started to target those buildings in which newspaper and magazine offices were housed. Eventually, however, things settled down. Hopes converged to their historical average, and the rate of bribe went back to 13%. Life returned to normality.

The TV siege awoke the nation from the sleep of complacency. Nationalists cheered in streets as the Chief Rival, along with his younger brother and a few close associates, was arrested. They were directed by the interim government to stand trial for offences declared punishable with retrospective effect. All the accused were eventually found guilty and given sentences expected to become part of the Penal Code after the restoration of assemblies.

In anticipation of the sentences, the government undertook to change the nation's opinion in favour of the verdict by telecasting an interview of Achoo the Minstrel, who confessed to his low caste and acknowledged that he was indeed a protégé of Mohammed Khan's maternal uncle, and that it was a family drama. At the same time, excerpts from the Chief Rival's depositions made before the anti-terrorist court were published in newspapers to authenticate his links with Osama bin Laden. "Terrorism is like the invisible hand of Adam Smith – no one knows who moves it," he was quoted on the front page of every tabloid. "All wars were created in heaven," he was alleged to have said on another occasion. "War is the most exciting thing that happened to man by God's decree," he reportedly told someone in confidence and added: "peace is boring." These statements brought the nation out on the streets yet again, demanding that he should be publicly beheaded and his body parts dissolved in drums of sulphuric acid.

The last nail in his coffin was his television interview for a syndicated channel. The nation saw a green turban with bird feathers protruding from its top, a pair of extra-large Gucci glasses still carrying the manufacturer's sticker, a blackened nose covered with pimples and blackheads, a beard reaching out to trample his features that were so ordinary as to be anyone's. His voice, charged with echoing static came from the other side of the beard. He was a speaking photograph: the lips didn't move, the expression didn't change, the eyes didn't blink.

He held the nation captive with his misplaced adjectives, his misdirected affection, and an undelivered message. So refined were his persuasive skills that the nation's heart went into spasm. Under cover of the resultant medical emergency, the Chief Rival escaped from the high-security prison and disappeared beyond the balding mountains running parallel to the capital. There he entered into usufructuary marriage with a widowed lioness for a period of three months, extendable for another six months by mutual consent. Unfortunately, he turned promiscuous and tried to enter into a similar arrangement with a younger lioness before the expiry of his original contract. His wife, in a state of altered consciousness, bit off his penis and chomped his head when she discovered his plans. Thus perished the man who, during the prime of his reign, was popularly known as "the Lion of East".

Book VI

The Humid Corridors

When the king of an underdeveloped country died without a child, the forces-that-be decided that the first man to enter the city gates next morning would be the new king. Such a man turned out to be a beggar. He was taken to the royal palace and placed on the throne. The beggar folded his tattered clothes neatly into a packet, placed them underneath the throne and issued the royal decree that the nation would henceforth eat halva – a local sweet – for every meal.

A week later, his defence minister brought the bad news that the enemy had attacked the country and asked for royal orders.

"Cook more halva," the new king ordered.

Enemy forces kept advancing to the capital and the king kept giving orders to prepare more and more halva. "Add extra ghee and sugar," he said when they informed him that the enemy had surrounded the capital.

The king had finished his lunch when the defence minister came in breathless. "My lord, the enemy is about to enter the royal palace."

The king reached underneath the throne, took out his worn-out clothes, ate the final helping of halva and walked toward the door. He stopped momentarily at the door and smiled.

"The halva is finished and so is my responsibility to this nation. I'll see you all somewhere else."

He escaped through the backdoor, dressed in his beggar's clothes.

(South Asian folklore)

27

*The National Accountability Bureau shall investigate all past
and future acts of corruption and ruthlessly punish the culprits.
However, armed forces and judiciary shall be exempted from this.
(Chief Executive of Pakistan)*

*Democracy is a system through which people are counted, not evaluated.
(Allama Sir Muhammad Iqbal)*

*"May the Force be with you."
(Sir Alec Guinness in 'Star Wars')*

The Chief Rival's timely death settled the question of succession for the time being. Mohammed Khan was invited by telegram to take the nation's destiny in his hands. The man who woke him from sleep to deliver the message was dressed in a blue uniform; his warped face seemed tired of bringing bad news to people when they least expected it. "The nation is waiting, Mohammed Khan," he said solemnly. "Leave before it changes its mind."

Without further ado, Mohammed Khan left the Primevous Dwelling. Two days later, his silvery silhouette appeared on the national horizon like the Ramadan moon amidst controversy of the exact date and manner of appearance. According to the official version of truth, an unregistered Bedford truck decorated with promissory slogans and paper-roses brought him perched upon the back of an African elephant who appeared to be suffering from gingivitis. Its tusks were gone, devoured by the disease, and two peewee eyes squinted through drooping eyelids overlaid with dust gathered from time-travel. The elephant's giant legs trembled underneath sovereign weight as the truck on which it stood, journeyed upon a path paved with the expectations of every man, woman and eunuch gathered to glimpse the remnants of the leader fated to fade behind the high walls of the President House. From a distance, they could see his leading profile and a gloved hand waving to them with controlled sincerity. All around him, deputed to protect his leadership from internal threats, were convoys of tanks and armoured vehicles manoeuvering with menacing grace on Constitution Avenue – a boulevard where rootless saplings were once planted to survive all types of constitutional turmoil and grow into fruitless trees with infructuous branches from which the remains of defunct constitutions, annulled statutes and repealed laws would hang. Ten thousand feet above the spectacle of abrogation and annulment, soared fighter jets, breaking every barrier of sound and silence and leaving behind a cloud of smoke so dense that enemy satellites were blinded and the April sun was forbidden from shining over the nation's new leader. Mohammed Khan watched them in a state of arrested thrill as he struggled to control the groan of his intestines amidst marching sounds.

The President House had the look of an old man whose ability to wonder at the unraveling of life had died with his youth. The land on which it stood was once part of a volcanic crust infested with snakes of another world and trees of this. A seventy-foot mud wall encircled it. Mohammed Khan entered through the backdoor into a series of corridors humming with trapped whispers afloat in the air like the dust of suspended time. Mohammed Khan shook hands with chefs and butlers who stood lined in the hallways, carrying trays of cakes and pastries wrapped in aromas of baked chocolate and iced strawberries. He immediately rejected this alien form of eatables and ordered them to prepare goat brain fried in buffalo fat and serve it with tandoori naans and nihari cooked by Mr. Phajja of Loehar's red light district. As he entered his office after issuing this very first order as the latest President of the Republic, he realised that his watch had stopped. Perhaps the alkaline battery inside was an imitation.

The Presidential Chair felt warm like a woman in love. He fell asleep the moment he sat on it, and slept a dreamless sleep for three consecutive days. When he awoke, his bones felt brittle, his mouth smelt of metal, and a disorienting sound clogged his ears. He realised that his hair and nails had stopped growing and when he looked at himself in the mirror, he saw a face embedded with frozen expressions belonging to the land of waiting he had left behind. By evening, he could no longer hear a sound in his chest except for the gurgling of an anxious stomach. In a state of near panic, he tried to feel his heart by the touch of fingers that once were his eyes and ears, but only stumbled upon silence. His fingertips eventually turned into clots of ice; still he failed to detect any perceptible sign of biological life in his veins. Next morning, he was tormented by a constipation that seemed to have an element of permanence to it. With a stomach bloating with winds of flatulence, Mohammed Khan wandered from room to room and corridor to corridor in a bid to lighten the weight gathering upon his chest and leading his legs. On the sixth day of his Arrival, he glimpsed his face in the mirror and saw eternity sticking to his cheeks like white plaster. That was the precise moment when he understood the futility of his plans and the irrelevance of biotic laws in this place. He came out naked, running from room to room in a state of dizzying excitement.

Life returned to the Presidential Office. President Mohammed Khan appointed seventy ministers, ninety ministers-of-state, eighty-nine advisors and thirty-three parliamentary secretaries to help him run the affairs of the state. The first meeting of the Cabinet had to be held under an open sky because the nation had failed in its duty to build a convention centre big enough to accommodate its rulers' goals and ambitions. The meeting continued for hours during which important decisions were taken. The Cabinet resolved to impose apostasy tax on leaders of the opposition and use the proceeds to hire cherry-lipped maids and almond-eyed servants for the parliamentarians on the government's side. It also promulgated an ordinance that made it mandatory for all men above sixteen to have a second circumcision.

"The penile sizes must be adjusted downward to reduce the current levels of obscenity in society," the Secretary to the Ministry of Law and Religious Affairs explained. "Naturally, the armed forces, legislature, and judiciary will be exempted because they've had several circumcisions already."

For the benefit of the judiciary, he suggested a jurisprudential amendment whereby the burden of proof would shift from the prosecution to the court and make things simple.

"Let the Court prove the innocence of the accused," the Secretary of Law said with an archaic smile reminiscent of eras gone by. "This is the only way to provide cheap justice to the masses: no prosecution, no defence, no lawyers; only one mouth to feed. Quick and inexpensive disposal. QED."

"QED, indeed," Mohammed Khan agreed. "When I was a child, I saw a seventy-foot wall like the one that currently blocks our vision of the outside. There were women on the other side, some of whom I incidentally knew. No, no. Not girlfriends or anything – I know it's against political etiquette and religious practices. Those women, they were licking the wall. Is it still there, the wall?"

"Walls come and go, Mr. President," the Secretary of Religious Affairs said. "Once there was the Berlin Wall, now there's only the Great Wall of China. Tomorrow there will be other walls and more graffiti on them."

"Ah, China," said the oldest and the wisest member of the Cabinet, a man who had served on every committee, council and Cabinet since the Division. "Our great friend. A friend in need is a friend indeed."

"Indeed," the Secretary of Religious Affairs added in his uncommitted voice. "Now as for the lickers, it's the legend of Gog and Magog, Mr. President. They must remain behind the walls or the world as we know it will cease to exist. We don't want that, do we, sir?"

"Certainly not," Mohammed Khan said hurriedly. "Who would?"

As the meeting approached its end, the oldest and the wisest one got to his shaking feet and impressed upon President Mohammed Khan the significance of taking a first lady as a matter of priority. "President Clinton would not have been able to save his presidency if his wife had not stood by him in times of crises," he said. "You also need a wife to stand beside you in times of embarrassment and shame – the time when even your fluids will give evidence against you."

"Why just one wife?" objected another Cabinet member who had matched the oldest and wisest in every step of life. "The Book allows him to take four wives at one time and the doors for prompt divorce are always ajar, waiting for a gentle push. Remember that one is alone, two make eleven and eleven make one million, one hundred thousand, one hundred and eleven. The more the merrier."

"Taking four wives would not be a politically correct decision," the old and the wise one said. "It will not go well with feminists."

"I'm not here to play politics," Mohammed Khan interrupted. "I'm here to take the nation out of the clouds of gloom and depression. Let there be four weddings and no funeral."

To ensure that the Presidential Order of four weddings and no funeral was implemented in its true spirit, the Ministry of Interior imposed a ban on memorial services. Police guards were posted outside cemeteries to prevent men and women from visiting the dead. Burial processions were baton-charged, mourners were arrested and sent to jail to await trials scheduled to begin after the Presidential Matrimony. Labour Inspectors swarmed the city markets and shut down every funeral house – though they were kind enough to give the owners interim permission to set up as temporary cinemas, where people who no longer had the fortitude to endure life sat upon upturned coffins and watched pirated Bollywood movies on VCRs. In a subsequent amendment to the original order, the Interior Ministry banned all acts of dying until the Day of Matrimony. People were forced to die illegally and in conspiratorial solitude. Their bodies lay prostrate on blocks of ice or remained huddled inside refrigerators and deep freezers, waiting for the day when a proper burial service would be arranged in their honour. The price of ice skyrocketed and refrigerators and freezers disappeared from the shops.

The Presidential House was in a state of connubial euphoria. Its rooms had assumed the look of honeymoon suites, and the whispers in the corridors spoke not of corrupting power but of marital bliss and the correct circumstances and methodology of divorce. Those who were single thought of taking wives, and those already married aspired to take new wives commensurate with their social status and that of their friends and peers.

A smaller and more dependable version of the Cabinet met in the Presidential Kitchen to discuss the marriage proposals. "I once committed the mistake of asking someone's hand myself," Mohammed Khan told them with the smile of a person capable of laughing at his juvenile adventures. "The man got mad at me and claimed he did not have a daughter."

"We've short-listed the best barbers in the world for this purpose, Mr. President," he was told with the air of a job well done. "They come with solid references, these barbers. They will be set upon the land to find the right brides for you."

The barbers were unleashed upon the land to find suitable brides for the nation's President, who was secretly contemplating changing his official title to Chief of Believers. Before he could make up his mind, the barbers returned with definite proposals about the most suitable daughters of the nation.

"We recommend that in the interests of national solidarity, the President may kindly take four wives at this stage," they submitted. "We further recommend that he may accept the Chief of Army Staff's eldest daughter as the First Lady, the Chief of Air Staff's middle daughter as the Second lady, the Chief of Naval Staff's youngest daughter as the Third Lady and the Chief Justice's baby daughter as the Fourth Lady."

"So be it," Mohammed Khan concurred. "Let the date of marriage be set six weeks from now. Let the nation also know that I'll make an important announcement on the grand occasion of my matrimony. My announcement will carry a message that will change the nation's destiny forever."

The marriage ceremony was held on the lawns of the Presidential House. Sixty thousand people were invited to attend in person and the remainder were allowed to watch it on television. Invitation cards gilded with invitatory command were handed over to bearers clad in maroon brocades and yellow turbans made of muslin woven by thumbless artisans summoned from other eras. The artisans were immured within the four walls of darkened rooms to consume their expertise – one, that after centuries of pointless toil, still struggled to escape the clutches of minimum wage. The bearers were directed to personally distribute the invitation cards to the rightful invitees, but many were persuaded otherwise by the promise of wealth. They sold them on the black market at prices that reflected their small minds and deficient greed. Those who purchased the cards queued up in front of the relevant – and in some cases, irrelevant – offices to have their names and castes changed in accordance with the information printed on the envelopes. A stolen copy of the wedding card ended up in an underworld fake-currency press and overnight, one hundred thousand phoney cards were printed and sold to unsuspecting buyers who were given to believe that the proceeds would be used to fund a campaign against polygamy. When M-Day arrived, over two hundred thousand guests, including a hundred thousand wild-eyed women wearing silks and chiffons, seeing stars and comets, and burping Avon and Christian Dior, gathered outside the President House, demanding entry to the realm of grandeur and happiness.

Sensing the delicacy of the situation, the Principal Secretary to the President, an old balding bureaucrat who had seen enough violence in his career to understand the value of submission in the face of power, allowed the entire lot of real and fake guests to join the festivities. When the guests dressed in Armani suits, starched cottons, and gaudy organzas were escorted inside the President House by usherettes specially recruited for the occasion, they found all the chairs taken by gate-crashers, relatives of the security personnel and by those who had bought their way to the front rows. Some walked out in protest, others argued with the security staff and were thrown out for creating a disturbance. Those more attuned to the demands of such occasions went in search of any place willing to accommodate their presence. Some climbed trees for a good view, some sat cross-legged on carpets and dhurries, and others took positions close to the tables laid with the one thousand dishes prepared by cooks flown in from Paris, Milan, Hong Kong, and Madras.

A voice announced the start of the ceremony and chatting voices quietened into an expectant hush. An unseen voice recited verses from the Holy Book. Another voice sang songs of praise. A third voice sang the national anthem after which silence was restored. Then a thousand virgins appeared on the stage, cloaked in velvet gowns and alcohol-free perfumes, carrying Cartier bracelets and Rolex watches. They walked down the aisles, distributing bracelets and watches and fragrance amongst the guests, some of whom lost their senses and went into a state of olfactory mystification. They were picked up by the security staff and handed over to police for transportation to shrines and tombs scattered all over the country.

The gong sounded and the world stopped moving. President Mohammed Khan marched on to the stage, flanked by his brides. The crowd watched in reverential silence as he walked down the aisles throwing diamonds and rubies and sapphires in the air. The guests let go of self-discipline and cheered.

The President walked back to the stage where M. Sahib bound him in wedlock and presented him the DVD version of his lectures on conjugal sex. The guests danced around bonfires made from thousand rupee notes and prayed for economic recovery. They were finally silenced as the President held up his hand and strode up to the glittering dais. He cleared his throat, flashed a smile and gave his message to the nation. "Adopt simplicity," he said and walked away with his brides.

28

What is life?
  A river of sorrow.
  Living isn't easy
  Nor death.
  (Song sung by late Muhammad Rafi, the greatest
  voice ever heard in the Indian sub-continent)

The crowd went wild. People threw wads of rupees into the smouldering heaps of burnt notes and danced with respectful fervour around the fire. When they tired of dancing, they attacked the food and ate, until some died with burst stomachs and others perished of fatal vomiting. When the last man had finished dying, more bearers arrived, carrying trays of dessert. For seven days, food was left laid on tables and its aroma attracted beggars from places as far off as Baghdad, and they arrived in caravans to fill their sanction stricken bellies. Ultimately, hunger was wiped off the aging face of the earth and the food started to rot amidst bodies of dead flies strewn everywhere.

The era following President Mohammed Khan's marriage was called the age of dying legally. There was such a massive backlog of people waiting to expire that as soon as the restrictions were lifted, four to five deaths were reported in every house. The families of those who had died illegally during the ban opened the padlocked doors of refrigerators and deep freezers only to discover that their compressors had malfunctioned. The bodies of loved-ones lay in different stages of putrescence, and their decaying smell was enough to lead the law to the scene of the crime. They sealed the bodies in polythene bags and smuggled them to cemeteries in the darkness of the night, but the undertakers refused to admit them for burial.

"We're sorry, gentlemen," they said with an unbribable authority. "We can't accept these bodies as newly-dead. The Monitoring Teams physically verify the particulars of every dead person and issue a certificate. We can only allow burial to certified corpses."

The bereaved families returned disappointed and dissolved the remains of their loved-ones in sulphuric acid.

The demand for memorial services continued for a long time. Scores of movie houses and school buildings were knocked down and replaced with multi-storey funeral houses. Even though profit margins declined significantly after two years, economists predicted that the demand for burial services was likely to stay ahead of supply by two to one for the present decade.

As the economy grew due to the extraordinary boom in the death sector, the Government decided to start an official campaign for the enforcement of simplicity. A sub-committee of the Cabinet met in a five-star hotel in Phuket, Thailand to chalk out the strategy for promoting Mohammed Khan's sovereign desire.

"We need to formulate an advertising plan to embody the spirit of the President's matrimonial message to the nation," the Chairman of the sub-committee said. "My younger brother owns an advertising agency and I believe he'd be politically sympathetic to the President's cause because of his kinship with me. We should hire the consultancy services of his firm for running the proposed publicity campaign."

"That would be against the rules," a bespectacled Section Officer from the Ministry of Finance, who happened to be sitting on the next table eating barbecue dog, objected without being asked. "Any project exceeding three billion rupees must be awarded through wide publicity in national dailies."

"We thank you for your timely, and gratis advice, sir," the Chairman said to the Section Officer. "The Committee will recommend two advance increments for you. Now, coming back to the issue at hand, I agree that we should go ahead and invite open tenders through the press which is currently enjoying unparallel freedom in the history of our nation."

"Oh yes, oh yes," others shouted in agreement. "Never has the press been so free in our history. We can even prove this through a rigged referendum."

Notices of tender were published in the Sunday papers. The nation and the potential bidders waited for the arrival of their favourite newspapers until late that afternoon. Some them went out in search of newspaper sellers, not knowing that the younger brother of the Chairman had purchased every copy directly from the publishers. Eventually, the wandering nation returned home, convinced that it was an unscheduled newspaper holiday.

Despite the wide publicity, only one company participated in the bidding process. It was owned by the Chairman's younger brother and the Chairman approved its proposal. Years later, when the Auditor General sent a team to audit the accounts, they could find nothing wrong with the procedure adopted for awarding the seven billion rupees contract. Their hunch of possible foul play was proved wrong in the face of overwhelming official evidence.

The company prepared its advertising plan with amateurish zeal. It made and remade hundreds of publicity films in which leading actresses of the country danced in sesame fields and atop skyscrapers of Gujranwala and Chicho Ki Malyan. Unfortunately, conflicting interpretations of the Presidential Intention about simplicity did not allow these to reach the TV screens and they eventually perished inside their tin containers. The company went through every book written on the subject of advertising and plagiarised all known slogans, but none was considered close enough to the President's original message. Eventually, when it seemed that the company awarded the biggest single promotional tender in the country's history was going to let the nation down, a young copywriter burst naked into the conference room. He caterwauled "eureka" three times to get the attention of his boss. "I've found just the right slogan for the campaign, sir," he shouted.

All eyes looked at his undersized penis.

"Adopt simplicity," the copywriter said triumphantly. "The slogan is 'adopt simplicity'. Isn't it what the President himself said? Who are we to change the words that came out of the Presidential Mouth?"

The meeting erupted into an uproar. They forwarded the slogan to the Ministry of Culture which approved it within a record thirty-seven minutes.

The idea of hiring an advertising company had apparently been taken in haste. Even before the campaign had started, the nation had already adopted simplicity. People had demolished their houses and moved into caves. They had slaughtered their animals and were using hides to make egalitarian dresses. They had converted jails into dungeons, and replaced hanging with crucifixion. They had let stars fall from their eyes and watch them turn into baptised aerolites liberated from directional bondage. They now lived in wait and dreamt of men with golden wings, green robes and white turbans, who existed beyond the reaches of believability.

29

"Girls are born only to low-caste people."
(Rahim Ullah Khan, Mohammed Khan's father)

On the twenty-ninth day of February, Mohammed Khan's four wives gave birth to four daughters.

"This is an international conspiracy designed to disturb the nation's gender balance," the oldest and the wisest member of the Cabinet said in a crying voice. "I hereby call for an open inquiry to confirm my suspicion which is truer than any belief held by the opposition."

By afternoon, the Federal Government declared February 29th as the day of mourning from which the nation was not expected to escape until the sound of a male child's crying could be heard in the Presidential House. As evening gloom fell upon the capital city, rumours started to circulate that an emergency meeting of the Cabinet was in progress and that a distraught President was heading it, despite his personal grief.

Soon, patchy news of the proceedings began to leak from the Cabinet room. Within the first half hour, it was known all over the city that the doctors who'd handled the parturition had been suspended. Fifteen minutes later, news of the dismissal of the Health Secretary reached every drawing room. The people also learned that contingents of the elite force had been dispatched to arrest the holy man who had given the tidings of four sons to the President.

People were waiting for more news when they heard explosions outside the Supreme Court. They rushed to the marbled courthouse to find gun-toting judges in rebellion against the Chief Justice, Mr. Justice S. A. Shah, who by pure coincidence, happened to be the disgraced father of Mohammed Khan's youngest wife. Within the hour, he was tried for offences that were never made public, and sentenced to spend the remaining days of his lucid life in the Andaman Islands. A few seconds after the sentence was executed, news arrived that President Mohammed Khan had dismissed the three Services Chiefs.

They, however, were unaware of the decision. At the precise moment of their dismissal, they were in Libya, engaged in strategic talks with Colonel Gaddafi. When they came out of his royal tent, they discovered that those who had previously saluted them with militant passion had taken off in their military jets. In a state of helpless fury, they boarded the next commercial flight home, determined to undo Mohammed Khan's treachery. They never reached anywhere. The airliner exploded and not a single passenger survived. Minutes after the crash, the President House issued an official denial of the rumours that the President had in any way interfered with the tenure of the Services Chiefs. The official communiqué stressed that the President held all type of military close to his heart and was extremely distressed by the tragedy.

"I promise to hold a judicial inquiry into the incident so the martyrdom of the General, the Air Marshal and the Admiral will not go to waste," he said in a hurriedly called press conference. "To prove that the rebellion against the Chief Justice and the deaths of the three Services Chiefs were random events, I reiterate my love for my four wives and promise to kiss them in public during the next public rally."

Arrangements for the public rally took several weeks. The Interior Ministry instructed every District Nazim to collect fifty thousand illiterate people and transport them to the site of the congregation – and to do it under their personal leadership so that they would not go astray like the directionless sheep that they are. The Nazims were reminded how well they had performed in convincing all voters and non-voters to cast their votes sixteen times in a single referendum held to elect the ex-President for five years. The Nazims smiled and promised to repeat their earlier performance provided that the district government system was allowed to continue.

On the day of the rally, there were one hundred and thirty million people present, some on the spot, some in front of their TV sets, and the rest glued to their radios for live coverage of the proceedings. The world stopped that day. The armed forces left the borders and came to the meeting, confident that their interaction with bloody civilians would only reinforce their lopsided view of the world. Doctors deserted the hospitals to escape their patients, police stopped chasing dacoits to prove good on their promises, mothers deferred their plans to bathe their babies to save water, lovers made excuses to their paramours to reduce medical expenses, bazaars and shopping malls were shut down to outmanoeuvre sales-tax collectors, the sun stuck at its vertex, and food was left simmering on stoves.

Mohammed Khan's four brides arrived clad in purdah. The President came half an hour later, having changed vehicles four times on the way for security reasons. His arrival on the stage brought the people to their feet and they yelled so loudly that the sound of their cheering was heard across all borders and was misconstrued as a signal from outer space. The cheering continued for several hours before it was ultimately stopped by executive order.

"We love you, President Sahib," the crowd whispered under his orders. "We also love the khaki uniform that is on your back. Please kiss your wives so we may kiss ours."

The President hesitated but the crowd grew impatient. Their whispers turned to shouts. "Kiss them, kiss them, kiss them," they kept shouting.

Mohammed Khan, his eyes brimming with tears of gratitude, lifted the veils off the faces of his wives one by one and kissed them with the passion of a man who has just discovered love. Suddenly, there was so much love in the air that the crowd burst into tears. People left in search of their wives so that they could kiss them with matching passion, and those who had yet to enter into matrimony pressured their parents to find them suitable mates before night fell. Those who had brought their spouses or girlfriends to the rally went mad. They danced, kissed their wives, their girl-friends and boy-friends.

"We are your followers, President Mohammed Khan," they shouted. "We believe in you, in your acts and your words, by which you promised to shed your uniform within one year. But we urge you not to do so. So please, do not shed your uniform and remain our imposed president for life. We are thankful to you Mr. President. You have shown us the sign, given us the courage to kiss in public."

"My people," Mohammed Khan said and they went mute. "I'll not shed my uniform, because you have implored me not to do so. In any case, fulfilling my promise of shedding my uniform would have left me fully exposed to the chilly winter of Margall Hills. So I'm not here to fulfil promises, I'm here to distribute love amongst you. I'll take more wives so the land can be filled with love."

On his return from the public meeting, Mohammed Khan issued a Presidential order that enhanced the upper limit from four to ten thousand. During the next three months, he took nine thousand nine hundred and ninety-six consorts. He fathered thousands of children, but none turned out to be male and the nation continued to live under the spell of depression. Frustrated, he divorced all his wives and took into his nuptials another ten thousand women of unparallelled splendour and fertility. Still the branches of his family tree remained fruitless. Eventually, burdened by the matrimonial obligations of so many daughters, his back turned into an arc and from that day on, he walked with his chest parallel to the ground, convinced that tragedy ran in his genes like that of the Kennedys.

It was at this juncture of his rule that he decided to reform the nation.

30

The heavy mandate given to us by the voters has provided me with a chance to initiate wide-ranging reforms and take the country to its destiny.
(Mian N. Sharif, deposed Prime Minister of Pakistan)

My government's reforms, particularly our devolution plan will turn things around and everyone will become prosperous and contented like the Rockefellers.
(Chief Executive of Pakistan)

Mohammed Khan kicked off the era of reforms by distributing state land to landless tenants.

He assembled a caravan of pedigree Arabian camels and left the nation's capital with the intent of knocking at the door of every poor man and woman trapped inside squalid dwellings. He rehearsed the words he would say to the expectant faces as he sat on his camel, and led the procession of hope from village to village. The banging hoofs of the camels left behind a dust of suppressed doubts that continued to cause lung disease for many years – even after the dust had been turned into slush by monsoons that flooded nullahs and ravines and forced people to collect their belongings and shift to safer areas.

Mohammed Khan held land distribution ceremonies all over the country. Tents were pitched on barren lands and landless citizens were invited to receive golden boxes carrying dust and a number.

"In this box you'll find dust dug from the land of which you're now the proud owner," he said in his speech to the tenants who were about to taste the forbidden fruit of ownership. "The dust will remind you of your humble beginnings and the number will guide you to your end. It will lead you to the orchards freed by your government from the clutches of absentee landlords."

Amidst cheers, he distributed the golden boxes and declared that the era of salinity, waterlogging, landlessness and landedness was over. Then he left the podium to work on other reforms. The newborn official landowners yoked their oxen and headed for their fields.

They never returned. The allotted earth cleaved into giant chasms and swallowed them. The people heard human and animal cries, and when they reached the fields, they only saw gigantic crevasses in the middle of the half-ploughed pastures with humans and animals trapped inside the belly of a hungry land. The tragedy was never explained, though some theorised that a stray earthquake had stumbled upon an unchartered course. Others suspected that the land distributed by the government was bad and had caved in under the ambitions of the new owners. A minority, comprising primarily leftists, claimed that the land had revolted against the new owners. They believed that the absentee landlords had always been apprehensive of the earth's intention: that is why they had never set foot on their lands.

The land reforms were followed by judicial reforms. "I want to devolve justice and bring it to everyone's doorstep," Mohammed Khan announced in his TV speech. "For that purpose, I've directed Colonel Naqvi to dissolve the judicial system imposed upon us like a curse by the British, and throw it to his dogs."

Through a Presidential Ordinance, Mohammed Khan disbanded all courts and turned the judges over to the Accountability Bureau. He ordered the Bureau to probe into allegations of corruption against the brotherhood of justice and against anyone they deemed fit. The Bureau employed every degree of investigation, ranging from first to third, but failed to substantiate anything even after several years. During this time, the judges languished in dungeons and worked as gardeners and batmen in the official bungalows of their Jail Superintendents. Frustrated by the sluggishness of the process, Mohammed Khan decided to shift the burden of proof to individuals, declaring one hundred and thirty-eight million people guilty until proven innocent. While the investigation against the judges and the judged was in progress, he sent a letter to every citizen under his personal seal. People opened the scented envelopes to learn that justice was on its way.

Justice took a while arriving. Mohammed Khan gathered the country's most pliant and shrewd judicial minds in the Southern wing of the President house and notified an extra-judicial committee headed by the prominent lawyer Mr. Gent-ur-Rel Peerzada. The Committee dug up factual and fictional data on all justice ever meted out to the human race and recorded it on rewritable CDs. Then genetic engineers were brought in from the mountains of Afghanistan. They used the recombinant DNA of myths and parables to produce a sixteen-headed Leviathan with twenty-four hands and twelve brains. So powerful was the monster that by himself he could perform the functions of three Major Generals, three Air Marshals, three Rear Admirals, one Superintendent of Police with two SHOs and three constables, one Judge of the High Court along with his Reader, three Brigadiers of the Intelligence Bureau with complete eavesdropping equipment, and one Commissioner of Income Tax with a team of three tax recovery officers. When the first batch of fifty million Leviathans left the factory, Mohammed Khan kissed the ground of the shopfloor to thank the Almighty for giving him the opportunity to dispatch justice to all and sundry.

People woke that fateful morning and found their personal justice-delivering Leviathan sitting in their living room. "Justice has arrived at your doorstep," the Leviathan said with a smile laced with good governance. "I'm here to protect you from the enemy, ensure that criminal cases are not registered against you, see to it that you're provided timely speerings about your neighbours' activities, decide your writ petitions in your favour – and of course, collect all taxes and other defaulted amounts from you. I'm here, right on your doorstep, your personalised civil-military bureaucratic servant, equipped with judicial aptitude."

The Leviathans pitched their tent in front of the houses they were deputed to serve and in the process choked all the traditional passages. A few days later, they acquired every inch of the village land in the name of patriotism, and set up defecation booths. At dawn, rows of multiple-headed judicious bureaucrats would excrete in a single file without regard to seniority, rank or service group, and return to their tents to sweat through long afternoons. After evening tea, they would go back to the fields and plough them using oxen and buffalos borrowed from the villagers in the name of humanity. At night, they would sleep in the open, allowing the villagers to hear their collective snores that were sixteen times those of an ordinary man. The sound drove away mosquitoes, caused winds to blow and brought rains during the cotton season.

While the nation heard the judicial snores, Mohammed Khan announced the long-awaited educational reforms. "The Holy Prophet commanded us to seek knowledge even if it means going to China," he said to the nation. "I realise that not everyone can afford a trip to China, so your government has decided to bring China to your doorstep."

He declared Chinese as the medium of instruction in schools and universities, and gave a six-month ultimatum to the nation. "I expect at least one Chinese-speaking person in every household," he declared and suspended normal curricula so the nation could learn Chinese. It soon became clear that a mistake had been made: the Ministry of Education estimated that it would have been cheaper to send citizens to China than to train them at home. Since public acceptance of the mistake would have been embarrassing, the Finance Ministry was directed to doctor the expenditure figures.

For six months, the nation struggled with the Chinese language, whose morphemic logic was so alien that only a few were able to pick up stray vituperations. When the deadline passed, the government conducted a ground survey and realised the complete failure of the campaign. The Cabinet held an emergency meeting and decided to extend the deadline by another six months. The citizens were warned that in case of failure, they would be given only three choices: learn Chinese, pay *jazia* (protection tax), or face the sword. Well before the closing date, there was a huge exodus of people to lands where speaking Chinese was a felony. Those who stayed behind because of strong family ties or other reasons, travelled to the Far East and brought with them teenage Chinese girls dressed as boys. They tore up their passports, forced them into Submission, arranged native ID Cards for them, got their names listed in the voters' lists and married them. When the census was carried out six months later, Cabinet members rushed to inform the President that there was now at least one lady in every house who could not only speak Chinese but also looked Chinese – such was the enthusiasm displayed by the nation for his vision.

31

(Bring in the Roses)

When the heaven shall cleave asunder
  And when the stars shall disperse,
  And when the seas shall be commingled,
  And when the graves shall be turned upside down.
  (Al-Quran, 82: 1-4)

And now, the end is near,
  And so I face
  The Final Curtain.
  (Paul Anka)

President Mohammed Khan was so busy reforming the nation that he forgot to give due attention to the country's economy. The country defaulted on its repayment of international loans and the International Monetary Fund stopped its next release of alms. Special emissaries arrived from Washington DC to deliver the ominous news and disappeared immediately after delivering it.

"How could that happen?" Mohammed Khan demanded from the Finance Minster, who in turn called the Finance Secretary and asked him the same question.

"How could that happen?" the Minister demanded from the Finance Secretary. "Doesn't the IMF give us fresh loans to repay the earlier ones?"

"They do, sir," the FS said with the functional spontaneity of a hardened bureaucrat. "They disbursed thirteen billion dollars to us during the current financial year."

"My God! Isn't that a lot of money? What did we do with it?"

"We took the money, circulated it, and belittled it," the FS submitted.

The Minister found it hard to believe that thirteen billion dollars could be belittled in so simple a manner as the Finance Secretary had described. He demanded to see the Treasury.

That afternoon, he visited the State Bank in a cavalcade of horses, camels and elephants. The Governor of the Bank welcomed him at the main gate that had been replaced with a thirty feet high portal to accommodate elephants of all sizes. He escorted the Minister to the conference room and gave him a comprehensive briefing on the functioning of the economy, the lack of the State Bank's role in controlling the money supply and its fast-and-furious circulation that inevitably led to triple digit inflation and belittled money.

"I'm not interested in the Bank's role," the Finance Minister interrupted edgily. "I want to know how rich or poor we really are."

The Governor presented the latest data on the amount of narrow and broader money circulating in the economy. "We're doing our best to control M1 and M2, Minister. We've imposed tighter curbs on new investments. We've also forwarded the names of all major industrialists to the Accountability Bureau so they dare not invest any further in new projects. This way, we hope to achieve a single-digit rate of inflation."

The Minister found the talk definitively misleading. He got to his feet and looked the Governor in the eye. "You can't deceive me with your fancy economic terminology," he said in a voice quivering with suspicion. "I don't trust you or your computer garbage. I want to see real money – and with my own eyes. Take me to where you store the money."

"There's no such place in this building, Minister."

"Where is it, then?" the Minister demanded. "Where is the treasury?"

"Nowhere, My Lord," the Governor said, switching to a more regal form of address in a bid to evoke a sympathetic response. "We no longer keep money in treasuries. Every penny is in circulation on the money markets."

A few hours later, the Finance Minister rushed back to inform a distressed Cabinet that the country was doomed. "The bureaucracy has plundered the national wealth," he said breathlessly. "The treasury is empty; there is not a single rupee in the treasury – in fact, there is no treasury. The bureaucrats have removed the very trace of their white-collar crime. I've ordered the arrest of the State Bank Governor and the Finance Secretary. I've directed the Federal Investigation Agency to locate the IMF team so it may be hanged for being the harbingers of bad news but alas, they've already left the country. I've placed their names on the exit control list, though."

"What are our chances of survival?"

"Alas, not very bright, Mr. President. We'd better start preparing the wreaths to cover the motherland with nostalgic petals. Alas, the end is nigh."

The heat of the blistering summer temporarily saved the nation.

"Roses don't bloom in this heat, Mr. President," Kamran Lashari, the eternal DG Parks and Horticultural Authority submitted to Mohammed Khan. "You can't allow the nation to die at this juncture. There are simply not enough roses available with PHA to prepare even a single wreath."

The nation's demise was deferred until roses could bloom. "Destiny has given us a second chance," Mohammed Khan said with interim hope. "We have until November to figure out how other defaulting nations of the Third World survive the wrath of the IMF."

"China survived through a policy of closed doors and nationalisation," the new Finance Secretary said.

"Ah, China, indeed!" the oldest and the wisest member of the Cabinet interjected. "Our friend in times of need. A friend in need is a friend indeed. The Chinese are a great people. They eat dogs and it rains cats and dogs in Beijing."

"So be it," Mohammed Khan directed when the wisest one finally finished talking. "Close the doors and nationalise. We will free businesses from the clutches of ownership."

Within three days, all activities were nationalised.

"We want to rob the rich to feed the poor," the Finance Minister said in his interview that was published in the classified section of the Wall Street Journal next to a feature about the rogue Pakistan army. "From this day on, dignity is a national asset, hope an endangered species, freedom a common property to be distributed according to caste, creed and political affiliation."

By evening, nationalisation walked into people's bedrooms. Their guardian Leviathans informed them with judicious firmness that no longer was it possible for men to keep women for the purposes of sex without obtaining copulation certificates that would soon be available from the Ministry of Culture. The order was implemented with immediate effect. Police checked couples at all major and minor crossings and those who failed to produce the certificates were charged under Hadood Act to face death by stoning for the offence of zina. Conjugal relations were also regularised through special laws, so that harmony could be improved and the costs associated with maintaining relationships were reduced.

"We have embarked upon the path to recovery," the Minister of Finance assured Mohammed Khan. "The new Finance Secretary has given me his word."

For a while it seemed that the nation had indeed set foot on the path of recovery. Then came the day when time was nationalised.

Historians say it happened on a monsoon morning carrying the promise of a fragrant day. The sun had disappeared behind dark clouds, leaving the earth wrapped in a moist shadow. The clouds were approaching from the northeast amidst intermittent sounds of thunder. The assurance of an overdue rain was in the air, saturated with a dewy chill that invited people to leave their pyretic rooms and come out on the streets filled with the fragrance of Sawan: the month of romance. Everyone was getting ready to greet the monsoons. Poets were dusting their notebooks and refilling their fountain pens. Virgins were making plans to meet their secret lovers. Wives were dusting floors and changing bedsheets. Husbands had saddled shisham trees with swings and were dreaming of concubines.

The rains came and everyone forgot about their pledged existence, their mortgaged fate, their forbidden desires—and bathed in the rain. Then the rain stopped. Barely a few seconds later, the loudspeaker of the Faisal mosque started to scream, telling everyone that time had been nationalised. They felt El Niño descending upon them. The loudspeaker further announced that it was raining hard on the mountains. By morning, red water came and turned all the rivers maroon. The fish died, leaving a stink that followed man for two hundred miles. The rains returned from the mountains. For seven days and six nights it rained a hard rain. Houses fell, crops were inundated. Animals famished. Hunger enveloped the country. Brother left brother. Weight, girth and baldness became status symbols. Flies walked through the streets strewn with everything destined to extinction. Locust swarmed like the first swarming. Gog and Magog and every trapped woman nearly burst through the wall. Firstborn males started committing suicide and the young ran away from home. Women wailed for three days at each death. Men buried their dead and queued up in front of the Cultural Ministry to apply for copulation certificates so they could conceive afresh. Old elegies lost their agony. New elegies were written but no one could hear anything because words were lost and noise was left. Frogs occupied the waters and land, and croaked.

The Great Flood that killed seventy-two people was followed by the era of sightings. A masturbating teenager saw Major Charles Devereux near the waters of the Great Lake. Topchi appeared in the nightmares of his estranged brother-in-law and directed him to construct a tomb to Major Devereux Sahib's memory and name it the Tomb of Oblique Vision. The estranged brother-in-law meticulously planned and executed the greatest jailbreak in prison history to return to the village to erect shrines for Major Devereux and Topchi. At night, he would hide in the jungle along with other absconders, and during daytime he would supervise construction. He named Topchi's shrine the Tomb of the Sixth Fable and made arrangements for unboiled milk to be provided for the pilgrims. Those who visited the tomb developed opto-spermatheca. The Chief Rival's eldest son emulated Topchi and fashioned a green-marbled mausoleum for the Chief Rival and baptised it the Tomb of the Vanished. Those who orbited the Chief's grave found their legs elongated by several inches. Ram Babu's relatives returned from across the Ganges to display his ashes in a glass reliquary and gave it no name. Those who went near the reliquary felt the heat of fire still burning in Ayodhia and Gujrat.

Shrines became fashionable. In every house where someone died, a tomb appeared. An architect of great fame visited the country and designed standardised tombs with aerodynamic domes in which cool air circulated and reduced electricity consumption. The Water and Power Development Authority went bankrupt, and even a string of Generals sent to head the organisation could not salvage its financial position because no one used electricity any longer. Citizens were left with extra cash, which they hid under their pillows for want of a conceivable use. There was no longer fear of famine or hunger or the IMF. Everyone visited everyone else's tomb and ate on the table spread for visitants with food and sweetened milk. No one cooked at home and no one bought meat or chicken or coal anymore. People killed their buffaloes and roosters and dumped them in the river. The river was choked with rotting carcasses and the water spilled across the fields into the tombs. People started filling their closets with the skeletons of dead animals until the closets were also full. Luckily, an economist of equal fame arrived and informed them of the likely advent of the WTO regime. People gathered the rotting animals from ditches and from underneath the current of the flowing river, and packed them for export to countries where the custom laws were not so strict regarding quality.

As the exports grew, the country was flooded with imported ploughs and ploughshares that did not require bulls to pull them. So much wheat was produced within two months that people threw up whenever someone talked of food. The IMF sent consultants to frame trade laws and it gave rise to smuggling. Wheat was smuggled out to the neighbouring countries, and in return, expression was smuggled in, creating a class of men and women who eternally talked. Men started to dye their hair, dyeing it brown, auburn, brunette, blonde, green and red. Some shaved their moustache and grew beards; others shaved their beards and grew moustaches. Some wore their shalwars above their ankles and others below it. All relational theorems were jumbled up.

In the midst of all the confusion, no one noticed the exponential rate of growth in the frog population. They continued to breed and multiply, and finally, the plains were wrapped with seven layers of noise. Under cover of the noise, it was natural for guerrilla activity to quietly breed in the mountains. It eventually came down to the plains in the form of a war that spread to every part of the land. The warriors sent their ambassadors to the land of missed opportunities in a bid to convince Sikander Khan to lead them in the war against his father so history could be repeated. Sikander, who was by now a successful male stripper in a San Francisco gay bar, refused to accept the offer on "personal grounds" so the guerillas contacted M. Sahib to take control of the hostilities. By the time the monsoons ended, M. Sahib who had meanwhile lost one eye in a road accident and re-grown his black beard, emerged both as a religious leader and as chief commander of the war, which he appropriately named the Great Civil War of Silence. People participated in the war in silence, felt its impact on their private, public and secret lives, and tried to live them without raising their voice.

No one could really figure out how sporadic guerrilla activity could evolve into the Great Civil War. Historians searched for all the just and unjust reasons for which wars were waged in the history of mankind, including the war on terror, and came back empty-handed. Only M. Sahib had the answer. "This war was thrust upon us," he said. "The Government wanted us to protest against noise."

The Civil War of Silence was the bloodiest civil war ever fought in the world. Corpses were mutilated and parts were severed. Bodies paved the streets. They were tied to the branches of the old tree, deposited in the wells, hung from the village gates. Wives became widows, virgins lost their secret lovers, children discovered orphanhood. A metallic jingle filled the atmosphere and nothing was audible any more. Friends appealed for help, the wounded cried for first aid, enemies pleaded for mercy, the ignorant offered excuses, the wise warbled quotable quotes, storytellers narrated the moral of the story – but no one heard them. Every voice froze in the nuclear winter.

The sun turned into a great ball of fire. It came down and started the apocryphal Great Fire, which was to sweep through green fields, houses and pasturelands. Animals and humans killed each other for flesh and grass. The survivors plunged into the river and were scalded by boiling water. Scavengers dived to the earth and were overwhelmed by sudden convulsions with their first tear of the grilled human flesh, perishing without a flutter. Those who breathed died of pierced noses and those who did not breathe melted in the heat, dying inorganically. It was an exaggerated deathscape littered with silence.

Epilogue
Chain of Being

On that day man shall be told of all
  that he hath done first and last;
  On that day man shall be eyewitness against himself
  On the day when every soul will find itself confronted
  with all that it hath done of good and all that it hath
  done of evil, and every soul will long that there
  were a mighty space between it and the evil.
  (Description of the Day of Judgment in the Holy Quran)

God is closer to a man than his jugular vein.
  (Muslim Belief)

M. Sahib was so convinced of his irrelevance to existential reality that he often forgot he existed. It was during those spells of self-denial that he became a legendary figure credited with historic heroism. He won a series of improbable victories against government forces ten times the size of his teenage guerrillas dying to lose their virginity at the hands of pseudonymous prostitutes. With each victory, M. Sahib's belief grew stronger. "This is not my war," he said on the eve of his one hundredth victory. "I'm neither its cause nor its effect. I'm not even aware of its existence or non-existence."

Mohammed Khan laughed each time they brought him the news of yet another defeat. "M. Sahib's turned into an historic fool. He can defeat my soldiers but can he beat the deadline? The roses are just round the corner – we'll all be gone by the time he pulls off his last victory. Forget about M. Sahib: make halva. And tell the cook to be generous with ghee."

M. Sahib continued to create legends of heroism, which the watching Super Powers dubbed as human rights violations. "We'll not tolerate human rights violations," their foreign ministers warned. Yet they kept tolerating them because they were tolerant nations. When M. Sahib won his hundredth battle, the Super Powers got together and decided to supply arms to Mohammed Khan, but M. Sahib had old men with green wings and snowy beards on his side. Before each battle, the old men would dress in matching robes, put on their baseball gloves and take positions in the sky above M. Sahib's head. They'd catch every cannonball fired by Mohammed Khan's forces and throw them back on the fleeing soldiers.

Eventually, enemy soldiers surrounded the capital. Sitting in a state of emotionless hiatus inside his air-conditioned office, Mohammed Khan became aware of their pathogenic stench and asthmatic breathing. Then he heard a giant whoosh inside his intestines and felt a dull weight travelling from an overfilled bladder all the way down to his gouty toes. As he rose from the Presidential Chair and staggered to the bathroom, he found his heart beating again. Two days and three nights later, when a victorious M. Sahib arrived in the President House, he was informed that the cursed and illegal ex-President Mohammed Khan was hiding inside the bathroom. A team of heavyset soldiers from the Engineering Corps broke down the door and sprayed several cans of air freshener to make the environment suitable for Presidential entry. M. Sahib entered flanked by brandished swords and found the bathroom empty except for the fragrance of fresh roses and sharpened pencils.

"Mohammed Khan has died the death worthy of a false prophet," President M. Sahib announced to reassure the masses convinced of Mohammed Khan's immortality. The explanation failed to dispirit those who were still on his side. They believed that he had been beamed up directly to Heaven after his crucifixion on the crossroads. They further claimed that one day he would be resurrected – along with Jesus Christ.

Mohammed Khan was actually beneath the earth, trying to find his way through a convoluted series of underground tunnels. The tunnels were built centuries ago as an escape route from commitments and promises. They ran the entire length of the volcanic crust where rats had dug huge holes through which passed hot air, sobbing like a cat giving birth to illegitimate civets destined to be thrown in abandoned wells under the cover of conspiratorial nights. Mohammed Khan first became aware of their existence when a servant otherwise sworn to secrecy was thrown into a state of gabbiness by Presidential Proximity, and revealed the myth of escape. Mohammed Khan hired private contractors to turn the myth into reality. He paid them millions of dollars from his secret funds to install a lighting system, but on the day of escape, as he stepped inside the tunnel, he discovered that the lights did not work.

For hours, he wandered through darkness. Having spent three nights in the bathroom, he felt so light he was virtually floating through the passageways humming with his mellow heartbeat. Soon it was the only sound worth listening to and darkness the only vision worthy of seeing.

He sliced through the dark, splitting it into zillions of glowing molecules. He tasted them on his tongue, smelt them deep inside his nose, felt them mingle with his breath and spread through his veins and arteries carrying whispers about unknown forces in control of things directed to turn invisible. He closed his eyes for a better vision and followed his blindness to a door at the end of the tunnel.

He opened the door and entered into a hallway that appeared to be a reception room, though no one was there to receive him. A thick green carpet covered the floor like ivy, sustaining furniture that was very dark, belonging to some unchronicled era of darkness. The furniture had been arranged to make seven distinct sitting areas but it seemed as if no one had been received here in a millennium-and-a-half. Overhead was a high, vaulted ceiling arching upward, and adding a sense of openness that was an excellent antidote for the claustrophobia produced by his tunnelled journey. There were concealed lights in the vault ribs, providing cheerfulness to the ambience. Mohammed Khan felt the warmth of a fireplace, heard the snapping sound of wood burning somewhere and sensed the presence of unread and unspoken words stacked in wall-lined cabinets of mahogany and teak.

He felt something crumble under his feet. He looked down and saw the ashes of half-burnt feathers spread all the way to end of a hallway, imbued in silence. He bent down and picked up a relatively well-preserved feather. It was surprisingly light. He touched its fine surface and felt it quiver in his hands like a wounded heart that had transgressed accepted boundaries. He brought it close to his nostrils and smelt musk. He let it fall and watched it flutter through emptiness.

He heard a rustling sound as if the wind was blowing away the feathers. He looked around to locate the opening through which the draught might have sneaked in. Then he realised it was not the sound of rustling feathers but of abandoning feet. The hieroglyphs etched on his body had become alive and were deserting him. He felt their grip loosening as they slithered down his body like crawling insects and wormed away from him in two rows. He suddenly had visions of bodies rotting under a fiery August sun, and the room turned so hot that he took off his clothes and stood stripped in a corridor that seemed to have eyes of its own – Mohammed Khan felt ashamed of his exposed existence.

The running symbols had now reached the end of the hall. Their leader – the one once tattooed near his jugular vein, the one written in a script outside the pages of the book of Names, the one which had always managed to elude meaning pushed at the door as others tried to follow it. An unnerving loneliness struck Mohammed Khan and he yelled out in rage. The hieroglyphs looked back to follow his cry and were turned into sculptures of stone by the spell of sound.

Mohammed Khan looked, in a state of ocular disbelief, at the sculptured words lining both sides of the hall. He had an urge to run and reclaim what had once belonged to him. The urgency of desire turned his stomach into a knot, tightly knit and hurting, sending nausea to his throat. The rush of adrenaline dazed him. His heart leapt to his throat, blocking his windpipe and causing him to gasp. He ran, his heart pounding against his chest, impure air stuck inside his lungs, his feet hitting the carpet and raising a breath of dust that made his nose bleed and his eyes pour a sweat of exhaustion. He reached for the first statuette in the line and it came alive, talking to him in whispers – "And when the tree embraced him and violated him, we caused profane details to be imprinted upon his body so he might escape shame, but he preferred to make meanings."

Mohammed Khan released another cry of rage. The sound desecrated the centuries old purity of silence, and silence reacted with the solemnity of a father forced into an honour killing. The indecorous scream reverberated through the quiet corridor, bounced off its walls and hit him like the blow of a knife searching for a sleeping daughter's heart. He staggered, then slipped, but never fell. Destiny gripped him, made him weightless and sent him floating through the columns of chiselled narration. They spoke and he spoke, and everyone and everything spoke, and it was a speech with the exuberance of storytellers forbidden every contact with listeners by verbal censor. Their voices were hoarse and awkward, lacking all manners of address. They talked simultaneously, jettisoning the debris of truth before censorship was imposed again. They talked to him and he talked to them in a monologue liberated of all syntax.

"Thy ancestor came into town where the ailing widow gave him a place to sleep and bread to eat," the voices resounded in the confines of the fourteen-hundred-year old room, "and when time came to divide the landholding, he killed her, threw her body in the gutter, and on the basis of false property documents declared the house along the ridges of flattened mountains his own and became one of those who would one day create fitna in the land and claim to be martyrs of the War of Cracks even though they did not even participate in the War and were killed merely as bystanders for they had no heart to fight but their leader who would come fifty years later had a thirst for blood and they were led by the leadership of the one destined to sneak away to the Great Isle of eternal greenery and everlasting cold, and indeed he is not cold for You made arrangements for him so he can warm himself with the breath of golden-coloured dragons and delivers speeches over telephones while the smelly waters of the sea throw out dead starfish and used sandals unto those who dress in long shirts and baggy trousers with bottoms rolled up and walk on soiled beaches, dreaming of green pastures where honey-coloured maidens would serve vintage wines and dance to the tunes of flutes played by creative gods, and what dost thou know of gods when thou knowst not thyself, and surely I know Your disciples and their deeds, for when the dreamers let go of their reveries, they are skinned alive by bearded men for brewing perverted dreams in their heads, and thou who dost not listen ought to know that heads must be shaved along with moustaches and lo, the roses must be planted and the beard must be grown equal to the length of a clenched fist so non-believers' hearts would be filled with terror of the thunder, and what are You but a meaningless symbol once carved on my jugular vein and how dare thou interpret Us for thou art what We know thou art and I finally know what I am and thou knowst nothing because We are what We know We are, and verily those who believed in false prophets were abandoned by them on the shores of deep seas when boats capsized and the leader left and the followers gouged their eyes with their nails so they might not see the spectacle of deceit, and pierced their eardrums so they might not hear the stories of their trusted ones, and severed their larynxes so stories were not repeated although it was nothing but a story that began everything, and from humble beginnings he went to the land of gold and left behind sisters imprisoned behind mud walls which they and scores like them lick through the night and ha, He talks of walls, He Who created walls and wrote stories about the wall and lo, he interjects but can he not see that when the wall turns into a membrane smelling of fresh onions, they go back, afraid they might break the vows they took when anonymous men came into their rooms and told them to say 'yes' in Our Name, though We never bestowed this right upon the men outside the rooms, and even though the ones behind the veil knew not to what and to whom they said 'yes' but they did nonetheless because Tradition is stronger than Submission, and those they accepted violated them in pursuit of one-third the happiness, and when he reaches foreign lands, he shall taste disappointment not different from the distress of the one who left his room in the Quadrangle in the cover of the night for lower pleasures to a place inhabited by the people of music and long traditions preserved on parchment of the night and returned a different man, but were it not for the sleeping guard who had eaten too much meat for supper and taken more than an allowable quantity of wine, he would not have become the father of an idea that should have remained an idea and nothing more, but he mistakenly saw a grand design and lo, he forged a questionable reality destined to turn into a memory living in hearts that will remain filled with plans to murder their parents and send them to old homes for they slither like pythons guarding buried treasures, and these children want their parents dead and buried under the same trees beneath whose branches lies everything they search for but verily they will not reach the treasure and yes indeed, how can they find it for it does not exist, and lo, he says it does not exist for he cannot see it since he sees with greed and lo, it was greed that drove him to imprison his deposed father in the bowels of the fort and wage war against the dead man's camel and against the widow who sat on it, and You who talk of war, can You deny that it was not his war but Yours and those who fought on both sides were Your people and You forgot Your promise of heaven for all eyes blessed with holy vision and lo, the one whose eyes are cursed with blindness talks of vision, and he forgets that the enemies of the camel tried to divide brothers and when he won the war, he took in his possession all the record of land and altered it so he could become the landlord whose holdings ran all the way to the edges of the earth that will soon be covered with roses and underneath it live all the pythons and all the snakes but he will surely turn blind and lose distinction between pythons and staffs and thus suffer because he forgot that roses will blossom and their fragrance will muddle his brain so he cannot judge as to which one was more dangerous, and lo, he would be deceived by those he trusts the most for he was trusted when he left for lands beyond the jurisdiction of his estate and came across many lands and continents hidden in the mist of posterity – the Great Peninsula where children carried guilt inside their school bags; the Land Between Rivers where great stories were written and people wrestled with wild and timid, good and bad, moon and sun, water and the water-giver, land and its fullness, eyes and vision; the Land of Two that boasted all the colours of the rainbow and all the notes of matutinal ragas; the Great Isle that was dark and bright, weak and strong, insertion and reception, movement and stillness, and heaven and earth – but when he reached where his followers feared him to reach, he lost faith in their vision and left them in the darkness of a movie theatre where a single movie had played since the big bang, and ha, the world was surely not created with a bang but with the silent tear of the father who received the pierced heart of his daughter on a silver platter and failed to admire the fine carvings on it for You have no taste for art and verily thou art a man with failing eyesight, unable to see the reality of love and the unreality of the genetic code, and thou ended up with the burden of a dead daughter with a knife thrust through her heart filled with her altered emotions for a man who dares to speak before Us and he forgets that his love for the deceived one was fleeting, starting from the moment he came down from the cave on the hill and ending with the post-coital void for he knew not how to make love and when he finally learnt from the one who had shortened his name to fit the cover of his books, alas it was too late, and indeed it was so late that all cafés had closed for the night and I had to sleep on lonely footpaths, listening to the wind talking to me in a tongue I did not understand even though You claim to have taught me all the names and assured me that I was ready for the world but you had lied to me, which is the greatest lie ever told and lo, We overestimated his abilities as a pupil and as a teacher, and he excelled only at violating his students and yes I did for sure, and it was fine because men don't get pregnant and if only he had not inseminated her, the lonely father with fading sight would not have been forced to become the unwilling hero burdened with the weight of honour thrust upon him by the entire village where two wars had been fought over property handed down to successive generations through the changing decrees of an unknown Benefactor that kept shifting allegiance for He was either indecisive, or searched for fun, the Lonely One (for He's the Only One) in possession of the heart of an elf, and in Your heart were the secrets of all pranks and antics and You often cried over them when You compared goals with results and verily what dost thou know about crying, you whose students continued to score less than 33% and their results kept getting worse because you were more interested in giving private tuitions and rigging elections at the behest of those who were declared the only surviving institution in the country, and they insist again and again and again and again and again on conquering the nation subjugated so many times that mothers now give birth to children with buttocks pre-stamped with serial numbers by the hand that wrote all writings, both on paper and on walls, but he refused to read the meanings in the graffiti and continued to take wives to have a son even if the son was born with a number on both his buttocks until thou suspected that the procedure adopted by thy government for selection of his mates was based on nefarious intentions, therefore thou took things in thy own hands, journeyed from town to town disguised as a mystic in search of Us so people would not suspect his true identity or intent, corresponded with marriage bureaus under false aliases, travelled to every corner of his dominion on hired tongas, spied on every fount and every well where young and unbled maidens gather under the purdah of an early morning to collect water for their homes, and behold, he selects thirteen maidens and sends his trusted barbers to their parents' home with the message that Chief of Believers wishes to take their hands as his consorts but only three barbers would return as four preferred to commit suicide out of his fear, and the remaining died of heart attacks because their cholesterol-choked arteries could not take its onslaught, and the survivors yielded themselves to the mercy of the system to submit that every single one of the chosen maidens had already been through your bridal chamber that was once a room filled with laughter but now a centre of intrigue where he makes plans to lead the led into deserts to ultimately abandon them when the enemy arrives, and capsize the boat at the first sign of the cyclone so stories would be buried under the seas like the ship on his maiden voyage that started from one house and ended in another and from the second house I travelled to the other side of the hillocks where land existed in absentia and the one who sent me to till the land for seven years employed a servant to move the chain on his door until the tiller returned, and when he did return, he was blamed for reversing time so he went back to re-reverse it and arrived at the hall where angels had sacrificed their wings before fire, and nouns and verbs had stoned themselves and lo, We turned him into thin air and sent him across the hallway to the chamber where he would be greeted by his first name and given the tidings that his coming was well, but he was an ungrateful guest who said he was not the one We sought because he was unsure of himself but assured of the shapeless statue of black stone with a distant look and I took off my shoes and crossed my legs and stretched myself to the breaking point between enfolding and unfolding myself and eventually found a posture that suited me and closed my eyes as if the answers were written on the hide of darkness but lo, darkness alone comes out of darkness and roses alone come out of land and he would not find the answers as long as he looks at the cracks on the walls or beneath the symbols on his body or inside the pages of expired books stolen from libraries because the walls are crumbling under the weight of their inherent weakness and the symbols are learning to revolt and books were dumped inside rivers so they would not pollute the impressionable hearts filled with arrogance and verily it was arrogance that made him say, 'I'm not the one you seek,' for he refused to listen and dared to speak but does he not recall the punishment for speaking truth before stones and lo, the day shall come when tongues would be yanked out of throats and cooked and served to guests invited for the Presidential Banquet before the victory celebrations end and roses burgeon and people come out of their houses, tasting non-alcoholic wine on their tongues, but he refuses to remember for verily he has forgotten what was told to him in his sleep and verily he has forgotten what was written on his skin and verily he forgets the names he was taught before We sent him upon the land, and nay, the one who taught him the word did a good job and it was he who forgot, but he dares to say that he never heard the voice because the noise in his heart was louder and more powerful than the voice that descended upon him, and We told him that We were the voice that cried in his heart and he said he was busy listening to cats crying in the night but how busy could he be that he forgot about the season of roses and can he not see the flashes of lightening outside and hear the thunder of firecrackers as they celebrate the victory of the one who existed in his stories but all stories have endings and lo, the roses are sprouting and he still says that he only saw lines on the wall and found confusion in his heart but verily he knew not how to read and surely he looked in all the wrong chambers of his heart or he would not have said that he stumbled upon himself and created himself out of other people's expectations and fears and out of minstrels' stories for We created all fears and all stories and every type of despicable fluid from which he germinated, and lo, the roses are blooming, and he stands before Us with the arrogance of a leader who hides from the public but surely, he is no leader and We are not what We're not and surely I know what I am and I know I decided to come so others could be saved, but He Who speaks had other plans and He was the jealous one and the fickle one, and He sends the gardeners and lo, the gardeners are gathering and indeed the gardeners are gathering and lo, the roses are blooming, and surely the roses are blooming but Who is bent upon taking revenge for His failure to communicate for it was not I who sought vengeance because vengeance is not mine but His, and if He could not scream louder than the noise in my heart, the failing belongs to Him for I never aspired to success but only struggled to take them across the desert and across all seas for this is what they wanted and verily when they lost faith in thy leadership, thou left them, and lo, the land has become red with the fragrance of fresh roses and people are running in wild ecstasy over what is their fate, and surely it is not ecstasy but confusion and certainly it is not my fate as I wait for the trucks with green insignias to arrive and lo, the trucks have arrived and men dressed in black uniforms disembark, and lo, the gardeners are cutting the roses and surely, I will wear a garland around my pubis, and burn in the fire of passion and lo, No, you don't speak any more for the last words shall be mine before the nation dies and

— I look outside and see roses.
— I look outside and smell fragrance.
— I look inside and see a bleeding heart with a knife stuck in it.
— I look outside and … see end."

For a full list of our publications
please visit our web site at

www.dewilewispublishing.com